Leana looke[...] [...] upon her. Hi[...] [...] the back of her booth, and he seized the table's edge for balance with the other.

"Excuse me. . ."

Slowly Leana released her sharply held breath while gazing into the darkest, most brilliant brown eyes she'd ever seen. Eyes so dark and gleaming with such lovely sable lights, they could be labeled midnight romantic.

"I hope I didn't hurt you." His voice was deep and soft with wonder.

"No-o," she stammered, as he leaned over her, his eyes wandering over her flushed cheeks, shining jet hair and trim figure.

"How long have you two kids known each other?" Leana's friend Brenda asked between giggles. "Patrice, my friend Leana Claremont. Leana, my friend Patrice Jackson."

Distracted by the aura of raw masculinity, a shiver Leana had not felt for a long time rippled through her body. "How are you?"

"Quite fine," he answered.

Made In Heaven

Amberlina Wicker

PINNACLE BOOKS
WINDSOR PUBLISHING CORP.

PINNACLE BOOKS are published by

Windsor Publishing Corp.
850 Third Ave
New York, NY 10022

The P logo Reg U.S. Pat & TM Off. Pinnacle is a trade-
mark of Windsor Publishing Corp.

First Printing: March, 1995

Printed in the United States of America

I dedicate this book with thanks to:
My agent, Eugenia Panettieri, who saw before her time
and to Earlean MacMillan,
the first to put her money where her mouth was.
May you rest in peace.

Acknowledgment

The author would like to acknowledge for his invaluable assistance and contribution to this book, Mr. Sidell R. Corley of the Corley Detective Agency of Mobile, Alabama.

Chapter One

Leana dressed carefully. She sat down on a slubbed silk chair in the long, luxurious room with white Japanese irises embossed on the delicately papered walls. Long vertical aqua blinds at the window with softly puffed valances over each streaked sunlight into the room that touched her hair as she pulled sheer pantyhose up long poster-girl legs, then slipped her feet into three inch red spiked heels.

When she was done, she crossed the thick pale carpet to examine her reflection in the enormous triple mirrors above an ivory double dresser in the aqua and white bedroom. She looked gorgeous, all slender supple curves and even-tone brown skin the color of dark honey. She'd chosen a strapless drop-dead-red slip dress, bottomed with ruffles, for Brenda's party. Showcasing the trim, graceful length of her legs in the skinny red heels, it was short enough to allow for a peek at big, creamy-sleek thighs when she moved. Twisting her full hips as if in dance, watching the bouncing tails ruffle up, she muttered smugly, "Thunder thighs, my foot!"

She turned her head to look at the pink cocktail dress

she'd discarded on the bed. It had been her first choice. She had been thinking about the handsome stranger who had nearly fallen into her lap at the restaurant when she first took the dress with precious hands from the closet.

How tall she remembered him. Standing six feet or better, his shoulders were broad, his hips slim. He was dressed roughly, in a black cotton Tee stretched tautly across his torso that emphasized its hard tapering length and his well-defined chest, the tight faded jeans, she recalled with a warm shiver, bulging at the apex of his long, well-muscled legs, a heavy ripe weight. Even the diamond stud in his ear and wary, street-wise way in which he moved, imparting an overall, if slightly thuggish impression of a man who could take care of himself, brought a soft look to her face.

Suspicion had altered her features, she remembered, moving toward the dress on the bed, when Brenda said he was a private eye. Too fun-loving at times, it was only when with a deflated kind of reluctance, as if it somehow detracted from the glamour of his profession, she added that he owned the detective agency, had Leana believed her.

Desperately wanting him to remember her, she had chosen that particular dress because pink was the closest color to the coral suit she had been wearing when she met him. 'And so,' she thought wryly, as she rehung the pink cocktail dress in her cedar-scented closet, 'you pick out a *red* dress to wear.' Smiling to herself in a dreamy sort of way, she went over that magical day in her mind, detail by detail, that unbeknownst to her, had in actuality, started with her secretary, LaDonna's day.

Chapter Two

"It must have been Leana."

The plump, brown-skinned girl cut her eyes around the coffee shop. LaDonna was one of those 'broken record' secretaries when it came to her boss. Setting her Coke on the table, she heaved an exasperated sigh. "Anytime anyone says they saw a really pretty woman at the Edward Blyden Center, you say," her voice turned mincing, ". . . it must have been Lee-na. Girl, come off it! I'm sure there are plenty of other pretty women where you work outside of Leana Claremont!"

Her friend, LaDonna, nineteen years old and so slender that the young men still called her 'Slim', fluffed her hair with supercilious calm, the colorful bangles on her pale arm clinking. "Sure there are, Trish. But none as sophisticated as Leana, none as beautiful, as glamorous, as . . ."

"Oh, puh-leeze!"

LaDonna laughed when with a flick of her hand, Trish dismissed the glittering parade of attributes to her boss. She was still laughing when she remembered she had to get back to—as she and her co-workers referred to their place of employment—'The Center'. Taking her leave, but not without a sassy, "... and smart, too!" she hurried back to her office.

The Edward Blyden Center was housed in a three story greystone turn-of-the-century mansion donated by a wealthy admirer of the Center's work with minority youth and needy or destitute adults. She entered through a side door, then took the back elevator to the third floor. Thanking her lucky stars that she wore the clinging, bright orange mini-dress—nipped in the waist by a wide, plastic, hot pink belt—that freed up her legs, she ran madly through the corridor. She raced in a last ditch effort to beat the clock then crept into the empty offices of the Assistant Director. She was sneaking her purse underneath her desk when she heard the sound of the door opening behind her.

"Well, who do we have here? It couldn't be my secretary LaDonna, could it?" The humor-filled voice belonged to a tall woman in her late twenties. Arms folded loosely over her chest, shapely legs crossed at slim ankles, she was leaning against the door to an inner office. A striking woman, possessing large, almond-shaped eyes set in a delicate oval face, and even black brows. The classy coral designer walking suit which she wore with aplomb lent a soft glow to her clear brown complexion, making even warmer the elfin smile that plumped out her cheeks. She looked every inch as glamorous as her secretary had pronounced her.

"Leana!" LaDonna squealed. There was a guilty, half-frightened look on her face. For the third time that week, she had been caught coming in overdue from lunch. "I thought you were taking late lunch!"

"Good grief! I'm *late?*"

LaDonna jumped at the voice now coming from behind her. Her supple torso bending like a young willow, she turned swiftly. "Miss Martin! How are you?" There was genuine pleasure, even relief in her voice.

"Leana!" she cried, swinging back to her boss with a chiding look before the visitor could respond. "Miss Martin is here for your lunch date and here you are keeping her waiting!"

Rushing past Leana into the sunny, pleasant interior of the inner office, then out again, LaDonna pressed a pink and beige leather purse upon her. "You don't want to keep Miss Martin waiting!

"Don't you worry, Miss Martin," she went on in a breathless advocate's rush, an almost comically earnest look on her face as she laid seige to her arm. "Leana didn't mean to keep you. She just forgot her purse. See, Leana's been working real, *real* hard. All day. Probably a touch of indigestion, too," she suggested in a whispery, unduly concerned aside. "She drinks *way* too much coffee."

Hyped up with guilt, LaDonna became even more so when her boss laughed out loud. "Ooooh, Miss Martin! Your collar's puckered!" she cried, ignoring the throaty laughter behind her, and although feeling utterly foolish, unable to stop herself. "Here," she said, her nimble fingers rubbing, patting, straightening at non-stop speed, "let me fix it."

Leana grinned as her friend Brenda Martin, a stunned expression on her face, stood at attention while the young girl patted her scarf, smoothed down her collar and then, the tan lapels of her braid-trimmed suit.

Taking pity on her stupified friend and by the arm pulling her stumbling toward the door, Leana laughed.

"Come on, girlfriend. Let's get out of here before she pulls that pretty scarf from your neck and shines your shoes with it. Oh, and LaDonna," she requested, calling back over one shoulder sweetly, "since I might not be back until late, keep the break down to fifteen minutes. Okay?"

"Where did you get her?" Brenda laughed. "She was like a whirlwind, running around and talking and apologizing for you all at the same time. She blew me away!" They were seated in a well-lighted booth in Glady's Restaurant.

Leana laughed. "LaDonna's okay until she gets caught sneaking in late. Or," she recalled with a wry look, "asking her to make coffee. That's a *big* no-no. She and the other secretaries at the Center have decided it's beneath their dignity to even go to the canteen for their bosses' coffee."

Brenda saw nothing odd in that. "Well, you have legs, don't you?"

Leana shrugged. "Don't bother me. I've tasted LaDonna's coffee." She took a nibble of the tossed salad piled high in the salad bowl. "This is good." She bent forward, one hand cupped beneath her mouth to catch a piece of lettuce that threatened to escape her pouty, coral-lined lips.

Brenda sighed whimsically. "Not as good as a good man, though."

Leana smiled as she chewed. "I haven't been looking lately but I guess they're still hard to find, huh?"

Brenda pointed with a fork at Leana's salad disdainfully. "Well, if I sat around eating rabbit food all day like *some* people, I wouldn't have to worry, either."

Leana cocked her head, flashed her a look. "Men aren't exactly falling in my lap, you know." Her brow puckered. She pursed her lips, thoughtful. "Assuming, of course," she squeaked, gleams of mischief slanting the lovely, almond-shaped eyes as she looked up at her, "you're talking 'bout lil ole skinny me?"

"Hrump! Skinny my foot! If I had curves like yours, I'd have every man in here falling all over me," Brenda sniffed, looking around Gladys, her favorite restaurant situated in the soul of Chicago's teeming inner-city on Indiana Avenue. The noisy restaurant was packed with men and women of every race and economic class. Renowned for its down-home cooking and friendly efficient service, Gladys's attracted every strata of society—from movie stars and politicians to garbagemen and domestics. Gladys's clientele was accustomed to beautiful women. The appearance of one, who if she were only a few inches taller could have passed for a megabucks model, was nothing remarkable for this crowd. Still, when Leana passed into the dining room, heads turned; eyes, openly stared—some appraising and a few, looking out from female faces, apprehensive—all admiring.

"Hm-m-m," Leana murmured, leaning back in the booth, her eyes closing rapturously as she savored the vinegar and oil dressing on the tossed salad. "Dee-li-cious!"

When Leana saw Brenda's face pinch with traces of envy, it was all she could do to restrain the chuckle gurgling up in her throat. It was Leana's own private joke on her best friend since high school that no matter how much she ate, she remained slender while Brenda's baby fat seemingly settled in her hips—for life.

The truth, if it were to be told, she detested salads. Crunching forever on lettuce leaves, carrot slivers and tomatoes—the mainstay of restaurant salads—made her jaws weary, her teeth ache for something meaty to tear, to pull, to crush. She ordered them only when lunching with Brenda. Brenda, whom she loved like a sister. Brenda, the self-proclaimed matchmaker who arranged blind dates with her thousand and one cousins for her pretty, but incredibly shy friend from school. Funny, popular Brenda who once, after Leana had polished off an extra large order of french fries, shoved the first salad in her face, then to the amusement of the Chicken Shack gang, had with sisterly ruthlessness told her, "You're getting thunder thighs." It was her punishment.

Chuckling to herself, Leana looked up briefly. Her face tightening with fear and surprise, she stiffened in her seat and fell back against the wall when the man came crashing down upon her. His fall broken by an out-thrown arm on the back of her booth, he seized the table's edge for balance with the other. Her hands upraised defensively and flattened against his chest, when he lifted his head and stared, embarrassed, into terrified eyes.

"Excuse. . . ."

Slowly, she released the sharply held breath, all the while gazing into the darkest, most brilliant brown eyes she'd ever seen. Eyes so dark and gleaming with such lovely sable lights, they could be labeled midnight romantic.

". . . . me." His voice was deep, soft with wonder. "I hope I didn't hurt you."

Leana, staring beguiled into his eyes, slowly opened her mouth. "No," she stammered, suddenly conscious he still leaned over her. A stunned radiance had crept into his glance, wandering now over her flushed cheeks, shining jet hair and trim figure. Interested eyes that slid up, and with a magnetism she could neither understand nor deny, engaged hers. The air between them seemed suddenly full of feeling, and for a space, she swam in the mystic depths of those turbulent, romantic eyes. She was pulled from her trance by a loud thumping on the table. Her shattered gaze shifted to Brenda. She was grinning from ear to ear.

"How long have you two kids known each other?"

The question caught her by surprise. It made no sense. Blinking, she stared hard at Brenda who burst into loud, raucous laughter, her mirth joined by smothered outbursts of giggles at nearby tables.

She relaxed back into the booth, dropping her hands from his chest as the man with midnight romantic eyes levered the upper half of his body away from her and stood up slowly. The dark brown-bronze of his face was tinged a deep mahogany red. "Patrice," said Brenda when she finished laughing—talk about thunderstrokes!—"my friend, Leana Claremont."

Leana's eyes grew even larger in her face. "Your . . ."

"Leana," she went on, biting down on her lip to keep from again laughing, "my friend, Patrice Jackson."

"Leana," he murmured with a brief nod of his head. Upright, he was tall, lean and strongly built, with wide hard shoulders and snug, faded jeans that molded to his thighs like a second skin. Standing with his weight balanced evenly on both feet, he regarded her intently from between a smudge of black lashes.

Distracted by the aura of raw, uncompromising masculinity he exuded, a shiver, a warm excitement rippled through her. Leana swallowed. Hard. "Um," she murmured in an unsteady attempt at nonchalance as she looked up into beautiful, solemn brown eyes gleaming through the most sinfully thick black lashes she'd ever seen on a man. "How are you?"

He had also silky black brows. One of them winged now, and the dark finger stroking the mustache above his chiseled upper lip dropping to his side, he relaxed, and a slow smile spread on his face.

"One of these days," he murmured staring at her warmly, "I'll get it together." Looking down suddenly and around, he stooped to retrieve the big leather purse that had tripped him up. A fierce, wanton charge of emotion lanced through Leana. Oh God! What was happening to her? Her eyes narrowed, tilted at the corners, she pressed a hand to her erratically beating heart. This was so unlike her. This . . . instant attraction. This wild fluttering of her heart she thought, watching in confusion his six feet plus of handsome male physique rise.

"Your suitcase, I presume?" he said, Brenda's purse clutched in his hand.

"Put that down!" She snatched the purse from his hand and scooting over, patted the vacated space in the booth beside her. "Sit next to me," she ordered him fondly.

He shook his head. "Like to, but I can't. I'm on my way out of town." His hand climbing back to rub across the soft thickness of his mustache, he turned a luminous, soulful gaze on Leana.

As if all the breath were slammed from her body, Leana sat perfectly still, her eyes cast down, her heart beating like a triphammer.

"I'm glad I caught you here, though," he mumbled, tearing his gaze away from Leana reluctantly to address Brenda. A certain firmness of purpose hardened his jawline. "I won't be able to make it to your party tonight. We're having labor problems again."

Brenda screwed up her face. "Oh, shoot! And it's going to be such a fun time, too!" She looked her disappointment across the table at Leana who was tense, and strangely silent, and her expression cleared. She looked back at Patrice. Her face was full of caprice, "Too bad. Leana's going to be there."

Two pairs of startled brown eyes looked at her.

Patrice hesitated, cleared his throat. "Well, I'll see what I can do. I might be able to come," he said in a deep voice. "For a few minutes."

"Oh no, you have business to attend to," Brenda reminded him quickly, "and it's really too far from the city to just stop in for a few minutes. Maybe we'd better just make it some other time." The sly grin inching its way across her face at his sudden sharp intake of air halted midway when she felt the blunt toe of Leana's coral pump make contact with her ankle.

Although unaware of the silent, if painful, communication beneath the table, Patrice, too, was not amused. He cast her a sharp glance, and Leana was surprised, and not a little unnerved, to see how hard those brilliant eyes could become.

"Don't push it, Brenda," he snarled, heavy brows snapping together. "I'll be there." Dismissing her with a glance, he turned his attention to Leana. As if he found pleasure in just the looking, his gruff expression relaxed and his voice softened. "It was nice meeting you, Leana. I hope to see you at the party."

Afraid to trust her own voice, her lips curled up slightly, and she nodded. Taken with the sweetness of that almost shy smile, so arch and delicately contained in her flawless complexion, his expression leaned to a tenderness so palpable he might well have reached out and touched her. Leana felt a swelling of joy that was almost unbearable fill her chest. Forcing a light, upbeat note to her voice—she could not risk this gorgeous male creature leaving her life; she had to detain him—with a brave little laugh, she asked, "What did you mean when you said you'd get it together?"

When a dark brow lifted briefly, she repeated, her voice feathery and uncertain, "You said one of these days you'll get it together when I said 'how are you'? That was strange." Her voice trailed. Aware of how lame she sounded, yet unaware of just how winsome was the dusky rose flush that darkened her creamy-brown cheeks, she dropped her eyes.

The puzzled look on his face cleared. Playfully, the corners of his mouth lifted. "Oh. Right." His voice dropping to a husky, low-pitched tremor, he leaned toward her, and she again felt a shiver ripple gently through her. "How do you do?"

When dark lashes fluttered up, and her head tipped to one side, he ceded, "That should have been my line."

"Your . . . ?"

"When a person says 'how do you do?' " he explained, regarding her with a quiet soft intensity as if they were only two in the room, "the accepted answer is 'fine, thank you'. My line should have been 'how do you do?' Then, when you responded 'fine', I could have truthfully said . . . you *sure* are.''

"Patrice! Stop ignoring me!" Brenda pouted, school-girl fashion. "You know you can sit for a minute. Come on," she insisted, patting again the space beside her.

"Wish I could," he lamented, then his tone turning matter-of-fact, looked back at Brenda. "But I have to find some help."

"Help?" Leana, the do-gooder, asked quickly. Too quickly. "Uh," she temporized, gently, charmingly smiling, "what kind of help?"

"Security, no doubt." Brenda hrumped.

"Shore you're right!"

The erratic beat of Leana's heart calmed as an idea formed. "If it's security you need, I can probably help," she injected, an excited edge to her voice.

What had started out all wrong had turned into a fortuitous meeting, indeed. Part of her responsibilities as Assistant Director was to develop contacts with business people for the Center's unemployed. A large number of their job seekers were high school dropouts with few job skills, and aside from their immediate families, fewer contacts. For those interested, the Blyden Center had set up a training program for security guards.

"The organization I work for has a training and employment division. Brewster, the supervisor for security training," she explained, warming to the subject and, at the recaptured interest behind those shadowed lashes, continued, "reports to Lawrence who reports to me, so I'm sure I can get you all the security people you might need."

The boyish grin faded, the interest in his eyes replaced by a hard, narrowed look, as if he were assessing something. Something unexpected. Something weighty. . . .

"If you'd like my card . . . ?" Leana began tentatively, sensing in him a kind of drawing back.

As if having resolved the issue, the grin flashed back. "No thanks," he said, breezily dismissive. Looking into his quickly shuttered eyes, she got the unsettling impression that the lightness was forced. "I've already got a couple of men lined up. I appreciate the offer, though. Ladies," he lauded them respectfully, then flashing another, anticipatory smile at Leana, took his leave.

"He's not married."

Leana looked up, startled. "I beg your pardon?" She had been watching the springy lightness of his thread as he negotiated the closely packed tables on his way out.

Brenda gave a whooping laugh.

"And just what party were you talking about?" Leana asked her, suddenly wary. Brenda bore watching. A good friend, but one with terminal foot in mouth condition, she loved her little jokes, especially those Leana had dubbed the 'setting up the victim' kind. Everyone was fair game—including her best friend. That episode in the Chicken Shack was not an isolated event. Even in her best moods. . . .

No, she reflected, as with a slight shifting of her head, she eyed the high-spirited woman across the table from her, *especially* when in a good mood, Brenda would have her fun. Her jokes, no matter how embarrassing at the time, tended to be for the other person's good—as she saw it.

A major part of Brenda's attractiveness lay in her sunny personality. She was so upbeat, she just couldn't seem to get it into her head that some people were sensitive. Possessing a frankness that was at once aggressive and humorous, meddlesome and friendly, she couldn't stand moody people, and didn't mind at all jolting them out of their moods—or their skins. Her idea of how to fix other people's problems was by forcing them into situations where they had either to sink or swim.

Leana remembered one 'blind date' she had not been even aware of. She had been feeling down because one of the boys on the basketball team that she liked and whom she thought liked her, had started going steady with one of the school's cheerleaders. Brenda had become impatient with her lingering funk. To lift her spirits, she suggested they go to the movies. When Leana arrived at Brenda's house, to her embarrassment, Brenda's boyfriend, Maurice, and one of her cousins, Carl, 'just happened' to be there. 'A foursome!' Brenda had cried gleefully. 'Good. Let's go.'

"This is the first I've heard of a party! And stop that silly laughing. Nothing is *that* funny!" she snapped, her lips pursing in disapproval. She turned her head, when Brenda laughed even harder.

It had been a long time since a man had so unnerved her. She thought of the way he had looked at her, wonderingly, intently. There was danger, yet in that unguarded moment, there was promise in the way his gaze had held and warmed hers. Those incredible eyes! Those lips! Full-fleshed, a deep dark purple in a face as nearly dark. They were firm, inviting cushions of sensuousness made for kissing.

Leana's dreamy remembrance was invaded by a soft frown as that 'drawing back' impression came to her mind. She had only wanted to help.

Sure, a little voice smirked. Like when you wanted to

help your old boyfriend Kerry. Kerry who took everything you had to offer and gave so little in return.

Spacing the dresses in her closet neatly, Leana sighed. For all her faults, Brenda had good instincts. She had not disliked Kerry; she had simply expressed her feeling that he was wrong for Leana. And she had guessed Leana's reason for even entertaining romantic notions about such a stuffed shirt.

With the exception of Brenda, all of her old friends were married. She had a good job and was earning more money than she'd ever dreamed. She wore the best clothes, lived at the best address and somewhere along the way, had shed her painful shyness. She was no longer thought of as just a pretty, brown-skinned girl; she had acquired a poise and confidence that forced others to glance her way, then turn back for a second look.

The only regret in her life was that her father had not lived to see the success she had made of herself. It was he who had inspired her to get her education, to strive for the best she could be. Her mother was more traditional. She worried about a daughter who, it seemed to her, would never marry and give her the grandchildren she craved. Somewhere in her mid-twenties, that fear had transferred itself to Leana. So when Kerry came along, she was ready to settle down, get married and have babies.

He wasn't a bad sort. Not really. But God, was he needy! Not ready for Prime Time socially, it fell upon Leana to make Kerry look good before his peers—to smooth the way in uneasy situations, to supply the gentle bon mot that breached awkward pauses in conversation, to take up the slack if the conversation faltered. It was she who introduced him to the better things in life—

restaurants other than Taco Bell, clothes that didn't come off somebody's rack. But although he had acquired a surface polish, Kerry remained in a fundamental way, penurious. She had tried to overlook it, for he was stable and she felt, would be a good father; and even if somewhat critical, a faithful husband.

The last straw had come when they were dining at an exclusive Gold Coast restaurant. Mr. and Mrs. Thomas owned a manufacturing company that was expanding. She was wooing them in a business capacity, as well as socially. Looking over the leather-wrapped menu, Kerry's eyes had bulged, and to her humiliation, countermanded her order. He had insisted to the waiter, and before the Thomases, that the lobster was ridiculously overpriced and *she* would have instead, the six ounce steak.

'Cheap, cheap, cheap!' Leana thought, experiencing a resurgence of annoyance. And that lack of generosity extended to his lovemaking. He had almost succeeded in making her think there was something wrong with her. Almost. She smiled. Good ole Brenda. She'd sensed something was wrong and wormed it out of her. It was Brenda who pointed out after listening to her story that as her giving and passionate nature extended to the bedroom, so did Kerry's cheapness. They were totally mismatched, she reflected sadly.

But this man! Why just one look at that mustache indicted there was nothing prissy about him. Thick and utterly masculine, there was nothing, she felt certain, that made a man look more masculine than a mustache. His was lustrous, coal-black. As black as the kinky, square-cut hair springing from his high, wide forehead. He excited her. Everything about him excited her, stirred up in her feelings that Kerry would blanch at as wicked. Just thinking about him made her heart beat faster.

She had never really been satisfied by a man—not heart and soul satisfied; certainly not by Kerry. Was he the one who could fulfill her craving for love, love in all its textures, measures and dimensions—great noble love? He certainly had the body for it, she mused wryly, her thoughts turning earthy as she recalled how flexed, how taut and hard the wall of his chest had felt, the wild beating of his heart beneath her fingertips.

Closing the white louvered doors, Leana shook her head mildly, as if exasperated with herself. What strange desires arise in the human heart. . . . Feeling an impatient desire to get it on, she picked up and flung round her throat a slender silk scarf of the same drop dead red as her dress, its richly ruffled tails floating full-length down her back.

So you're attracted, she said to herself fliply, throwing up her chin as she gazed upon the enchanting picture she made on three sides. You're not some awkward sixteen year old going on a blind date. And he's not the first man you've ever been attracted to, either. So he's got strong white teeth, midnight romantic eyes and a body that won't wait. You have poise, confidence. You're a mature, sophisticated woman of the world. Everyone says so. A second later, she found herself turning, a sudden quivering in her stomach as she stared at the closet door.

Chapter Three

Brenda's family home was just outside Momence, a largely black farming community a couple hours drive south of Chicago. Turning off I-55 at the Kankakee exit, Leana drove the short distance to the outskirts of town, then turned and wound her way down an undulating band of state highway past miles of dense, golden-spiked corn until she saw shimmering in the distance, lights in jewel-tone colors, glitter into the night.

The house was built by Brenda's parents in the late 1940s when Mr. Martin, an inventor, sold a patent to the Sears and Roebuck catalog company. Sears, Jewish, and Roebuck, an African-American, were one of the great success stories in what was then thought of as the 'melting pot' of America. Inspired by their example, Mr. Martin had thought to merge his talents and profits from the patent with a similarly talented Yugoslav immigrant, but once he saw the blueprints for the house, he fell in love, pouring all his profits into its construction.

And it was well worth it, Leana thought, as the ten year old Mercedes slipped effortlessly through the twi-light onto her destination. She remembered the first time she saw it. It was a house of distinction, with rooms that flowed one into the other. Designed by a naturalist of the Frank Lloyd Wright School, sheets of clear and beveled glass with abstracts of grasses native to the Midwest were coordinated into the overall architectural design. Panes of artglass in the shades of nature—lime green, mocha, red, golden yellow and burnt orange found in ceilings, behind plaster frieze boards at the tops of ceilings, in skylights, alternating with clear glass panes on every door—were carried throughout the interior. The strong color motif in the stained woodwork, as well as the appeal and aesthetic beauty of the artglass, distinguished the house such that there was no need for pictures on the walls. Indeed, Leana reflected, pictures on the walls would stand out as garish, clash with the simplicity of the artglass, and detract from the coordinated symmetry of the house's design. Although the family no longer lived there on a full-time basis, the deadly sameness of country life soon wearing on the city-bred people's nerves, an elderly couple maintained the house and the twenty remaining acres.

Leana pulled up into the gravelly driveway before the large fourteen room farmhouse surrounded by gardens, the painted, fired glass in its windows glimmering in the moonlight. An aged, gnarled elm, thick with summer leaves, flanked the traditional red gambrel-roofed barn with big overhangs that had been converted into a guesthouse, beyond which stretched a vast field of corn.

Picking her way across the uneven footing of white-speckled gravel in the grosgrained heels, she passed up the walkway lined with johnny-jumpups and petite, ghostly white yarrow. At the leaded glass inset on the handsome oak door, its goldenrod abstract evoking warm memories, Leana pressed the chimes and waited.

Wearing a white frilled apron over a gray gabardine uniform that matched her steel gray wig, Mrs. Eulalia Benson, the cook and female half of the house-maintenance team, opened the door to admit her, her face dimpling in welcome.

"Little Leana Claremont," she cried with arms outstretched. "Come heah, chile!"

Falling into her embrace with a wide grin, Leana hugged her old friend tightly. When they parted, Miss Eulalia as she was called, took both of her hands and showed her into the foyer. Stopped in the brightly lit one and a half story anteroom, she looked around and smiled, a slow impressed smile.

The earthy hand of Brenda, the weekend gardener, showed in the abundant and varied floral arrangements that decorated the spacious foyer. Stands of dried flowers with thin spike stalks splayed artfully beneath a quadrangular chandelier, its muted, multi-colored panes glittering romantic jeweled light wherever their reflections fell, welcomed her to the hall. The handsome staircase to her right, an imposing cantelevered sweep railed in heavy red oak, climbed to a thirty foot long, ceiling-high skylight of artglass behind the musician's balcony on the second floor.

"You've been away too long!" Miss Eulalia chided maternally. "I told Brenda if she gives one more party and don't make you come, I'm not working it. So there!" Her porous brown cheeks plumping out cherublike, she beamed her a warm smile.

"Oh, Miss Eulalia," Leana moaned blissfully. "I've missed you!"

"It has been some time," the kindly-faced woman nodded, gratified by her response. Pushing wire-rimmed glasses with a forefinger up her soft round nose, flattened slightly at the corners, Miss Eulalia looked her over in a critical, but admiring way. "I always did think you was the prettiest little thing, but now," she murmured, shaking her old head solemnly, "you has turned into a *real* beauty!"

Leana's eyes misted over. She had been too long from Miss Eulalia, she thought, recalling how welcome she had made the shy, serious teenager she had been feel in her first forays into the rich people's home. Miss Eulalia had taken Leana under her wing and, like a doting mother hen, clucked over her comfort. It was Miss Eulalia to whom she had turned for succor when she felt intimidated or out of place within the big and boisterous Martin household. She touched her cheek now to the elderly woman's dearly.

"Thank you, Miss Eulalia. You have no idea how much that means coming from you."

"I remember when you first come here. You shore ain't the shy one now!" she said, giving her strapless, red ruffled-tailed dress, a thick sidelong glance.

Leana rolled her eyes heavenward and sighed. "Boy, was I shy! I remember thanking my mother for making me take Trigonmetry. Otherwise, Brenda and I would never have gotten to be friends." She laughed, charmingly apologetic. "We were the only two girls in class."

"Girls ain't no good in those kinda classes. I tried to tell Miss Vinta that, but she wouldn't listen. Best Brenda ever got was a "C"," she added with the satisfaction of the one who knew all along.

Leana smiled indulgently. She didn't have the heart to remind her that she had earned a ''B''.

''Well, it shore is good seeing you again, Leana. Miss Vinta told me how good yall are doing in your job and all. Said she knew you had it in you all along.''

''Well, thank you for remembering me, Miss Eulalia,'' she said, lifting her head as sounds of muted laughter drifted with the mingled scents of hair-dressing and perfume wafting from a crush of warm bodies through the partially opened doors to her left. Taking her leave and moving in that direction, Leana turned on impulse and gave the stout, elderly woman another big hug. ''Oh!'' she squealed, ''I just love seeing you again!''

''You just gone on and have a good time, now,'' Miss Eulalia scolded, dashing a sudden wetness from her cheek. She shooed Leana off. ''Gone on with yourself, now. I'll bring you your special drink, so don't you go far.''

''Thank you, Miss Eulalia,'' Leana called as the old lady scuttered off, swiping at another tear sliding down one plump cheek.

Passing through one of a pair of French doors, several of its panes decorated with the artglass motif, Leana stepped down into the family room. Stained in earth-tones of burnt orange, lime green and brown, there was a festal haze to the country classy room that sloped 18 feet upwards to where a skylight, inlaid with goldenrod abstracts on lime and mocha borders, loomed over a wood-burning fireplace over six feet tall. Her eyes sweeping the rustic, sunken interior, Leana saw more flowers from the gardens—delphinium, phlox, and daylilies in bursts of orange and yellow—set in tall vases and disposed randomly with Queen Anne's Lace, Black-eyed Susan, Ironweed and other prairie wildflowers about the room.

Paused on the bottom step, she cast an appraising eye over the party, already in full blast and, as it was being thrown by Brenda, a guaranteed success. 'Ole matchmaker Brenda,' she thought with a gentle inward smile at what she deemed a proliferation of singles. Some, she knew, would be staying overnight. As her best friend, Leana had agreed when Brenda insisted she stay the weekend and act as unofficial hostess for the duration. As a result, she brought no date. But, she saw to her satisfaction, it was unnecessary.

A glitter of expensive jewels sparkled in the gentle chandelier light. One guest, splendidly gowned and dread-locked, wore a jewel in her nose. The party luminaries crowded the room, sitting or standing in clusters, sampling hor d'ouerves and getting acquainted. The majority came as couples, but Leana knew that a large number were 'looking'. She shook her head fondly. Would Brenda never learn to mind her own business?

Leana hovered near the front entrance hall with a brandy snifter filled with weak tea because she did not drink. Leana accepted Miss Eulalia's recommendation with a smile. Gently swirling the glass in her hand, she continued her idle survey of the party.

A dark, petite woman, slim and startling beautiful in a black lace sheath that exposed a delicately boned back, seemed overwhelmed by a blond giant of a man with watery blue eyes with flabby pouches beneath them. Prevented from bellying up even closer to the woman by his capacious paunch and the champagne glass she clutched in long thin fingers protectively before her, Leana recognized him as Christopher Volk, a German businessman-friend of Brenda's father. Her lashes lowered briefly. Chris was trice married—once to an East Indian woman; his last two wives were African-American. He was currently divorced.

Her glance shifted to a far corner of the room where a tiny, octagonal pool, built into the floor and floating gardenias in a two foot basin, was the focal point of an intimate conversational grouping. Sitting on one of the stained oak armchairs around the pool—its gently running waters fed through a pipe behind a backlighted glass aquarium set in the wall which lent light to the corner and showcased colorful goldfish swimming—was a striking woman in a peplum evening suit, the wrist length sleeves of her white taffeta jacket puffed at the shoulder, her teal blue skirt with a long side split just brushing the tops of her insteps. Smoking a cigarette, one shapely leg curled underneath her, she looked alternately at her companion, a thin intense man whose earnest eyes gazed at her longingly from behind thick glasses, and then thoughtfully, at the water in the basin.

Leana stood there a long time, studying them. Sensitized by the drama unfolding before her, she soon wrenched her eyes away, feeling restless, as well as neglectful of her hostess duties. Moving purposefully into the party arena, greeting old friends and throwing smiling glances at strangers, dusty old dreams of a man, strong and brave, who would sweep her off her feet, into his arms in wild, glorious abandonment, tugged at her heart like a hunger. 'Will a man ever look at me like that?' she wondered wistfully as she walked the room slowly, nodding, smiling, occasionally lifting a languid hand and waving. Kerry certainly had not. He was too self-absorbed, too controlled, his desires too anemic.

She had not been joking when she mentioned to Miss Eulalia that bit of information about her mother making her take Trigonometry. Muh-dear had the idea that the smart boys, the ones going places, who would be good providers, took the tough classes. It was precisely because most parents felt as Miss Eulalia that girls were not mentally equipped for the 'hard' mathematics that Muh-dear had pushed her into Trig in the belief that her socially backward daughter would have no competition for such boys. Her displeasure when she learned that one of the most popular girls in school was in Leana's class quickly disappeared when she and Brenda became friends. When Miss Vinta, Brenda's mother, urged Leana to make the most of her intelligence and go to college, Muh-dear had concurred. Only Muh-dear didn't give a fig about Leana using her brain—boys who would earn lots of money and be big shots went to college. She was sure that with her help, Leana would snag a good prospect.

Leana's father, a construction day laborer, had been killed in an accident on the job. The company claimed it was his own fault, a case of negligence. Intimidated by the men in dark suits and carrying briefcases who drawfed her tiny apartment, Muh-dear had signed a piece of paper promising not to sue the company in exchange for burial costs and $10,000. Forced into menial jobs to support them, Muh-dear, as pretty as Leana and with little formal schooling, but as much native intelligence, had determined her daughter would marry well.

'Poor Muh-dear,' she thought, smiling admiringly at a woman in an electric-blue satin-back jacket with portrait collar, posing such that a glimpse of well-shaped thigh in shimmery hose peeked through the sequinned slit of her miniskirt, 'how terrible it must be to have to live through one's child'.

Leana saluted her mother with the brandy snifter silently. 'I tried Muh-dear. I'm sorry, but I did try,' she reflected, smiling sadly into her drink glass as she thought of Kerry. She had no intention of following in Chris Volk's footsteps, marrying people for whatever reason, then getting rid of them when they proved boring, worrisome, inconvenient, or whatever.

Divorce was not for her. Indulging herself briefly in a fantasy of being held in two strong arms that would cherish her forever, the man who fell into her lap in Glady's Restaurant flitted into her mind. And hung there. Him of the black form-fitting Tee and tight faded jeans . . .

Leana looked up quickly, a flush rosying the dark honied-hue of her suddenly tingling face. Twirling the stem of her glass with an increasing zeal, she looked across the room with darting eyes and a nervous smile. As the erratic beating of her heart abated—no one seemed to have noticed—her attention was arrested by similarly searching eyes at the open French doors.

Finding his target, the tall, trim man came from the foyer, walked to within a few feet of a group of bejeweled, ebony-throated women and pleated-shirt men surrounding Marie Henderson, owner of the Henderson Group, a private investment firm, and stood there, staring toward her. Lowering the glass and holding it about the curved bottom absently in the palm of her hand, Leana watched as the model-thin woman, the silver metallic gown plunging and glittering with her every movement, glided from the small gathering to meet him. He held out a hand and the jeweled fingers of her own clasped his lightly. Wordlessly, they began to dance.

A small sweet smile pulled at the corners of Leana's mouth. During the brief episode, once their eyes met, they never broke contact. By sight, by heat, they felt out each other. It was so romantic. Almost as romantic, she thought, feeling light-headed and suddenly dizzy, as midnight . . .

"Excuse me," the seductive masculine voice coming from behind her, asked, "May I have this dance?"

Leana's breath tangled in her throat. She turned, looked up soft-eyed. "Uh, yes. Of course," she murmured, staring into the tan, clean-shaven face. Stifling her disappointment, she set the glass on top of a tall planter beside her.

The five man band had stepped down and a slow song was playing. Reaching a quick arm around her, Leana felt herself being drawn, and as if in protest, to the highly polished dancefloor.

Her head held high on her slender neck, Leana betrayed none of her inner turmoil. He had said he would come! Resting her hand on the stranger's shoulder lightly, she schooled her features to serenity, went with her partner's lead and the flow of the music. 'Maybe he's just late. He had said he was going out of town. But for what?' she wondered, showing none of her agitation as her lips curled in recognition of another couple moving up beside them. A small frown crossed her soft brow. That detective business was all a crock. A T.V. fantasy! Just like her fantasy of a strong man who would cherish and protect her with his life, if necessary. . . .

The fluffy ebony curls on her head bounced as she shook her head to clear it. The man who said his name was Otis King was speaking to her and staring at her as though she were a choice piece of candy.

"I said I noticed you standing by yourself. Are you here alone?"

"I'm acting as Brenda's hostess for tonight." Leana replied with polite detachment, "And yourself?"

"Available," he smirked, his hazel eyes lingering over her lissome body in the suggestive slip dress meaningfully at song's end. It was nothing she had not guessed. Throughout the entirety of the dance, he had thrown off vibes of interest as unmistakable as the fact that he was on the make. Before they left the floor, he managed to convey to her that he was single, drove a BMW, owned a computer software firm called—what else?—King's Software, and since he found her attractive, that they should go somewhere to talk—somewhere private.

Leana's lashes lifted to the man whose ego was the size of a small house, but with arms only slightly bigger than hers. "I'm sure you'll find whomever it is you seek. As you can see, Otis," she said, turning impressively, a flattened palm sweeping the party, "there are lots of lovely ladies here. Please excuse me," she smiled, already moving back to the drink she'd left on the planter.

Leana suddenly became very popular. She turned down two more offers to dance while she scanned the room, seeking out *his* face, for she had the disquieting sense that if he didn't come, she would die from the ache of it; failing death, to be made useful, for only by immersing her consciousness in the problems of others could she relieve the inward tension at his absence, put a brake to her yearning thoughts.

Evoking an air of faded beauty, a woman of late mid-dleage, nicely dressed in a yellow dress pinned at one shoulder by a green topaz brooch, looked lonely. Fluttering in a corner, a smile pasted on her lips and a drink glass in one hand, there was such a vulnerable quality to the woman that Leana's heart went out to her. At one time, that could have been her. Taking her hostess duties as seriously as she took her job as Assistant Director of the Edward Blyden Center, she picked up her drink, and red spiked heels sinking into the deep pile of the patterned carpet edging the dancefloor, sauntered over to her.

"Hi!" she said, making her voice bright, and because the woman was short, smiling down on her. Although she looked in control, even aloof, Leana was not fooled. She knew shyness when she saw it. Swirling the weak tea in the snifter with a rotary motion, she looked out over the crowd and observed, "Nice party, isn't it?"

When the woman in saffron smiled her agreement, Leana went on dreamily, "but then, Brenda always throws good parties. Oh, excuse me!" she exclaimed warmly, as if just remembering her manners. "I'm Leana Claremont."

"Martha Eggleston."

"Pleased to meet you, Martha." A scent of Arpege drifting with the tinge of apology in her manner up to her. Leana's voice was friendly, full of warm welcome, and as she anticipated, the little woman responded in kind.

"I'm pleased to meet you, too," Martha replied with a smile, and the smile was genuine. "How do you know Brenda?" she asked, her voice hesitant as she attempted to keep up her end of the conversation.

Leana laughed. "Oh, Brenda and I are friends from way back!" Just then she saw the subject of their conversation advancing upon them. Brenda's full figure flattered by a lovely satin gown with drifting turquoise panels, she held the arm of an elderly, short-necked gentleman with dark, piercing eyes beneath an intimidating pair of gray tufted brows.

"Martha!" Brenda called out before she even reached them. "I'm so glad you came! This old flirt, Arthur," she said, smiling coyly at the man she pulled forward beside her, "has been playing with me, talking about how pretty I am. My great, unparalleled beauty. I thought I'd introduce him to a real beauty just to keep him from making me blush!"

While Martha looked down self-consciously into her drink, Arthur was non-plussed. "As dark as you are?" He sniffed. "I should hope not!"

Leana's brows rose. Brenda laughed. "Martha! Help me!" she cried, falling upon her with an air of hopelessness. "He's one of a kind. A truthful man!"

Martha smiled up at him tentatively. "I can think of nothing more refreshing than a man who tells the truth."

For the first time, Arthur smiled, a little crooked smile that turned up one corner of his mouth and popped out an Indian-high cheekbone. He made her a courtly bow. "Thank you, my dear."

Brenda chuckled, looking pleased. Moving away unobtrusively, she looked around, then called back, her voice lunging at her, "Leana! Come help me find where Miss Eulalia hid the caviar. The Andersons are positively screaming for it."

Leana turned her head, a frown puckering her soft brow. "Oh, yes. Yes, of course," she managed. Taking her leave of Martha and Arthur, who seemed not to notice, much less to care about her departure, she followed Brenda. "He's kind of . . ." she struggled for the word, ". . . *strong,* isn't he? I mean, Martha's so *shy!*"

"Why do you think I invited them?" Brenda replied in her best professional match-maker's voice. "Martha is shy. She needs a strong man, one who's not afraid to make the first move. Even carry the ball, if necessary."

Leana was unconvinced. "You sure he won't steamroll her? She's a nice woman, Brenda," she objected.

Turning her head, Brenda emitted a dramatic sigh. "Leana, Leana, Leana," she said with weary repetition. "Are you forgetting my cousin, Carl?"

Leana started, then, her fingers caressing the wide bottom of her glass, smiled. "We did get along well, didn't we?"

"Leave the match-making to us experts, girlfriend. Okay?" Leana smiled at the tone of professional disapproval in her voice. But when in her conceit, Brenda, like the cat that got into the cream, purred, "After all, I did tell you Mr. Right would fall in your lap at Gladys', didn't I? By the way, where the heck is he?" Leana found herself rubbed on the raw.

"You're not 'Hello Dolly', you know," she said, unable to prevent the slight tartness that crept into her voice as carefully, she set her glass on the silver tray of a passing waiter. "People *are* capable of meeting, dating and falling in love without your help.

"And furthermore," she went on, hardening her chin, and already bothered by his absence with a testy surge of resentment at Brenda for pointing it out, "you said no such thing. You said something about *men* falling in my lap, but *nothing* about any 'Mr. Right' doing *anything!*"

Brenda's only response was to raise her brows and stare at her in a supercilious, pitying sort of way. When she sighed and brushed an imaginary speck from the immaculate bodice of her gown, Leana steamed over.

''I, for one,'' she declared in a low voice tight with indignation, making a sudden sweeping turn to face her, ''couldn't care less if I *never* see him again!'' And to prove her immunity, she proceeded to do the most childish, ungracious thing she'd done since high school. Folding her arms over her chest and rolling her eyes, she sucked her teeth.

Brenda's shout of laughter caused heads to turn. When she bent nearly double, hooting herself to tears, jabbing now with a shaky finger at a point behind Leana, Leana's jaws tightened, and her teeth clamped together. Her hands had dropped to her sides and were curled to tight little fists when she felt the heat of a hand at her waist, sensed the big body beside her. Rearing her head angrily, her hot eyes flickered, widened and turned limpid, the pupils suddenly enormous as she looked into the dark, arresting face of Patrice.

''I like a good joke as well as the next one,'' he said, an insinuating smile tugging the corners of his handsome mouth. ''How about letting me in on it?''

Standing there looking self-possessed and prosperous in dark evening clothes, his body yet strong, straight, and as virile as she remembered, when those midnight romantic eyes took an admiring turn over her face, the air seemed suddenly turbulent with scents—pungent wildflowers, a cacophony of perfumes, his uncompromising maleness. Her anger unraveling, dissolving in a curl of heat in the pit of her stomach, spreading rapidly to her every extremity. Leana, feeling giddy, and too full of emotion to speak, smiled weakly. When his chiseled, full-fleshed lips pulled slowly into an answering grin, the first wet thrill buckled her knees, and her dark eyes smoked.

Tears popping, Brenda laughed even harder when Leana, visibly shaken, passed a nervous tongue over suddenly dry lips.

Drawn by her uncontrolled merriment, other party-goers gathered round. Leana's expression was composed of two parts embarrassment and one part outrage when finding Brenda's mirth contagious, they laughed along with her. Clutching her sides and gasping for air, Brenda's little tremoloes of laughter pealed up loud, robust, and an ironic arch lifted the left of Patrice's black brows.

Bending to Leana's ear, for he was indeed better than six feet, he suggested quietly, "I think she has enough company."

Her consternated gaze locked on Brenda, Leana's full red lips tightened. "I think you're right, Mr. Jackson. Excuse us, please?" she inquired cuttingly of Brenda, who howled.

"Do you know where we're going?" he asked. Skirting around dancing couples and shouldering his way through the crush of others who would separate them, he caught up with Leana, her footsteps quick and tense as she forged, straight-backed and furious, through the floral-scented corridor.

"Yes!" she retorted, fiercely. "Away from that *crazy* woman!" Stopping in a mosaic-tiled alcove, momentarily deserted, before a bank of doors open to the terrace, she whirled about to face him. Her color was high and emotion charged her voice.

"You know what I'm going to do? I'm going to turn LaDonna loose on her! Ha! She can handle her! You should have seen her yesterday. She wasn't laughing *then!* Why do you think I hired LaDonna in the first place? She's only nineteen years old—I could have hired someone with *real* experience for my secretary. At the least," she sputtered, LaDonna's flashy outfits flitting through her brain, "a more *conservative* dresser. But no! I chose LaDonna because she reminded me of my so-called *best* friend, *Brenda!*"

There was a huffy, breath-catching pause where Patrice regarded her in a detached sort of way, full of wonderment.

"Well?" she demanded of him hotly, lifting an impertinent chin to gaze up at him.

"Um . . . ?" he mumbled, blinking rapidly. He smiled suddenly. Disarmingly. "Excuse me. I was looking at your face. Your cheeks," he touched her flushing skin gently, "reminded me of old roses. What was it you were saying?"

Her soft lips parted as anger fled her instantly. Who was this man, Patrice, that by his mere touch the heat of her anger cooled, the rage pounding her heart stilled, his brushing touch gentle, so soothing it washed her with a peace she could neither understand nor deny? Feeling vulnerable, she flinched away from his hand; turned back searchingly, and looking into the magnetic beauty of his eyes, was lost. Swallowing a sudden lump in her throat, she lowered her lashes. Self-consciously, she muttered, "Thank you."

Tucking a hand under her chin and tilting it, turning

her averted face to his, Patrice stared into her half-closed gaze. "Thank *you*," he said, his voice a husky, soft tremor, "for staying so sweet."

His dark face lowering, his lips were only a hair's breath from hers when Leana drew back, the muscles of her stomach tensing. Things were moving too fast. She was an experienced woman, yes, but not an easy one. Flattening her palms against his chest, she lightly pushed. His glazed eyes narrowed, hardened, and when a heavy black brow quirked, she unconsciously shifted her weight, turned her back against his all of a sudden overwhelming masculine presence.

Soft strains of music floated out from the party, eddied through the hallway to reach their ears, breaking the silence that descended upon them. An old standard, 'Moonlight Becomes You', sung by Johnny Mathis, was playing. Finding its way through the French doors of the terrace, silvery moonlight spilt into the secluded alcove, shimmered in Leana's hair, and set her red dress ablaze. Tracing with enthralled eyes the silvery effulgence along the graceful curve of her back and breathing in her perfume, Patrice thought the sentiments issuing from Johnny's throat in round dulcet tones, apt. There was a gentler note in his voice, a softening of the night-dark eyes when extending his hand, he asked, "May I have this dance?"

Lifting her gaze from the floor tremulously, she turned, and as if plucked from a stupor, nodded numbly. With dreamlike slowness, she crossed the floor to be with him. Their eyes engaged, their fingers enjoined, his arm drew her near.

They danced cheek to cheek, their bodies pressed close, across the mosaic tiled floor. The master's dreamy voice a warbling caress to her ears, Leana felt weightless as a feather, graceful as a ballerina as Patrice whirled her about the narrow hallway, through the French double doors onto the flagstone terrace.

The night was warm, and having winged its way into the star-spangled heavens, the moon beamed its sheen on their entwined, slowly moving bodies even after the sensuousness of Johnny's voice had for long minutes been replaced by the lulling love calls of crickets in the night.

Chapter Four

Swayed pliantly into him, Patrice turned her in a gliding two-step into the deeper shadows along the edge of the terrace. The lilting, sensuous voice and lyrics reaching out to bind them to each other, to the night, to a whole cosmos of feeling and emotion, Leana closed her eyes, and with her soft length curved gently against him, breathed deeply.

Spinning her to a halt gently, Patrice wedged a knee of his leg between her thighs, and his body tensing, pressed forward, arching her supple spine back as if to command her in a dip. Secure in his strong arms, she was cradled against his lean hardness, ready to respond, when she felt his lips touch her neck, and the strong beat of his heart treble up wildly against her breast. His nostrils distended, breathing in her perfume, the skin on her back tingled, and a sweet ache trembled her sex. When, his mustache brushing against her ear, he murmured, "Moonlight really does become you," Leana shuddered, and her arms wrapped sinuously around his neck.

Tightening his grasp, he held her in his arms tenderly, stroking her back, twirling her slowly about the flagstone terrace while a warm night breeze riffled through her hair and billowed softly the ruffled tails of her dress.

"Patrice," she whispered, her voice tinny with emotion when just beneath the small garnet hoop in her ear, he kissed her neck, "the music has stopped." Aroused by the hard strength of his thighs riding her leg and the thick bulge in his trousers that lodged against her hip, when she heard his voice in her ear whisper softly, "Trust me, baby. Please, always. Trust me . . ." with a sweetly responsive gladness, she pressed her cheek longingly against his. But when she relaxed in his arms, as if to pull away, Patrice demurred.

"No," he muttered thickly. Strong brown fingers curved behind her neck while the hand possessive at her waist drew her closer. "Not yet. Not before . . ."

The last of his words were lost in her mouth as gathering up her soft, slender body into his arms, he kissed her. Kissed her with a sensuality so seductive that she felt weak with the intensity of it. His deep purple lips on her soft red mouth richer than wine. His kiss was deep, drugging, and Leana succumbed longer than she ought. She knew she should pull back—she was giving a false impression—but when an anguished trembling started up between her thighs, to assuage the ache, she tightened her arms around his neck and squirmed even closer into him.

Never had she been kissed like this. *Never.*

The demands of the kiss lessened. His hands clasping her shoulders lightly, his tongue rasped out, nudged the clinging softness of her lips gently, and Leana trembled. An alarm sounding in the haze of her desire. So much this soon, this was not her style. She wrenched away her face. Her neck arching back, as she panted shudderingly for air, he kissed the hollow in her throat where the pulse fluttered wildly, beneath one ear and then again the other. When she sighed and laid her head on his shoulder weakly, he lifted her short black curls away and kissed the nape of her neck, moved his lips back to her throat, the tender underside of her chin, all the while caressing gently the feverish skin on her back, on her tingling shoulders.

Swayed limply into him, every fibre of her being weakened, when he slipped a hand between them, cupped a taut breast, and with an exquisite tenderness, caressed her ripe fullness in the palm of his hand, Leana breathed slowly, as if she might faint, in soft panting gasps.

Oh, God. She clutched at his broad shoulders to keep herself upright. Dear God.

Her heart racing madly, her dark lashes drifted with slow, agonized pleasure over her half-closed eyes. But when his head dipped and she felt the warm wet of his mouth close over a stiffened nipple through the thin silk of her dress, the sensuous fog lifted and her eyes flew open.

Oh God, no! This was wrong. All wrong. Mustering the last of her reserves as the whipping heat of his tongue flicked her defenceless little nipple to pebble hardness, she spread her hands against his shoulders.

"Don't, Patrice," she begged him, her voice quavering. "Please, don't."

Shaking with passion, his dangerously exciting tongue stilled behind parted lips, he lifted his face to stare into tortured eyes that beseeched his restraint. His own eyes luminous pools of desire, she could feel the intensity of the passion that shook him as, relinquishing her waist, he surrendered with a sigh.

They strolled through the soft moonlight to a rose garden where damask teas and brilliant gloriosas twined in regal profusion over ghost-white frames. Patrice slowed before one such trellis, extravagant with pink pale blooms. Reaching out to examine one delicately furled blossom, its petals curled in sweetly on itself, there was a thoughtful look on his face as he noted: "Innocent-looking, isn't it? And yet, in its own quiet way, it's as showy as any of the red ones." He brought the flower to his nose, his bold nostrils distending as he breathed deeply of its fragrance. His lips pulled in a soft smile. "Smells sweet like you, too."

Flicking a curl in place with a negligent finger and looking off, Leana could at that moment have kicked herself for not wearing the pink cocktail dress.

They moved on a few steps more when he stopped before another trellis encrusted with roses of a vainer color, giving off an even more exquisite fragrance than the last. Carefully, he plucked from one of the thorny stems a magnificent, fire engine red bloom, its fleshy petals enfolding in velvet the exotic core of its essence.

"Moonlight and roses become you," he murmured, a stirring of warmth in his eyes. Taking her hand, he pressed it into Leana's palm. "Red roses." Recapturing the hand curled about the flower and lifting it to his lips, he kissed, then pressed his nose into the rose, his nostrils flaring wide as he breathed in its bouquet with such passion and fervor that she felt her knees buckle; when his olfactory senses satiated, and his lips moved up to caress the tender inside of her wrist, her pulse fluttered up madly and her legs turned to spaghetti.

Looking down, to cover her emotion, Leana smiled. "Thank you," she whispered moistly, touching with one finger the extravagant bloom gently. "It's lovely."

Resting a proprietary hand on her waist, he squired her to a wrought iron divan, its filigrees delicately forged at the back in the shape of leaves, at the edge of the garden. Soft strains of music and a low humming revelry floating from the party through the open French double doors of the terrace to their ears, he drew her down to the padded seats where they sat in comfortable silence, their bodies touching.

Breathing in the bracing freshness of country air, the strong earth smells, the woodsmoke scent of his after-shave, when he eased an arm around her and embraced a bared shoulder, Leana settled against him with a sigh of contentment, wondering how she had existed for so long without him.

Bending his head, he kissed her, first against the temple and then, warmly on her cheek. When she nuzzled her head beneath his chin and his tongue darted out, traced intimately the shape of her ear, she closed her eyes and breathed deeply of woodsmoke.

"Hmmm," she murmured, tipping her head back on his shoulder. The cool palm of her hand stroking the hard line of his jaw, she gazed tenderly into midnight romantic eyes. "Who are you, Mr. Man?" she asked softly, wonderingly, as if she had never before seen him.

"Patrice Lumumba Jackson," he murmured, kissing her hair, her eyes, the tip of her nose. "31 year old son of Mattie and Crawley Jackson. And you?"

"Where'd you get that name? Patrice La . . . La. . . ."

". . . Lumumba," he intoned deeply, and they both laughed.

Shifting his posture upright to a more comfortable position—the mood was broken, but not that painful fist Indian-wrestling his groin—he informed her. "He was a revolutionary. My father, among others, was a great admirer of Lumumba. He was assassinated for trying to free South Africa. They say on some parts of the continent, that as long as someone says your name, you never die. My father named me after him."

Leana looked at him indulgently. "Patrice Lumumba. There! He lives!"

"And me?" Tilting his head in order to see the face she pressed to his shoulder, a slant of moonlight threw the bold romanticism of his face into sharp relief. His dark regard unwavering upon the honied perfection of her features, she felt again the mystic wells of intensity in the man. Before, his arm like a band of steel around her waist, she had felt frightened by the eroticism in his masculinity. Now with that same arm pulled protectively around her shoulders, she felt only contentment.

"Always," she breathed, feeling her heart tremble.

Caressing with thoughtful eyes the glowing luminosity that was her face, gently he insinuated, "There's only one *real* way to ensure immortality, you know."

Leana opened her lovely orbs wide, and although she saw the seduction in his face, and heard it in his voice, her tone held innocent surprise. "Really?"

Patrice regarded her for a long moment before his tautened features relaxed, and he smiled again. "And who are you, Miss Lady?" he asked, adopting a lighter tone.

"I am Leana Claremont, and," she replied pertly, "I

invoke a woman's perogative to keep my age to my-self!''

A lazy brow lifted. ''That old, huh?''

''My mother is Mrs. Alfreda Claremont,'' she con-tinued, ignoring the crack, ''and my father, Lazarus, after whom I was named, if you can believe *that,*'' she grinned, then her face softening, added, ''is deceased. He was killed in an accident when I was 11.''

Patrice took one of her hands in his tenderly.

''It's okay.'' Leana shook her head at the sympathetic gesture. Unconsciously, she squared her slim shoulders. With the moon throwing shadow and illumination across their soft casings, Patrice thought she looked in-credibly young, terribly vulnerable and very brave.

She turned the conversation back to his family. ''What about your parents?''

He answered immediately. ''Divorced. My mother got the house, the car, alimony and me.'' At the odd look that crossed her face, his lips twisted in a wry, humorless smile.

Her hand, locked in his, Leana squeezed the larger one briefly. A dear expression covered her face.

''No sweat, baby,'' he said, his tone again flippant, but he dropped her hand quickly, as if her touch burned.

But as with Brenda, she was true to her breed. Thus, professional do-gooder that she was, Leana, who could never leave well enough alone, asked, ''Why did they divorce?''

Patrice made a funny noise in his throat, almost a laugh, but with a bitter edge. ''When he married my mother,'' he explained, ''my old man could barely write his name. But he was ambitious, so when he wanted to go into business for himself, my mom, who was a high school graduate, taught him how to read and write. And since he didn't know anything about records and ledgers, she did all the books for the business, as well.'' His voice was intense, and in the small silence that ensued, Leana noticed that his hands had clenched themselves into fists.

"What kind of business?''

Patrice regarded her with a curiously intent look. Black brows knitted over tilted brown eyes, her voice was soft, like summer rain; it washed over him and some of his stiffness dissolved.

"Printing. Mostly church stuff, club announcements, raffle tickets. Mom worked as hard as dad. Then, when she came home, she washed, ironed, cooked, cleaned the house,'' he chuckled hoarsely, ''. . . . and me.

"In the early days, because money was tight, she made her own clothes. I remember getting up late one night and finding her at her old sewing machine making a new dress for my speech at Sunday School the next day. Some big shot blacks from ritzy Pill Hill were expected and she didn't want to embarrass me.'' Having relinquished her shoulder, he stared straight ahead, his jaws tight, his eyes lustrous, darkening pools of anger.

"Patrice?'' Leana quietly ventured. She put her hand on his, her fingers caressed his wrist. He seemed to have forgotten her presence.

His black gaze glittered in her direction, then away. "The long and short of it,'' he said dryly, ''is that mom not only stood by him when he decided he needed that high school diploma by running the business almost singlehandedly while he burned the midnight oil studying, but she did it again when he decided he had to go bigtime.''

"College," he grunted. "Ole dad wanted it all. The big people like your Johnsons and your Travises, the people with the big money, don't go to small-time, nobody presses for their printing needs. They deal through their clubs and fraternities, their boards of directors."

"So what happened?" she asked, gently apprehensive.

His full lips curled to a smirk. "He did it all." The tendons in his neck strained, his tone turned contemptuous. "He was the oldest pledge his fraternity ever 'rushed'; he graduated magna cum laude and retook his place as head of the company. He got the big bucks contracts. He did that by changing the way he dressed, the way he talked and toning down the aggressive working class mannerisms," he added with a bitterness that made her heart ache, ". . . expanded the company, hired more staff, bought the house, the car, me a Corvette when I graduated from high school, retired my mother. . . ." He paused, his face screwing up as if he had just bitten into something nasty, ". . . . dumped my mother and married his new, 20 year old secretary."

Leana could feel the blood drain out of her face. "Oh, my God!"

"God didn't have anything to do with it," Patrice shot bitterly.

Conscious of a sick swirling in the pit of her stomach, moistly she whispered, "I'm sorry."

"Don't sweat it. It's been ten years."

Leana shook with the miseries. Then anger. Profound anger. She sat there, quivering with anger on behalf of a woman she didn't even know. It just wasn't right! A thought struck her. '10 years . . . that would make the spring chicken . . . 30!' Whirling about with pinched nostrils and in a voice that shook with righteousness, she demanded: "He left her, too, didn't he?!"

Patrice pulled out a cigarette, and with fingers that trembled slightly, lit it; then taking a long drag, exhaled smoke slowly from his nostrils.

"They live on Pill Hill. My new brother is named Martin. After Dr. King."

Her wrath deflated, silence hung heavy in the rose-jeweled garden as they sat, their shoulders touching, looking out across the moonlit lawn into the shadowy cornfields in the distance. Folding her hands compulsively, one over the over in her lap, Leana felt awful. She should have left well enough alone. Glancing at the taut figure by her side, the cigarette between his fingers smouldering, it came to her that he had not pried into her hurtful past. Most people would have asked about her father's accident, and once learning the circumstances, asked nosey questions about the 'settlement'. By his reticence, Patrice had spared her the humiliation, the defensiveness she always felt forced to assume at the astonished pity that puny ten grand effected. Tracing the hard line of his handsome, disconsolate jaw in the blue shadows with her eyes, she wanted to weep. Silently she vowed that somehow, someway, she'd make it up to him.

The strains of music starting up again, came to them. Flicking the cigarette to the ground in a disgruntled fashion and crushing it with the toe of a well-shod foot, Patrice glanced past his shoulder to his silent companion, a rugged smile of reassurance on his face. Looking into her face, made radiant by moonlight, Patrice saw the hollows beneath her eyes, underscoring a drawn look of sorrow. The breath caught lightly in his lungs, a swelling of tenderness flared briefly in his breast.

Some women would have shrugged off the tragedy of his mother's life as being just 'one of those things,' no concern of theirs; they would have expected him to feel likewise. Having long since forged his anger, pain and sense of betrayal into a burning determination to self-success, his harshness when he spoke had been directed not so much at his father's perfidy as anger at himself for allowing those emotions to surface.

"Forgive me," she said softly through a spasming throat. "I'm . . ." Her shoulders raised helplessly. "I shouldn't have been so nosey. It was none of my business. Oh, I'm usually more . . ."

Without thinking, he bent and tenderly kissed her mouth. It was a chaste kiss. One more of a desire to comfort than of passion. But when he drew back and she sighed, her silky lashes drifting above eyes holding within them a responsive light of warmth that played havoc with his senses, it was not comfort, but a proprietary passion that propelled him to lean over to kiss her again. To his consternation and disappointment, she angled her body sideways.

"It's getting late," she said, rising. Her lips curved in a self-deprecatory smile. No more than an hour ago, she had been filled with longing for an exciting man to come along and sweep her off her feet. This man would not only sweep her off her feet, but if she were not careful, carry her off to bed, as well. The soft, sibilant magic of the night had wakened in her a latent sensuality, and she knew that if she let him kiss her, she would be lost. "I'd better go."

Patrice sprang to his feet. "Can I take you home?"

Feeling compelled to keep her with him for one more hour, all night, if possible, forever if he could, the tension in his voice was overrode by an eager huskiness.

The throaty sound of her laughter filled the night with soft noise, gentle noise, possessing a tinkling, underlying sussuration that sounded in his ears like chimes in the wind.

"I'm staying the weekend. I only have to go upstairs," she explained smilingly, unaware of her effect on his senses. "Unlike Brenda, I can't party all night, then get up at the crack of dawn, fresh as a daisy." Poised for departure, Leana felt suddenly awkward. Should she kiss him goodnight? Or had she kissed him too much already? She experienced a giddy rush when Patrice settled all questions by positioning himself quickly in her path.

Chapter Five

Casting its luminescence across the fragrant garden, the moon caught and sparkled in Leana's eyes. Wavering tantalizingly before him, blocking her way, Patrice thought her beautiful. Beautiful, classy, and elegant he thought sighingly before the muscles at the corners of his mouth tightened.

Beautiful, elegant, classy, but definitely no sophisticate, he concluded, looking at the still, small face upturned questioningly to him, the eloquent eyes, the soft red mouth, now trembling. There was nothing cold or brittle about her. She was a woman grown strong and straight with a heart as warm as her beautiful, tip-tilted eyes. He had known from the first that she was The One. Something more than mere beauty had drawn him to her. Something inside her, something that yearned to be taken seriously, preciously. And it was this, her unspoiled femininity, it came to this most masculine of men, that was the source of her allure for him.

"I'll walk you to your room," he said, looking down at her tenderly, feeling that the gods were with him for almost as soon as he spoke, he remembered the pickup truck he'd arrived in. He was on a case and the pickup was a part of his cover. He had notified his assistant to bring his new Excalibur around the next day, for from the moment he laid eyes on her, he knew that Leana was The One and he wanted to impress her.

Her insides turning to mush, Leana, thanking the same gods silently, was barely breathing when she smiled her assent. Allowing him to take her arm—and even this casual touching caused her heart to flutter— she permitted him to escort her back into the house, up the oak stairway and down the darkened corridor to her room. After he had taken his leave at the door with a farewell of "take care"—which she took as a caress more so than a caution—she switched on the mock hurricane lamp, globed in red sumac artglass, then lying the rose he had given her lovingly on the night stand, undressed for bed. She would shower in the morning. She could not bear to wash from her body the scent of his passion, the wood-smoke of his aftershave.

Unzippering her dress, she let it slither down the perfumed sides of her body, the soft, sybaritic rustling recalling the pusillanimous passion she'd permitted herself to feel, an echo of what was to come, what sure as rain would come.

But not now, she thought, slipping out of the tiny triangle of her panties. Laying her undergarments neatly on the red oak armchair in the room she occupied as a teenager on her visits, she turned back the lightly quilted blanket on the four-poster bed, sumac abstracts, as on the lamp, carved into the filials. Her body an ague of emotion, she slipped into a black lace teddy, its satiny feel cool and soothing on her bare skin. Pulling the tap pants up over her hips, the elastic snapping on her waist when she released the band, she climbed into the bed and eased herself under the thin summer covers.

Remembering the rose, she propped herself on an elbow and reaching across the bed to the oak nightstand where she'd laid it, picked up and tickled her nose in its soft velvet petals. She had come dangerously close to responding to him with all her need. Although not a virgin, she was not promiscuous. One night of arousal was not enough to make a commitment. Sex, in and of itself, was only a release, a purely animal act. She would be made love to, and love required commitment. Yes, she thought drowsily, the blood-red rose of passion slipping from between her fingers to the pillow with her head, she would get to know this sexy man, this romantic man named after a revolutionary.

The moon sending its beams in ghostly sheets through the windows, blanketing the foot of the bed, reaching up to touch her, to kiss her lips with silver, Leana fell on her back, stretching her suddenly tingling body to its full length. Switching the lamp off, but unable to sleep, she went on thinking about him. He was a self-made man, and even more commendable, he loved his mother. She was a firm believer in the notion that if a man can't love his mother, he can't love any woman. Then again, there was his father. Now there was a man who went all out for what he wanted—and the devil take the hindmost. Uneasily, she sensed that the son shared that same trait. She shivered under the covers. He, too, was to be watched. Still, she could not forget how handsome he looked in his evening suit. Tall, dark, handsome and. . . . commendable, she reflected, yawning, a smile curving her lips as she drifted off into sleep.

* * *

"So-o-o?!"

"So?" she echoed in polite query.

They were seated on cushioned, wrought-iron lawn chairs on the south terrace facing across a round, similarly constructed table inlaid with tempered glass. Her hair drawn back in a bun wrapped in a skinny white scarf, there was a sly twinkle in Brenda's eyes as she slanted Leana a sidewise glance. "Still mad?"

Leana regarded her cooly. "I beg your pardon?"

"Oh, Leana!" she pooh-poohed. "You know I get carried away sometimes. Besides, I was right, wasn't I?!"

"I'm sure I don't know what you're talking about."

"Oh you do, too!"

Leana sighed gently. She stirred the tall glass of iced tea. Garnished with a bright yellow wedge of lemon, it was set attractively on a white lace doilie with serrated edges that centered a white, gilt-ringed saucer. The elongated spoon swirling the amber liquid in the frosted glass, crushed ice tinkled its sides delicately as she stirred.

Brenda's wide, good-humored mouth turned downward in a frown. When she had seen Leana seated alone on the terrace, reveling in the buttery effulgence of sunshine that blanketed the lawn, she had been ready to make up for her shameless high spirits of the night before. But when she pulled up a chair and joined her with a friendly, "Well, good morning lady-whose-lap-all-the-best-men-fall-into," Leana seemed unaware of what she was talking about.

Wearing with her inimitable style a simple eggshell

white sundress, its pleated bodice complemented by white on white high-heeled sandals and silver hoops in her ears, her manner was as cool as her dress. Brenda had felt hurt. Was it her fault if beneath that urbane poise, Leana was so thin-skinned? And, after a couple of distant "thank you's", she decided to assume a similar blasé attitude. But, unlike her more sophisticated friend, she could not keep up the pretense forever.

Snatching up the green, fan-pleated napkin stuffed in a water goblet, Brenda flung it aggressively across her lap. She was looking up from the glassful of tea she poured with a pout from the pitcher on the table when she caught sight of a tense, dark figure, sunlight glinting off a diamond stud in one ear at the edge of the terrace, glancing purposefully around, as if seeking someone special.

"Oops!" she exclaimed delicately, tipping the pitcher back, flat on the glass tabletop. "Almost overpoured." She dimpled up slyly at her best friend, but when she refused to even acknowledge her look, Brenda shifted the undamped excitement of her gaze back across the garden of summer annuals over Leana's shoulder. The identity of the lithe dark figure, once he began his graceful, wary stride in their direction, was unmistakable.

"Good afternoon, ladies."

At the intrusion of the husky-soft voice with the resonant timbre and fluid tone peculiar to the black male courting issuing from behind her, Leana felt her stomach muscles tense, and her clinking spoon clunked. Goose bumps were acquainting themselves intimately with the ridges of her spine when she glanced across the table to see the gleeful grin Brenda had been suppressing plump out her cheeks.

Darting her a swift, no-nonsense glare, a look of satisfaction covered Leana's face when Brenda gulped, then swallowed a long draught of tea. Steeling herself to face the man who with a single glance had the power to reduce her to silly-putty, at the same time determined to give Brenda no opportunity for further romantic mischief, to her inward relief, Leana's voice was polite, but friendly when she asked, "Won't you join us?

"Ah!" he exhaled ruefully, continuing in that same throaty timbre as she smiled up at him. His face shadowed against the blue arc of the clear country sky, huskily he intoned, "Nothing could tempt me more than to bask in the company of two of the fairest in the land . . ."

A coughing, choking rattle interrupted his tribute.

Falling over the table, her eyes slightly bulged and convulsively shaking, Brenda was gagging.

In three quick strides, Patrice was behind her, and after giving her a quick sharp slap between her shoulder blades, tea and bits of crushed ice spewed from Brenda's mouth in all directions. The iron legs of her chair scraping on the cinnamon-red flagstone, Leana scooted back to escape a drenching, and Brenda howled.

"The fairest . . . !" she gasped, wiping her grinning mouth with the green linen square. "You must have been taking lessons from old Arthur!"

Thinking privately that he might as well be taken for a tiger as for an alleycat, a sardonic brow arched. "Okay," he said, spreading his hands slowly, unaggressively, and although his mouth kicked up on one side in a smile, his voice had roughened, and Leana was again reminded that underneath that urbane manner was street-pride and temper.

"Maybe I did lay it on a little thick. I take it all back, and beg your pardon, Miss Lady," he said, sketching her a bow that was more mocking than apologetic.

"That was not *thick,*" Leana insisted loyally, feeling a flicker of annoyance at Brenda's lack of tack. "It was pretty!"

Sliding his glance to Leana as he straightened, Patrice was momentarily stunned at the beauty in her glare of exasperation for Brenda that he saw on her face. An angry flush covering the creamy texture of her honey-dark skin, her delicately feminine jaw set and gently flared nostrils pinched, he thought her beautiful. Rarely, wonderfully beautiful. But then again, he thought with a warming glance, she *was* The One.

Feeling the weight of his eyes upon her, Leana lifted a smiling face to him and made her tone light. "Thank you, Patrice."

One heavy brow quirked, the sable lights illuminating the night-dark of his eyes as intent on her face as the sun on her skin, Leana felt the pulse in her throat quicken when, picking up on the excitement of her dusky flushed cheeks like radar, a gentle half-smile tugged one corner of Patrice's mouth.

"Miss Lady," he began anew softly, the courting husk eloquent in his voice but no more so than his expression, "there is nothing I would like better than to bask in the company of the single most beautiful woman my eyes have been privileged to behold. . . ."

Interrupting, Brenda drew up in her seat, whooping in laughter.

The smile wiping from his lips, with great forbearance, Patrice ignored her. Bending his six foot plus frame over Leana, his brilliant eyes skewering her heart, quietly, he added, *"and that's God's honest truth."*

The dark eyes holding upon her, Leana's slender hand was visibly shaking as she reached for her glass of tea, but it was Brenda who, the laughter dying from her voice to be replaced by deep conviction, breathed, "I'm *impressed!"*

Her sentiment was drowned out by the screeching roar, then appearance of a long, sleek, low-slung, gleaming and sparkling chromed white Excalibur Roadster, the driver swinging into the gravelly driveway, skittering along the shoulder, then braking in a cloud of dirt and pebbles that peppered the air.

"Patrice!"

The two women watched as the pretty girl in designer jeans stretched tightly across slim hips jumped out of the monster two-seater luxury car that looked like something out of a fairy tale, and came hurtling up the walk, her Italian leather boots making crunching sounds on the gravel before she hopped onto the flagstone terrace.

"I brought the car. Man! It is too *much!"* she exclaimed breathlessly, white teeth showing in a sexy grin as she stopped before him. Ignoring the seated women, she looked at Patrice brightly. "You ready?"

"My ride, ladies." Slipping her arm beneath his, Patrice grinned sheepishly as the newcomer pulled him around.

"Aren't you going to introduce us to your friend?" Brenda asked in a suddenly crisp voice.

Patrice started, then laughed. " 'Cuse me! Mandy," he said, tugging her around and pointing with his head, "this is my hostess from last night, Brenda Martin. And this,'' he said, and unconsciously dropping the arm clinging to his, smiled, ''is Miss Leana Claremont.''

Brenda noticed that Mandy's bright observant eyes had traveled as he took her through the introductions from herself to Leana to Patrice, then almost in a double take, back to Leana. Speaking up in a not-so-innocent tone, she asked Patrice lightly, ''No, 'the most beautiful, fairest in the land'?''

Sooty lashes slitting his cynical detective's eyes, Patrice slewed her a sidewise look. Sliding a lazy hand into the trouser pocket of his tailored suit, he regarded her thoughtfully before a wry grin, almost a smirk, curled the full purplish lips and he rose to the challenge.

''I would like to introduce to you . . .'' His tone was again deep, elaborately soft, but in his reinvention of the black male courting voice, so fraught with meaning that Leana glanced up at him in surprise, and saw in the dark centers of his gazing eyes the warmth that had existed in the rose garden between them, open to the world to see, ''. . . . Miss Leana Claremont—God's gift to man.''

Wrenching away her eyes, Leana made a little rolling hand gesture, then crossing and uncrossing her legs, exposed a lovely length of nyloned thigh over which she immediately moved to smooth the full, eggshell white skirt of her dress.

Standing there, his hand in his trouser pocket while she fumbled with her skirt, Patrice moved his glance to Brenda. Pleasantly, he asked, ''Have I embarrassed your friend to your satisfaction?

''I may be many things, Miss Lady,'' he said, looking back at Leana in the awkward silence that followed, ''but a liar, I am not.''

''I'm sure no one who really *knows* you would be-

lieve *that,* Patrice!'' Mandy objected, slanting Leana an
arch look, then when he turned, made puzzled by the
shrillness of her tone, softening her conviction with a
smile.

Her skirt forgotten, Leana raised her eyes to Mandy
briefly. As she did so, a faint look of amusement came
into Brenda's. She, too, had caught the arch look.

As the two women took silent measure of each other,
then as if by agreement, looked away, Brenda murmured
softly, ''Mandy.'' Leaning back in her chair, she
squinted into the distance, as if conning the name over in
her mind. ''Mandy, Mandy, Mandy.''

Swinging her chin to Brenda and tilting it defiantly,
the younger woman spat, ''Yes?''

Three curious pairs of eyes stared in her direction.
And although one set of the varying brown trio glared
her a challenge, Brenda refused to be rushed.

''I've got it!'' She snapped her fingers sharply.
''Amanda! You're Amanda Parker, the one Patrice is
teaching to be a girl detective!'' Clasping a hand to her
chest and leaning forward with an expressive glance at
Leana, who returned her a dry look, she gave a little cry
of pleasure. ''Nice to meet you.''

An amused smile curved Leana's lips. There was a
reason heads turned for a second look when she walked
into a room, and she knew it had as much to do with
confidence and a personal sense of style as with her long
legs. And then again, one no more rose to the board-
rooms of corporate America than got through high
school without learning a little something about
women's in-fighting. The small smile settling on her
lips, she turned her head.

Unknowingly out of his element, Patrice continued to

dart puzzled glances at Mandy. Mandy looked greatly offended.

"I am not a girl," she shot back. "I am a woman. And I happen to be Patrice's *assistant!*" Glaring full into Brenda's unnaturally bright eyes, a sudden awareness seized the younger woman's features. Her own eyes narrowed, and then, she smiled. Smiled with such wholesome purity that she positively radiated friendly intention. Returning her attention to Patrice, she beamed up at him a klieglight smile.

"If I had known you had such funny friends as. . . ." Tipping her head in Brenda's direction, a charmingly distressed expression arose to cover her face. "I'm sorry," she murmured, making an airy gesture with skinny fingers, "but what was. . . . ?"

A taunting whimsical look came to Brenda's eyes, but by no means an unfriendly one. Returning her a game smile, she replied promptly, "Brenda."

"Excuse me." Silver hoops swaying against her elegant neck, the interruption came from the woman who was perfectly able to take care of herself. "Excuse me," she reiterated, throwing a smiling glance, "but I believe Patrice has an appointment to meet." She turned in her seat. "Thank you for taking time out of your busy schedule to come to the party, Patrice. It's been a pleasure getting to know you."

Looking down on her smiling face, Patrice enfolded the slender hand she held out to him in his larger one and fingering it reverently, promised, "I'll call."

"I think that Mandy girl hates you."

"Don't be silly." Leana, personally, was breathless.

"I think there's more to *that* than meets the eye! She wants him." Brenda sighed. She shook her head sadly. "Poor thing. Hasn't got a snowball's chance in hell against you."

Leana put out a hand, warm with the friendship of years, over hers. "Oh Brenda!"

Brenda's arched brows rose. "Not mad, anymore?" then laughed when playfully, Leana slapped her wrist.

Chapter Six

Leana sat behind the neat cedar desk in her office. There was a picture of her parents on its polished surface, a pen set received for her high school graduation and between book ends in the shape of ceremonial African masks was a dictionary, a speller, a Chamber of Commerce guide and several directories of small businesses. A month-at-a-glance calendar centered the desk's wide width, and a video display terminal took up space on one end. There were prints in black and white on the walls and ivy in planters scattered around the airy, if not quite spacious, office. A floor lamp stood before a red and maroon tweed chair which matched the one in which Leana sat, talking on the telephone when LaDonna entered her office like a house afire.

"Leana," she said, shouldering the door closed behind her. "A Mr. Grant from Training wants to see you. He says it's ur. . . . Oh, excuse me!" she exclaimed, noticing the receiver in her hand.

Leana made an apology to the caller, then putting her palm over the mouthpiece, looked up at her secretary. "See me about what?"

"He's having a problem with Lawrence Appleby. I've got his record here from files." She laid on the edge of the desk a manila folder with the name 'Horry Grant' typed neatly on the colored label.

Leana picked up the folder with her free hand, glanced at the label. Gray over white, she thought with an inward sigh. The labels were color-coded with respect to education and experience. The gray top meant some high school, but no diploma; the white bottom signified unskilled laboring jobs.

"He has a wife and two kids—the one in high school is his; the other is his grandson," LaDonna informed her in an urgent, whispery voice. "He's 52 years old; his last job was . . ."

"Thank you LaDonna." She cut her off. "I'll look his file over. Tell him to have a seat; that I'll be with him in about ten minutes."

She watched as the secretary scurried off to placate the trainee. Her hand releasing the mouthpiece, she put the receiver back to her ear. "Mr. Baxter. I'm sorry, but an emergency has arisen. Would you mind if I called you back in say . . ." she paused, looking at her wristwatch, ". . . half an hour?"

After she hung up the phone and replaced the tiny jade hoop in her ear, Leana read quickly through the paper file, then checked for updates on the computer. Lastly, she called Lawrence Appleby in Training. Ten minutes from LaDonna's departure, Horry Grant was shown into her office.

"Mr. Grant," she said, coming from behind her desk to greet him.

Dressed in brown twill slacks that bagged at the knees, he wore a threadbare white polo, its short sleeves fraying over ropey, still muscular biceps. She could see the Adam's Apple bobbing in the older man's throat as he swallowed, the tightening in his narrow shoulders as he stared at the slim hand she proffered uneasily before he took and limply shook it. Then, just as uneasily, but much quicker, he released it.

"Please," she smiled, indicating a chair beside her desk.

"Well, ma'm," he began modestly once they were seated, hands between his knees, thick, callused fingers laced together tightly and hunkered over, "Mr. Appleby has had me in that training unit for over a month now, and he ain't did nothin' for me all this time."

Rolling the swivel chair with her feet to one side, so there was no desk between them, Leana leaned forward and smiled. "Tell you what," she said in a low, conspiratorial, and perfectly kindly tone, "if you'll call me Leana, I'll call you Horry."

Horry's shuttered eyes peered up and saw crinkling back above the plumped-out cheeks of a gamine grin, a warm brown gaze of acceptance. His shoulders relaxed; he straightened in the chair. "All right," he nodded, tipping his head toward her, a slow smile splitting his careworn face, "Leana."

"You said you were in the Training section?" she asked, leaning a forearm on her right leg, crossed over the left, as if she had all the time in the world. "What job are you training for?"

"Well, right now I'm in Firearm Safety. But that ain't the problem!" he said feelingly, his deeply furrowed forehead corrugating in a frown. When she neither objected nor seemed turned off, he went on. "See, my wife works at this fast food place. She's been carrying the load ever since I come here when my un'ployment run out. It's too much for the woman. We got bills cain't no fast food job keep up with. I told this to Mr. Apple . . . uh, Lawr . . .''

Leana cut him off immediately. "Call *him* Mr. Appleby." She laughed in a wonderfully comforting way. "Some of us are not so down to earth!"

Horry grinned, nodded his head vigorously in agreement. "You know you right there!"

"So," she prompted with a smile, "you were saying . . . ?"

Horry looked back at his fingers, then up, his eyes harried. "I need a job. I gotta bring in some money. We got our grandboy living with us now. Mr. Appleby said we would get work soon. I cain't wait for 'soon'. I need to work now! I need a job!"

Leana sat back in the swivel chair; gazed at him musingly. She sighed. "I'll be truthful with you, Horry. Right now, Employment has more applicants than jobs. But," she hastened to add, moved by the look of dashed hopes contorting his features, "I'll be talking to some company heads next week. I promise you, if they have any openings in your field . . .''

"I'll take anything!" he blurted, impassioned. "I gotta git me some work, Miss Leana! We'se about to go under!"

Leana gazed at him, a thoughtful expression on her face. Quietly, she asked, "Are you sure, Horry? I mean, getting a job is one thing. Staying with it after you get a couple of paychecks under your belt is a different matter. The Center has a responsibility to the companies, the corporations who accept our referrals, too. And," she swept on, steeling herself against the poignancy in eyes that would unduly sway her, "if our referrals don't work out, they won't use our other people who need jobs." Her gaze, soft and dark, leveled on him.

"Miss Leana," he said, drawing himself up into a dignified posture. "Even if it's a job I hates, you just tell me how long I should stay—even if it's a year—and I'll do it. I wouldn't mess up a good thing for nobody. I won't let you down."

Leana was giving Horry's paper file a thorough going over when LaDonna popped her head through the door.

"Leana," she called in a loud whisper across the room, her eyes buggy with excitement, "there's a hunka-hunka man out here to see you!"

"I hope you didn't mind me dropping by your office. I was in the neighborhood when I thought you might want to join me in an afterwork drink," said Patrice as he held out a leather-padded armchair for Leana in the plush V.I.P. Lounge, a popular Southside nightclub.

"No. Not at all. To the contrary," she replied, smiling as he moved around her to another chair and dropped into it, unbuttoning his suede blazer and sprawling his long length to a comfortable position beneath their table.

Far from being 'in the neighborhood', he had been following a 'suspicious' boyfriend in Waukegan, close to a hundred miles from the Blyden Center, when the need to see Leana, to be near her, to touch her, had distracted him to the point where it affected his concentration and the boyfriend had eluded him. He had driven like a madman, weaving in and out of traffic, the speedometer edging 80, to get back to the city before five, shower, change, then try to look nonchalant when he appeared on her office doorstep. Looking at Leana now, as if for the sheer pleasure of looking, he grinned. And she was well worth it. Out loud, he said, "What's your poison?"

"Well," she sighed, mock supercilious, "I don't drink poison, so I guess I'll have to settle for orange juice. If you don't mind?"

"You're kidding?" A skeptical half-smile curved his handsome lips. "So what was it you were drinking at Brenda's the other night?"

Peeking up at him in guilty, girlish mischief, she tilted her head. "Tea?" she squeaked, and they laughed.

He capitulated. "Okay, orange juice, it is," he said, turning in his chair to snag with raised eyebrows the attention of a waitress who pushed immediately through the genteel, fast-filling lounge to take their orders.

"My, that was fast service," said Leana as she sipped the juice through a plastic straw slowly. Dressed colorfully with a marishchino cherry and a wedge of lime that matched exactly her two-piece suit, the fruit juice was disguised to simulate an exotic drink.

"They keep me happy; I keep them happy." Nonplussed, he curved a hand around his shot glass, took a swallow. He had ordered Courvoisier, water back. "Works out fine that way."

Leana's eyebrows rose slightly. "Really?"

"Oh, I'm not playing big shot." Reading her look, his grin was wry. "Bill Augustus owns this place. We're business associates as well as friends. The Jackson Agency provides security for him."

Leana lifted her head and looked around. The crowd seemed to her to be a mature, cosmopolitan one—the men wore suits; the women were dressed to the nines. It was a quiet elegant cocktail lounge, a little jewel of a place, dark and cool. A coffered, mirrored ceiling reflecting its black smoke glass and leather interior, it featured a geometrical mix of round and square tables faced by black leather-tufted armchairs and an assortment of leafy green plants. An aquarium with tropical fish ran the length of one wall, and with the exception of the dance area, good quality carpeting covered the floor.

"To keep out the kids," he said, answering her puzzled look. "This is an over-25 set and Bill wants to keep it that way. My agency can't stop the 'over 21 but under 25's'—we try to steer them down the street to 'All the Way Live'. The teenagers are the ones we've actually hired to keep out. Excuse me," he said, rising in response to a motion from the bartender. "Take care of the lady," he told the passing waitress, already moving in the direction of the bar. "Whatever she wants."

Leana watched him move agilely, pivoting sinuously from the hips around tables and patrons in pushed-back chairs. Noticing that several women were casting appraising eyes in his direction, their thick glances entirely feminine, she felt an instant surge of pride. His fit, athlete's body filling out the navy suede blazer collared by a black, open-necked silk shirt, his well-proportioned legs, long and thigh-muscled beneath dark, tailored gray slacks, Patrice was, indeed, a hunka-hunka man.

No slouch in the looks department herself, as she sat at the round table looking cool and lovely in a skinny, single-buttoned suit in electric lime green with slash pockets, Leana's demeanor was one of cool competence and assurance. With a calf-length skirt that showed to advantage her own trim figure, one high-arched foot in black pumps kicking under the table, she drew admiring glances from more than one quarter. By the time Patrice returned, two more glasses of orange juice that she did not order shared space on the table with her black clutch before her.

Frowning, Patrice slumped down into his chair. "Hm-m," he said. One eyebrow winged at the colorful drinks. "I see you're not the kind of woman a man can safely leave alone."

"Two very nice gentlemen sent these over," she said innocently, indicating the glasses. "That was sweet of them, don't you think?"

" 'Nice' is not exactly the word I would use," he replied drolly. His thick lashes narrowing beneath swooping black brows, when Patrice swung his head deliberately around the lounge, a hard, 'this is my woman look on his face', Leana felt a delicious thrill shoot through her.

"What was that all about," she asked, sipping the juice to cover her excitement. "If you don't mind?" she added hastily.

Patrice looked off, his scowl deepening. "One of my men didn't show up Saturday. This is the second time he's done this—taken off without calling in."

"We have an employment section at the Blyden Center," Leana, the 'Executive in Charge of Developing Employment Opportunities' suggested immediately. "If you want, I can get you all the men you need. Reliable, responsible men. Not only in security, but almost any opening you have, we've got someone who can fill it— from accountant to janitor. And for those who need it," she swept on, in her excitement, "we even provide the training!"

For a startled moment, Patrice sat still, utterly still, his dark eyes looking a hard stare across the table at her. Then, a heavy brow quirked, and his shoulders relaxing, an amused smile coursed his lips. "Are you always so enthusiastic about your job?"

"Well, yes. Of course," she said uneasily. Outside of that hard stare, which in itself was unnerving, there was something in his voice which she did not like. A lightness of tone which did not express the regard, the professional regard to which she was accustomed. Quietly, she asked, "Aren't you?"

"Don't sweat it, baby." He made a careless gesture. "The man was probably just sick. Happens all the time."

"But . . ."

"It's not your concern." Although the casual tone and his thickly drooping lashes gave him a relaxed look, there was a tensile tautness in the hard muscled body that warned Leana off.

"If you want," she said slowly, feeling slighted. Patrice had not struck her as one of those men who were contemptuous of women's competence, she told herself as she reached out stiffly for her glass. But that couldn't be so, she reasoned, remembering the pride she sensed when he had spoken of his mother's running the family business almost single-handed while his father attended college.

Sipping slowly through the straw, a tiny frown wrinkled her brow. She cast a surreptitious glance about the darkened lounge. Taller than average, with a buff male physique, Leana recalled in a sudden warm rush that she wasn't the only woman there who found his predator good looks fascinating. But when her lashes trembled up and she saw a warmth stirring in his eyes, easing the harshness of his expression as he watched her, she could not but conclude that even that was of her imagination, for although a bevy of elegant women were angling for his eye, Patrice seemed oblivious of them, his attention devoted exclusively to her.

"You look beautiful."

His voice reaching across the table like a kiss to her ears, a dark emotion, soft and beautiful in her eyes, complemented the dusky flush that crept up Leana's cheeks. Dropping her eyes demurely, she returned the compliment. "And you look very handsome."

For the space of a few seconds he said nothing. Then, leaning across the table, his posture was intense, his tone compelling as he suggested, "I'd like to see you again.

"Sure," she replied, and although her heart felt full to bursting, swirling the orange juice calmly with her straw.

"There's a stage show at the New Regal Theatre Saturday," he said with subdued gladness. "It's sold out, but I know the manager. I can get us a couple of tickets."

Leana's silky lashes lifted. "Excuse me," she said, laughing gently, "but you seem to know everybody!"

"Business," he said, expelling the held breath. "I worked on a case for his uncle down in Alabama. He had a contract with the state to provide the speed limit signs you see on the highway."

Leana leaned toward him with raised eyebrows. "You're kidding!" She shrugged a shapely shoulder, charmingly bemused. "Well, I guess someone has to make them. So!" she grinned, looking up and scooting her chair closer, girlishly eager. "What happened?"

His libidinous juices stirred at the firm jiggling of her

breasts beneath the fitted linen suit in her selfless enthusiasm. Patrice felt his body harden.

"Patrice?" Her smile was encouraging.

Blinking lustful thoughts away, Patrice cleared his throat, took a careful swallow of water, then replaced the glass on the table.

"Well," he said, and although carefully avoiding her eyes, oblivious of everything save the warm, classy woman across the small table from him that without whom he was fast realizing, all was meaningless, "it seemed that as soon as he put them up, someone would take the signs. At first, he thought that someone was uptight because a black man got the contract. But he couldn't find out who or even what was happening to them, so he hired me. I posed as a hitchhiker, someone whose car had broken down. I walked the interstate in Abree County between 11:00 P.M. and 4:00 A.M. for three nights straight. . . ."

Leana gasped, her hand clutching at her throat as an image of Patrice, a lone black man walking a deserted Southern highway in the wee hours of the morning in the middle of an infamous Klan county, rose distressingly in her mind.

"You're kidding?"

He shook his head. "You'd be surprised at how much one of those signs cost. I finally saw some white guys come by in a truck and take one down. I followed them. They took down all the other signs he'd put up that past week, too. To make a long story short, it turned out that this white guy who had the same contract with one of the adjoining states, was stealing my client's signs and putting those he could use up as his own.

"I don't know if I like that, Patrice. It sounds dangerous," she said, her stomach muscles knotting. So it was true. He actually was a detective. And, racial memories aside, it *was* dangerous.

Patrice waved her fears aside. "That's a part of doing business. It's not all sneaking around with cameras trying to catch some guy creeping on his wife, you know." Looking down with grim satisfaction, he chuckled, low in his throat. "I got a big bonus for it, too."

Leana looked off, still not liking it.

Patrice lifted somber eyes to her face when she fell silent. "That's what I do." He let out a deep breath. "That's why I'm trying to recruit more operatives. That's where I was going Saturday. They have a detective's school in Ohio. I interviewed some candidates there."

"You can't train them yourself?"

"I could, but we're too small for that right now. I can handle training security, but to train operatives is too time-consuming. Not only is there the actual detective work, but they have to be able to fill out reports in such a way that our clients' attorneys can take the reports to court and the opposing lawyers not shoot them down. It's a little more complicated than what you see on television. So it's easier to simply hire them out of school. Unlike security, where street smarts and a cool head are the main ingredients—I can train them to our methods easily. Although," he sighed heavily, "I wouldn't mind an assistant in that area. Someone who knows something about the business. He'd have to be an older man, though," he ruminated in a low voice, thinking his problem out loud. "Nobody listens to a young man."

"Well, I can help you there!" Plucked happily from her abstraction Leana pushed herself forward, propped her elbows on the table. "I know just the man. He even has firearms control!"

A pained look seized Patrice's features before his expression turned wary, then annoyed, as if he had permitted himself be lulled by a liquid sloe-eyed gaze, ensorcled by a seductively smiling mouth into discussing his difficulties too freely before her. His face shutting down, he flapped a deprecating hand. "Don't worry your pretty little head about it. I'll manage.

"So, pretty lady," he said, changing the subject, "what about Saturday?" Flashing strong white teeth, he bent on her a delicious, killer smile.

Her offer of help trivialized, then blown off, Leana looked at him with quickly hurt eyes. "I'll have to think about it. Thank you for the orange juice," she said, gathering up her purse with a slightly shaky hand, "but I think I have to go now."

Seeing the startled hurt in her eyes, Patrice got to his feet with alacrity and, reaching out, caught her wrist. "Leana." His voice trembled as he spoke her name.

Oh, God, what further insults would he heap upon her now? She flinched visibly.

"Yes?"

His extraordinarily deep, dark brown eyes troubled, his words in the soft shuffle of patrons moving about the quickly filling lounge for her ears only, were almost despairing in their urgency. "I think you're beautiful, beautiful inside and out, and I want to see you not only Saturday, but the Saturday after, and the one af . . ."

"Patrice sugar! I haven't seen you in a month of Sundays!"

Leana fell back as turning sharply, Patrice braced himself when the lissome, curvaceous body wrapped in a sequinned gray shirt and black velvet pants that belonged to the sultry voice calling his name, threw itself upon him.

"Monica!" He grinned foolishly, his eyes searching out Leana's pleadingly helpless as Monica's arms twined his neck and she stood on tiptoe to kiss him. But only for a moment.

It was an interesting moment. Using both hands, he had no more dislodged her hugging arms from his neck than the voluptuous woman was slithering her body against his, reaching a hand into the unbuttoned collar of his shirt and fondling his chest. Standing outside the pale and watching, Leana thought it to his credit that he'd had the grace to be embarrassed. Still, she could not help wondering how often this type of thing happened; how many women would push her aside to get to him.

"How have you been, Monica? Leana," he said, dull color staining his dark face darker as he turned to include her. "I want you to meet an old friend of mine, Monica McLeod. Monica, Leana Claremont."

"Hello Monica," said Leana, staring assessingly into the wide, heavily made up in shades of purple, eyes of the woman who, with equal feminine curiosity, stared back at her.

Turning sidewise, Patrice slipped a reassuring hand down her arm, his fingers dipping to catch and entwine her fingers gently in his. "Where's Sam? I can't believe he'd let you out of his sight for ten minutes," he said, grinning and squeezing Leana's hand.

Nervously? Leana wondered, darting a look up at him. Or, when he fingered her hand possessively, putting on her professional smile for the predatory female who painted her eyes in lurid shades of purple, anxious?

Having flitted a cursory glance around the elegant lounge, Monica had turned back to stare at Patrice's companion who obviously interested her more. Her eyes dwelled shrewdly on Leana's blandly smiling face, then waving the blood-red fingers of her hand in an airy arabesque, said disdainfully, "Oh, he's around. You can bet your life on that!"

"Well, we were just dropped in for an after-work drink. Nice seeing you again, Monica. Tell Sam I said 'hi'."

The pressure of his hand was firm, reassuringly protective, and felt strangely intimate curved on the small of her back as Leana allowed Patrice to guide her to the door. Although he gave her the low-down on several people they stopped briefly to chat with, he was not forthcoming about his relationship with Monica, nor did he offer any explanation about his reluctance to consider her offers of help. Lifting her head on her neck and smiling, she told herself she had just met him, it wasn't even a date, he owed her no explanations. But she still felt hurt. Moving on, it came to her that she had not given her goodbyes to Monica. Ever polite—no one could accuse her of being one of Bebe's kids—and with Patrice at her side, she reasoned wryly, nothing to lose, she swung about, moving from the protective circle of his arm. The farewell salute she was lifting faded mid-air. Monica had remained standing, stock-still, by the table where they left her, her eyes had fixed on the spot where Leana turned, filled with malice and envy.

Chapter Seven

Leana turned the Mercedes into Willow Grove's underground parking lot. Patrice followed in the Excalibur. Even though her pulse quickened whenever Patrtice touched her, and her heart stutted erratically when he leaned near, riding the elevator to take them to the 21st floor of the apartment building, there was an echo of the earlier strain of the evening between them. Casting a smiling glance his way to breach it, she remarked on the beauty of his car.

He let out a deep breath, as if he, too, had felt the strain, then of the hand-built, fiberglass automobile, its GM V-8 engine styled after the 1927 Mercedes, he said flippantly, "Better than the pickup."

"I wish you had called me this morning," she smiled shyly. "I would have taken a cab to work."

Patrice flicked the cuff of his sleeve, checked his watch. "I've got an appointment at eight." Flicking her a glance, a rueful, half-smile quirked the corner of his mouth. "We've got enough time to wow the denizens of MacDonald's if you want to drive through for a hamburger."

"Another time," she protested laughingly, then added, "and another place!"

They were still laughing when they arrived at her door.

Leana took out her keys. "Would you like to come in? I don't have any hard liquor, but I can offer you coffee or a coke. I think I have some tea," she said, her pretty brow puckering after she had unlocked the door and Patrice, lounging above her, one arm extended up along the doorframe, pushed against it with his free hand. "I definitely have water!"

"Coffee," he smiled as he walked behind her into the parquet-tiled foyer of the capacious, luxury apartment. She fumbled for the light switch. Lamps blossomed, softly illuminating the parquet-tiled foyer. Textured, contrasting whites on the walls and in the furnishings, mirror-brilliant surfaces reflecting the oyster-hued scroll of the ceiling, his lips pursed as if to whistle. "Classy!"

"Thank you," called Leana in as pleased a voice as if she'd had him in mind when she decorated the rooms. She put a tape in the CD player before moving further across the beige carpeted floor to the kitchen. "Make yourself at home."

Pushing back his suede jacket and hooking his thumbs into the belted loops of his trousers, Patrice strolled across the floor of the apartment, gazing appreciatively at the white and cherrywood furnishings as the sweet alto sax of a jazzy instrumental started up. He twitched back one of a wallful of burgundy, pleated drapes which fronted floor-to-ceiling windows, sucked in a sharp breath as a panoramic view of the sparkling dark waters of the great Lake Michigan, and beyond it, sheer space, greeted him. He stood there a moment, looking out, his admiring gaze sweeping the blurred watery horizon and the harbor to the north where the furled sails of luxury boats docked, before dropping the drapes back and retracing his steps across the carpeted floor.

Flinging himself down on an inviting white sofa with burgundy red pillows tossed in among the white, he leaned forward, appropriated a pear thoughtfully from a silver rose dish on the cocktail table. Leana returned with coffee for two, placing the silver tray carefully on the inlaid glass counter. He bit into the firm fruit as she poured.

"Real classy," he murmured, crunching as she draped herself elegantly on the sofa next to him. Smoothing her skirt beneath her, she bent lady-like from the knees, tucked her short straightened black hair behind an ear to display one of a pair of jade earrings, then picked up with slender hands the blue-glazed cup, bringing it to her lips.

"Do you like jazz?" she asked him after she had taken a sip.

"Some," he acknowledged, his expression lazy, but impressed. Watching her flutter her exotic dark eyes, he decided he liked the way she drank coffee, too.

"Me, too. I mostly like Theolonius Monk. I've been trying to find his version of "Wade in the Water". I heard it on the radio once when I was a little girl and I never forgot it. When that jazz piano rolled its way out, I thought my heart would burst, it was so moving." A quick apologetic smile flitted across her face. She brought the cup again to her lips to cover her embarrassment.

No hand at flowery phrases—Brenda's laughter at his pathetic attempt on her patio was a burning reminder—

he could still appreciate the passion of that affinity in others. Or was it just her? Stretching his long legs out and settling back against a plump burgundy pillow, Patrice grinned. "I've got some old Nat King Cole."

"What was the classic song that Natalie Cole remade? You know, the one where she dubs in her voice and sings along with him?"

Her eyebrows raised and leaning her slender body questioningly toward him, it came to Patrice that it was her. In the beginning, it was her; now and at apocalypse, it would be her.

" 'Moonlight Becomes You?' " he insinuated softly.

"No. Of course not." Her eyes falling before his suggestive glance, she picked up an apple from the silver rose dish and bit into it to cover her embarrassment. "That was Johnny Mathis."

"Oh, yeah! Another of those silver-throated old-timers," he teased, thinking how, with the sweet brown gleams in her eyes tilting at him over the rosy roundness of the apple, very lovely she looked. "If I could only sing," he lamented, his voice slowing lyrically to the swinging, romantically swaying tones of the alto sax on the CD.

"And what would you sing?" she asked prettily.

He slid an arm across the spine of the sofa. His voice was husky, doggedly singleminded, as he whispered, " 'Moonlight Becomes You.' "

Tenderly, their glances engaged and held. Charting the drift of thick black lashes with his lowering lids over midnight romantic eyes, Leana could feel his breath touch her face and her respiration quickened. His hands sinking into her hair, cupping her finely shaped head, his thumbs stroked gently across her temples, and feeling the tapping of the pulses beneath her flesh, his own breathing quickened.

Soft feminine stirrings strummed her insides like Circe's song; desire, like smoke, spiraled up Leana's spine. Fighting the sensuous fog, she shifted her weight as his cushiony lips pressing gently on her cheek, moved over her tingling skin to kiss the tip of her nose, and before she could turn aside, brushed her trembling lips gently.

"Oh, uh," she muttered incoherently, feeling goose bumps pop on her skin. She had to be more careful. She was entirely too responsive to him. She pulled away, skittered back on the sofa, away from her temptation. Twisting her fingers in her lap nervously, her heart was beating like thunder when huskily, she asked, "Who was your friend at the V.I.P. Lounge? She was pretty."

Heaving a muted sigh, Patrice straightened on the sofa. The moment was broken, the opportunity lost. Picking up his cup, he asked, as if bored, "Monica?"

"Yes," she concurred, her eyes wide, her voice breathless. "Her."

"It's like you said," he replied, holding the cup out for a refill. "Just a girl I know. Thanks," he said when she complied. "You brew a mean cup of coffee."

Leana experienced a fresh surge of uneasiness. 'Just a girl I know.' Was his assistant, Mandy, just a girl he employed? How easily he dismissed the women who loved him. Placing the pot on the tray, carefully, she asked, "Just a girl you know?"

Puckering his lips and blowing on the coffee, Patrice glanced over the rim of his cup at her sharply, assessingly. "There's no reason for you to be jealous of Monica."

Leana tucked her feet beneath her on the sofa, draped an arm gracefully over its spine. "I'm not jealous. I'm just asking."

Her eyes meeting his from beneath the curve of her bangs were gentle but unsmiling, and Patrice again had a sense of something deep inside her, now demanding to be taken seriously. He took a gingerly, but fortifying, little sip of his coffee, and then sat it down. "The guy Sam I told you about? He's her husband."

"Husband?"

"She thinks he's boring."

"But not you." As gentle as was her voice, it was not a question.

"Some women think that being a detective is on a par with being a rap star."

"Including Monica."

Damn! he thought, frustrated. There's more to her than meets the eye. While her probing indicated a welcome interest in him, it was leading into something that was none of her business. Something messy and hurtful to innocent parties, and he didn't want to talk about it. But there it was, he saw, looking at the graceful, glamorous figure across the sofa. That 'take me serious' look that demanded reassurance. He rubbed a heavy hand over his eyes. There were things he could not yet, dared not yet, tell her. Although he felt as if he were breaching a confidence, this he could do for her. This he could explain.

"Monica," he began, wondering how to put it delicately, "is a hugger. One of those touchy-feely people. But she's never been so openly . . . affectionate." Giving her a sidelong glance, when her face refused to yield, he looked off. "Believe me when I tell you, I was as surprised as you.

"Leana." His voice deepened and he looked up. "I don't play around. I'm a 'one woman' man."

"But Monica's not a 'one man' woman."

"That's Sam's problem."

"But she grabbed you," she prodded gently. "I mean, she really grabbed you."

Patrice groaned inwardly. She had to be the most persistent woman he'd ever met!

"Okay." His broad shoulders heaved. "This is the way it is. Monica, as you said, is a pretty woman. And she knows it. She's used to men falling at her feet. I met her at a party. I didn't have anyone, and we seemed to hit it off, so I took her out a couple times.

"Sam is a friend of mine. The minute I found out she was his woman—they weren't married at the time, but it didn't make any difference—I walked away. I never told Sam. He . . ." Patrice paused, chose his words carefully, ". . . knows how Monica is. He's a good man, Leana, a good friend who would give you the shirt off his back if you were in need, and I'll never tell him. Unfortunately," he sighed, "even though I put it behind me, Monica doesn't seem to be able to. I don't flatter myself that she's in love with me. I think it's the ole 'one who got away' thing for her. Maybe not," he shrugged when Leana shifted on the sofa. "I don't know. But I do know she's never been that blatant before. I think it had something to do with you."

Leana's eyebrows lifted a fraction. "Really?"

"I'm serious. Monica's pretty. You're," his eyes squinting on her face warmly, his dense brows knitted, " . . . past pretty. I think she was jealous of you, that she resented you snatching up the 'one that got away'. So she loses it and goes overboard." He tilted his head skeptically. "You can't tell me women aren't jealous of you."

Leana's lashes drifted sadly and she smiled. "Your friend Sam sounds like a sweet man. You're right not to tell him, you know."

Patrice took her hand, squeezed it lightly and smiled. "Yeah. Matter of fact," he said, falling into fond remembrance, "it was Sam who hooked me up with a friend of his, Richard Mabrey, who owns a detective agency down in Mobile where I was working on the 'Case of the Missing Highway Signs'. Richard—he's from Chicago, by the way—was running security for a rap group. We got together and he put me in touch with another friend up here who helped me to get my security operation together."

Leana experienced a fresh surge of uneasiness. All her offers of help he brushed aside. Every one. Yet he had not hesitated to accept it from a stranger. Evidently, Patrice was one of those people who feel that a man's opinion, no matter how spacious, is to be taken over any woman's. Her lashes drifted gently. Here she thought she had found the perfect man—generous, attentive, protective, cultured when he wanted to be, and utterly romantic. Perfect, except for one very important thing— he was contemptuous of women. For all Kerry's faults, he had valued her opinion, her contacts, and was proud of her accomplishments.

"Leana?"

She jumped, as if struck, when she felt the back of his hand rub across her cheek, heard him call her name gently. "I'm sorry," she said, shifting the position of her slender legs, forcing a smile to her lips. Looking at the man who would relegate her to the periphery of his life, hers was a small, but polite, smile. Small, polite and so sad and beautiful that Patrice blinked to see it. Hope sprang to her face when she saw in his eyes a flicker of conflicting emotion, as if he guessed its source. But. . . . what conflict? He seemed about to say something, as if to spare her some worry, then, as though thinking the better of it, rejected it with a shake of his head.

"I'd best be going," he said with a tired grin, unable to meet her eyes as he came heavily to his feet. "Got that eight o'clock appointment to meet."

A shine of unshed tears in her eyes, Leana saw him to the door.

It was over.

In the parquet-tiled hallway, Patrice hesitated, then unexpectedly, turned. She felt his big hands tremble as he took both of hers in his.

"Do you remember what I told you at Brenda's?" His dark face looked strained, as if about to beg of her something to which he had no right to propose. "To trust me? Please do. Please remember that no matter what happens, you can trust me to do right by you. I'm a good guy. I swear it."

Leana awoke the next day feeling tired after tossing and turning the whole night long. She lay sprawled on her back, one arm flung limply across the bed, the other over her eyes, shading them from the sun coming in through the window. Its bloody yellow rays blanketed the foot of her bed, sending a creeping warmth up the sheets twisted round her exhausted body. Groaning and rolling across the rumpled sheets to the edge of the queen-sized bed, she eased her stiff body from the mattress, flung her legs over the side, and dropped her high-arched feet to the floor. She slumped there momentarily, her sleep-heavy eyes closed, the toes of her feet digging into the soft shag that covered the platform.

She had dreamed fitfully throughout the night. Dreams that alternated between Patrice and Kerry. She shook her head lethargically, scratched, then shook it again, her short hair shimmering around her sleep-puffed face like a cloud in an effort at remembrance.

Dancing with Patrice. What were they dancing, she wondered groggily, a waltz? He was twirling her, spinning her round and round, the loose folds of her dress flaring out behind her. Gazing into her face with the eyes of love. Kissing her, his full lips thick with sensuality, as if there were no tomorrow. She was clinging to him, swaying pliantly into him, smiling, her eyes half-closed. They were on a mountaintop. His kisses were growing fierce, fierce, fiercer as their flying feet moved to the edge of the precipice, spinning closer and closer. An uneasiness flickered into her somnolent mind, then terror as she felt the ground weakening, giving way. Her eyes beseeched him: why? but his fingers only dug deeper into her softness as he continued to hold her, kissing her mouth, twirling her in the moonlight, dancing her to the edge of disaster.

Leana leaned over the bed, her hands pressed weakly to her thighs, her heart beating fast as the fear rushed back upon her, even in her waking state. As she sat there, breathing in deep draughts of air, Kerry drifted into her mind.

They were dancing in the moonlight, their footing secure as he moved her around the mountaintop. But his eyes were not on her face; he was concentrating on their feet. She made a misstep. She laughed. He scowled. 'This is serious business,' he told her. 'People might be *watching*!'

The dream shifted. She was on the mountaintop, dancing alone in the moonlight. She had on a white dress of a thin, gauzy material. The breeze the dance created flattening the flimsy fabric against her upthrust breasts, the ends of the dress flared, fluttered gracefully about her as she twirled on tippy-toes, her neck arched back, her arms outstretched.

She felt joyous, free! She twirled round and round. She stumbled, fell. She picked herself up, hesitated, then her arms flinging wide to embrace the starry night, pealed loudly in laughter.

The dream again shifted. She was on the mountaintop still. Moonglow washing her outstretched limbs, making even softer the cream-brown of her shoulders, molding in silver the flexing calves of her legs, the slim bones of her ankles, the exquisite architecture of delicate feet perched daringly on tip-toes. Unseen eyes watched adoringly as straining like an earthbound angel heavenward, she began to dance. Twirling her body a graceful dark flame captured in a blaze of white, she swooped and dipped. Paused mid-toe in dance, her tip-tilted eyes liquid, glowing in the night, were caught by a clump of feathery white yarrow, moonbeams shimmering their petals at the edge of the precipice. She was moving in slow enchanted dance toward them when she felt the earth tremble beneath her light-stepping feet.

'Leana! Come back! It's too dangerous—you'll fall!'

She turned, confused. It was Kerry calling to her. His

tone of voice was urgent. Her arms flung out still, she twirled back a step, spun and stopped, her eyes drawn with yearning to dainty white flowers that could capture moonbeams in their petals.

'You wouldn't let something so lovely slip through your fingers, would you?'

Her head lifted sharply. The grave voice, fraught with amused tenderness, belonged to Patrice. He was standing to the rear of the flowers. His brilliant dark eyes smiling, slowly, he extended a flattened palm to her.

'Leana, come back. Come back!' It was Kerry again, warning her. 'Those flowers are dangerous!'

She spun around gracefully. Moved lightly and at first hesitantly, in his direction. Then in an agony of emotion, turned back to look at Patrice, his smile and outstretched hand patient, the flowers between them. Only. . . . She tilted her head, confused. The flowers were at the edge of the precipice. So what then was he standing upon?

'If you can dance,' he told her, casting her his smile with a beckoning hand as he hovered in the black vastness of space, 'you can fly'.

Disregarding the jacuzzi in the blue and aqua tiled bath, hanging ivy in pots drifting above the tub, Leana took a cool, bracing shower. The needlesharp stream erased the tenseness from her body, unclouding her mind. She was drying off with a beach-sized towel when she heard the doorbell chime. Wrapping a blue silk kimono about her nakedness, she ran barefoot to answer the door. She peered through the peephole of the security door to see Josh, the delivery boy from Karlov's Florists in the building's atrium.

Unwrapping the green tissue florist's paper, she gasped when she saw the roses, a full ruby-red dozen, their blooms as big as her fist. There was another, flatter package with them. Tearing mist-delighted eyes from the flowers, she opened the box quickly. The mist swelled to a joyful flood of tears when she picked up carefully from the box, an old, barely scratched 45 recording of Monk's 'Wade in the Water'.

Chapter Eight

Leana was walking on air as she entered the impressive, turn-of-the-century graystone mansion which had been converted into the Edward Blyden Center. Bouncing into the high-ceilinged but less than opulent waiting room consisting of an orangish-pink pair of Danish-modern couches, a double row of orange plastic chairs hooked together at the base, and a heap of out-of-date Ebony and Jet magazines strewn across a coffee table done in wood laminate before the sign-in desk, she breezed past the receptionist with a cheery "Morning, Morning, Morning, Theresa!" Taking the elevator to the third floor, and grinning her thanks at old Mr. Gladowski, the elevator operator, when he commented on how nice she smelled, her high spirits carried her sweeping into her private offices where she greeted LaDonna with a "Morning, LaDonna!" and a radiant smile.

LaDonna went buggy-eyed on her again. "It's that man, isn't?!" she exclaimed intuitively. Running from behind her desk, her breasts in the push-up bra nearly bouncing out of the sweetheart neckline of the baby-blue sweater, she launched herself straight at Leana and hugged her, happy for her happiness.

"LaDonna!" she said sharply, disengaging herself from the suffocating embrace. "One does not hug one's boss!" she sniffed, and although the secretary looked properly penitent, her tone remained scolding, even arched up haughty when she said, "Now! I'm going down to the canteen for coffee. How do you want yours?"

The sun broke on LaDonna's face. "Oh, Leana!" she squealed, ready to rush her again.

"Stop!" Leana commanded, one arm thrusting out stiffly like a traffic cop's. "Number one, you're jumping to conclusions. Number two, this is a business office and your voice is much too loud, and number three, I happen to have a luncheon date and I'm not going to have you getting me all wrinkled! So just," she said, tilting her head towards her with a firm, yet reassuring look, stay back."

"Yes, ma'm," said LaDonna in a small voice. But although she held her mouth primly, a playful mockery lit her eyes. "I guess I did jump to conclusions," she said the words as if they were a mouthful. "Seeing as how happy you seemed when you came in. And," she added, her eyes holding an admiring gleam as they swept her boss, head to foot, "how very nice you look."

Leana, smart as a runway model that day and every workday, was wearing one of her many business suits—a white linen two-piece over a cool georgette blouse in pale pink with a high-notched collar—but in a fit of ecstasy at receiving the record and roses, she had flung a richly fringed tartan over one shoulder as she walked out of her apartment, then ran back for a second all-over spritz of perfume. A white pearl brooch pinned the fling to her suit; coral-colored pumps adorned her feet and real coral earrings weighted down her lobes. Thus, it was looking rich and smelling good that she was wowing them at the office.

Choosing to pay it coy, she informed LaDonna, "I really don't know what you mean. I try to look nice every day. By the way," she stopped in the doorway, "did I get any messages?"

LaDonna decided that two could play the same game. "No. Unless. . . ." She shook her head, as if at a foolish thought. "Nah."

Leana was instantly suspicious. Her eyebrows arched up. "Nah?" she repeated in the same broad accent.

"Well," she sighed, meaning to assume Leana's previous, haughty manner, "usually when one says 'messages', one means of the telephone kind. . . .

"*He sent flowers*!" Her loud squeal reverberated in the tiny outter office. "Flowers! Big, beautiful red roses!!" And before Leana's dropped jaw could close, she had thrown herself again upon her, disarranging Leana's scarf and wrinkling her suit.

Leana settled back in the tweed swivel chair behind her desk, staring with awed eyes at now two dozen long-stemmed, ruby-red roses with blooms as big as her fist. She sucked in a voluptuous breath of air, felt it fill her lungs—and laughed. Arched her throat back laughing, the sound so merry as it pealed from between her lips that LaDonna came bursting into her office.

"What's up?" she asked, her eager eyes dancing, clamoring to get in on the joke.

"Breathe, LaDonna. Breathe!" When she looked at her in amused mystification, grinning even as she awaited the punchline, Leana gasped through her mirth, "Me? The flowers? LaDonna, this has got to be the sweetest smelling office in the building!"

The description so amused LaDonna that after laughing for some time along with her, she proposed a thing she was notorious for avoiding. "You just sit tight," she told Leana bossily. "I'll get the coffee!"

Will wonders never cease? Leana watched, awed, as LaDonna's narrow behind switched off happily to the basement canteen. 'Maybe this is my lucky day,' she reflected, possibilities flitting through her mind. 'Maybe I ought to play the lottery.'

When LaDonna had returned with the coffee, two creams and sweetner for Leana, and left her office, Leana eased her head back against the chair, pitching it a little to one side, her eyes closed and thinking blissfully, 'it doesn't get any better than this.' She sighed. 'Pleasant things first.'

Checking her personal telephone book, she dialed the number to Patrice's office. The telephone made five impatient rings before a man answered with a most unprofessional, "Who's dis?"

"Excuse me," she asked apologetically, taken aback. "Is this the Jackson Detective Agency?"

"Yeah," came the impatient reply. "Who's dis?"

"Leana Claremont. I'd like to speak to Mr. Patrice Jackson, please."

"He ain't here."

"Well," she persisted, and in the unconscious hope that her tone might be catching, very businesslike, "could you tell me when Mr. Jackson is expected to return to the office?"

"Prob'ly when he wake up."

Her even brows tugged together; the man's telephone etiquette was inexcuseable. "I beg your pardon?" she asked, her tone taking on a clipped quality. "To whom am I speaking?"

"Henry."

"What?!" she blurted in exasperation.

"Henry. Henry James. I'm da jan'tor."

"The jani . . ." Leana did a double-take. "Uh," she ventured hesitantly, feeling as though she had wandered into the twilight zone, "do you always answer the phone when Mr. Jackson is not in?"

"Naw. Got a girl, sec'tary, do that. But she ain't here. She out checkin' up on a case he 'sposed to be on. Don't know why. Girl caint lie worth a nickel," he went on, unperturbed by his caller's stunned silence. "Called in sleepy dis mornin'. His other 'tectives outta town."

"Wha . . . Called in sleepy?!"

"Yeah. Da man out all night, runnin' round tryin' to fine some tomfool record." Then ominously, he added, "Woman involved."

Leana gripped the receiver tightly, her body charging with raw emotion. Leaned forward over the mouthpiece, trying to hear him above the sudden rush of blood pounding in her ears, she murmured, breathlessly sympathetic, "Oh, the poor thing."

"Po' my foot! Man jest 'bout bought out somebody's whole flower place, too. Den, he call all ova da country tryin' ta fine a record."

Goose bumps broke out on Leana's flesh. "All . . ."

The loquacious Henry James disregarded the interruption. "Got on a plane, mine you, 'n went all da way to St. Louis, Missouri ta pick hit up. Dint git back 'til four, five o'clock in da mornin'. Too tired ta come ta work. Had ta git some sleep, he sez. Woman. You kin bet on it! Ain't nuthin' kin make a man ack a fool lak dat but a woman!'' Then, in a drawling, amused voice, Henry James chuckled deeply, ''He in luv!''

Passing LaDonna's desk on her way out, Leana called back to the secretary, who having been caught in the act again, hurriedly pushed a Jet magazine under a stack of correspondence, ''I'm leaving. I won't be any good for the rest of the morning!''

The days leading to Saturday seemed to be of an interminable length. Unable to reach Patrice with her next call to his office, Leana left a crytic message with his secretary, saying 'Thank you. Saturday is great'. When she returned home from a lunch date with Brenda two days later, there was a message on her answering machine saying, 'No, thank *you*. I'll pick you up at six.'

By Friday evening, Leana felt so on edge she had to postpone a business dinner with Jack Gilmore, Personnel Manager of the Williamson Engineering Company, a black-owned firm that did a lot of business with the city. To pass the time while 'Maids on Wheels', a professional cleaning service, finished up in her apartment, she decided to get in a little shopping at the neighborhood Dominick's food store. Carrying an armload of groceries, she was making her way between slant-parked cars in the dark, unusually deserted parking lot when she sensed someone following. Turning her head quickly, she looked over her shoulder. A biker on a Harley-Davidson was coming up fast upon her. She was moving over, sagging her body against a parked car to let him pass when he stopped in a roaring screech on the black-top pavement before her.

''Want a lift?''

Ankle-booted and thigh-muscled under heavy leather chaps and possessing a formidable pair of shoulders on which hung a menacing-looking leather jacket with snakeskin insets, he had positioned the Harley only an arm's length from her.

City-born and bred, Leana's adrenalin kicked in big time. Her heart pounding madly, she braced her feet, automatically arched her back, and with the bag held protectively before her, jutted her chin. She was about to tell him to bug off when the biker pulled the black shielded helmet from his head, and the diamond in his ear winked.

"Patrice! What in the . . . ? You nearly scared me to death!" she cried, her bravado giving way to temper. Then, just as quickly, the pleasure of seeing him again, so unexpectedly, overwhelmed her.

"What are you doing here?" she laughed, dancing her head from side to side, thrilled to her toes. To cover her giddy/happy excitement, she flicked her gaze over his beat-up biker's jacket, the black leather chaps and scruffy motorcycle boots with wicked-looking steel caps.

Cradling the helmut in the crook of his arm and sitting back, straddling the bike, he grinned. "Take a wild guess, then tell me what you're doing here? I thought they had a grocery store in that apartment complex where you live."

"I decided to come out for a breath of air," she said, inwardly cursing the silly grin which refused to leave her lips. "I usually do my big shopping here. I'm on my way home now."

Patrice gave her grinning-to-bursting face a thoughtful, protracted look. Wearing soft suede boots cuffed

just above the ankles, gray pleated slacks and tweed
blazer over a silk white blouse, and a red kerchief tied at
her throat, she looked as if she belonged anywhere but at
a Dominick's. He glanced up at her, his brows climbing.

"I'll be done in fifteen minutes. Half an hour, tops.
Can I come over?"

"Boy!" she retorted, a flirtatious glint in her eye.
"You sure don't beat around the bush, do you?"

"Seize the hour, baby," he said laughing, and putting
action to word, leaned over the bike and the bag she carried, and kissed her lightly on the mouth. "There's more
where that came from," he whispered, and feeling reck-
less, licked suggestively across her lips.

"Hmmm," she murmured, shifting the brown bag in
her arms, the blood racing in her veins at a mile a minute. "Maybe it won't be safe for me to see you. Uncha-
paroned, that is."

He tugged at the beaten lapel of his jacket, made a
mock-pained face. "Don't let the clothes fool you. I'm
really a pussycat."

"Oh, yeah, shore you're right!" she snorted, and they
laughed.

"Well," he said, his fingers in the black motorcycle
gloves flexing over the handlebars as he revved the big
Harley up, "got to go. Can I come over?"

Her lips pursed in a mute smile, Leana nodded her
head, unlocking in his face a big grin that flashed white
and lingered in her heart long after Patrice had sped off.

She changed from the slacks and blouse to a drifting
hostess gown of slate blue, chosen for its scalloped
neckline trimmed in white satin which played up her
deep brown eyes, brightening them so that the attractive
tilt seemed even more pronounced. Pressed for time, she

stumbled out of the nappy suede boots, and discarding the knee-hi stockings, slipped her bare feet into white satin mules. Running a quick comb through her hair, then dabbing perfume behind her ears and on her wrists, in the last minutes, she checked over the apartment.

Smelling faintly of lemon wax, the cleaning people had given it a good going over and everything was in tip-top shape. Before she could check the time by the crystal clock on the living room wall, the doorbell chimed. Rubbing suddenly clammy hands down the front of her dress, a clingy silk-blend, then gasping dismayed when she realized what she had done, Leana was taking a quick worried look into the center mirror to check for spotting damage when the doorbell chimed again.

"Hi," she said, smiling up at him with a toothy nervousness that belied her sophisticated look as she quickly flung the door open. He hung there in the doorway looking malevolently handsome in his biker's leather, and to her surprise and further pleasure, holding before him a bouquet of carnations.

"Maybe these will excuse my appearance," he said, looking down ruefully at the scuffed tops of his steel-lashed boots, the black leather chaps that hugged his strong muscled thighs. "They were the best Dominick's had to offer."

"Come in," she said, taking the flowers from his hand. "Thank you. They're beautiful." As she sniffed the blushing pink and white carnations, the whiff of a more gamy odor smote her nostrils. Her eyes tilting at the corners, she looked up, surprised.

Unconsciously, Patrice rubbed his nose and sniffled. "I was kind of hoping these would camouflage my odor." He grinned weakly, pointing out the flowers. "Do you mind if I, uh, kind of wash up? I've been out for over 18 hours."

"Please do," she consented gladly, whisking Patrice through the foyer into the living room, then pointing him to the blue and aqua bath.

Grateful for the extra minutes as he showered, Leana busied herself in the kitchen, sticking a plate of store-bought muffins into the microwave and percolating coffee. He was standing at the open draperies before the window when she re-entered the room with coffee, sugar, a creamer and two demitasse cups on a matching porcelain service. Placing the tray on the glass cocktail table carefully, then straightening, she hesitated, staring across the room at Patrice.

He had showered and dried off hurriedly. Recessed lights from the ceiling falling upon his kinky, coal-black and slightly damp hair, droplets of water glistening on individual strands like the diamond winking at his ear, damp patches seeped through the sleeveless Tee, wet-spotting the open-neck shirt he now buttoned in decorum. Thumbs hooked in the girdle of snug, black leather chaps tied down long muscled legs, exposing the back-side of grungy jeans stretched provocatively tight over twin muscled buttocks, his was a commanding presence, that of the dominant male, the kind of man other men take serious and women find irresistible. Yet, despite his lordly self-assurance, Leana sensed beneath his blatant maleness, a basically lonely man.

With a lonely profession, she realized, thinking of him on a Southern highway, waiting for hours by his lonesome on a dangerous stakeout. She knew some women found him a glamorous figure in a glamorous

profession but other than the demons that drove him to
best his father, what in his mind was he looking for?
Love? The universal need for affection? But with all he
had going for him, why had he not reached out, seized
it?

Perhaps he doesn't know how, reflected the basically
shy woman, thinking of Martha at Brenda's party, and
herself before she knew Brenda, as she cast his face in
profile under the subdued illumination, a languid smile.
Caressing with infatuated eyes the thick winging brows,
brilliant dark eyes smudged by heavy dark lashes fluttering wearily on his cheeks, the straight bridge of nose
that flared boldly above the black male's mustache, and
treading softly up to him, her footsteps absorbed in the
plush pile underfoot, his sensuous, deep purple lips.

"It's something, isn't it?" she remarked, finding his
prescience thrilling as he pulled her elegantly-clad body
against his hard length when he first sensed her beside
him.

Aroused by the blatant maleness of him, the implaca-
ble feel of his thigh pressed against her hip and sidling
closer, although she longed to lean her head on that rugged shoulder at her cheek, to bury her face in the cove of
the thick masculine neck rising out of the network of
hard brown muscle she felt beneath his thin shirt, she
dared not. Contenting herself with breathing in the clean
scent of her shampoo in his hair and his personal, wind-
swept dark flavor through her nostrils, they stood there
quietly together, looking out upon the furled white sails
in Belmont Harbour.

She had made that mistake with Kerry. Her naturally
affectionate nature, she discovered, translated to one of
passion in the sexual arena. But because they were en-

gaged, she had taken a chance, and in an ecstasy of un-
bridled spontaneity, let herself go with Kerry. The first
time it happened, she had taken as a compliment what he
laughingly referred to as her 'wantonness'. But, when it
happened again, he had given her a stern look, and suggested that only 'whores' moved like that.

Stung, she had fought thereafter to keep the impetuous side of her love in check. It was when at a later time
he complained of her need for what he considered
'lengthy' foreplay and suggested that if a woman really
loved a man she would occasionally let him satisfy his
needs without requiring it, that she had talked her problem over with Brenda. Still, despite her reassurances,
Leana had been leery of expressing her amorous nature
to its full with any man since.

Schooling her body not to relax into him, when from
the corner of her eye she saw Patrice's languid gaze
upon her, her heart gave a little bump. His dark, broad-
shouldered form etched against a panoramic view of an
indigo night sky, he was studying her face as lovingly as
she had his, his gaze heavy-lidded as it moved slowly
over her eyes, her nose, a sensual smile tugging back his
lips when he traced with his eyes the soft curve of her
mouth.

No, she told herself, fighting the urge to return the
smile, to touch with her hand his face, to share with the
dampness of his skin her heat, to turn and with gentle
hands plow into the thickness of his crispy-kinky hair.
Conscious of a slow heat warming her insides, rippling
between her thighs in sweet pulsing waves, when his
glance drifted to the scalloped fabric framing the exposed tops of her breasts, Leana dragged a ragged breath

into her lungs and angling sideways, eased from his embrace.

She started back on unsteady legs into the room. "How about some coffee before it gets cold? You can look out the window anytime."

Although his words were casual enough, his eyes glittered with a half-amused, half-annoyed look. "I'll be looking forward to it," he said, charting the gently swishing motion of her hips and buttocks as she retreated into the kitchen to take the muffins from the microwave.

Pushing the pastry at him, Leana poured the rich dark liquid into the demitasse cups while Patrice sprawled, rubbing the back of his neck tiredly, in the plush depths of the sofa.

"What case are you working on now?"

"Checking up on a boyfriend. Ump!" he grunted, looking at her over the rim of his cup, the weariness of his eyes lifting as he tasted the French roasted blend, scented faintly with mint. "This is good."

"Thank you. Boyfriend?"

"Yeah. My client's parents think he's too good to be true. She claims she's tired of their yakking, but I think she's a little worried that might be the case, too."

Leana slanted him a look through narrowed lashes. "I've heard of wives checking up on husbands, and husbands checking up on wives. Now we have girlfriends and boyfriends checking up on each other?"

Patrice took another sip of coffee. "It's getting to be big business," he murmured as he swallowed. "My client just got a settlement. He turned up about that time. Has a business deal he says he wants her to invest in."

"What kind of business?" she asked, looking him

over skeptically. She had hung the beat-up leather jacket in the hall closet. Underneath, he was wearing a black nylon shirt shoved into the cracked leather chaps and grungy blue jeans. "A motorcycle dealership?"

Feeling the weight of her eyes upon him, Patrice grimaced under their scrutiny. "I can't go into specifics, with client confidentiality being what it is, it wouldn't be ethical but let's just say that when you're on a case, things sometimes get hairy, so it's best to make a respectable appearance. And, since clothes do make the man, respectable is whatever the crowd is wearing."

"I wasn't critici . . ."

He put up a restraining hand. "I know. But I don't like coming here dressed like this any more than you do. I just want you to why—that normally I wouldn't. But when I ran upon you in that parking lot," he said, his thick lashed eyes drifting temptedly to her lips, "I knew I could no more take the time to go home and change as I could wait another 24 hours to see you. That I had to see you . . . tonight."

His husky timbre of voice shook Leana to her core. Never had a man talked to her like that; looked at her in that way. She had the oddest sense that just as she could feel the vitality of the man moving inside him, he recognized beneath her gentle demeanor the kindred spirit of a passionate woman. Aware of the dangerous territory her imaginative mind trod, and that in her aroused state it would take little on his part to rocket her senses out of control, Leana took a quick, shuddery breath, lowered, then raised her eyes.

"Is it real?" Her emotions reined in firmly, her gaze and tone were serene, dispassionate. "The business deal?"

"We'll know that by tomorrow," he said, one corner of his mouth hooking down as he watched her, his tone all of a sudden testy. "At this point, he's not checking out."

"He's a confidence man?"

Patrice shrugged. "May be. I don't know." He glanced upon the small delicate cup he cradled in his big hand gently, and his expression hardened. "I'll find out, though. That's for sure."

He fell silent, mulling the case over in his mind, and Leana sensed anger simmering just beneath the surface. The tightened skin on his face, the dark lips pressed together, firm and unyielding, that relentless set of jaw she'd first glimpsed in Glady's when she had offered the services of the Center. And underneath it all, that sense of hesitation, that weighting as of some heavy matter.

A fierce look hardened Patrice's face. His head jerked up and his lips peeled back, showing a glimpse of clenched teeth. "If a man ever asks you for money," he ground out, glaring full into Leana's face, "for anything, you tell him to go to hell!"

Leana flinched and drew back, shocked and puzzled by his vehemence, yet perversely, thrilled at its extravagance. He felt things. Like her.

"Sorry, he muttered, putting the cup on the glass tabletop to run strong brown fingers over his hair, the thick, kinky-elastic strands crackling with electricity, in a frustrated gesture. "I didn't mean to upset you."

"No." Upset? she thought. Upset? Feeling a deeper rapport with him than she'd felt with any man, she hid her flush of excitement in breathlessness. She would liked to have joined him, run her fingers across the healthy black hairs on his head and, as exposed through the unbuttoned neck of his shirt, the hairs on his dark muscled chest, as well. But those were desires she knew she could not address. For the last thing Leana wanted to see in this proud man's eyes was that haunted look of 'maybe, just maybe, I don't measure up. . . .'

Moved by a selfless feeling of protectiveness, an overwhelming need to give him something, she rose suddenly from the sofa. The clingy silk-blend gown draping and unfolding about her legs, she moved with long determined strides to an antique rosemarble-topped console with brass fittings at the opposite end of the room. She unlatched the door hiding the turntable and put on the 45 disc of 'Wade in the Water'. Returning to the sofa and settling herself demurely sideways to Patrice, when the first notes crashed into the room, filled their ears, clutched at her heart with its passion and rattled their bones with its power, she smiled radiantly.

"Thank you. Thank you very much." Cupping his tense cheeks with her hands impulsively, gently she kissed his lips.

Capturing a soft palm pressed to his face, Patrice held it there, rubbing it across a rough stubbly cheek while his eyes devoured the sweetness of her face. "Leana," he said fiercely, his brilliant gaze running riot over her with the musical background of joyous, free-wheeling piano. "Leana. I love you."

Stunned, gentle brown eyes lifted, searched his. Roused to the feel of his rubbing thumb on the back of her hand, the prickly stubble of his jaw against her palm, little shafts of pleasure lanced through Leana. Melting with sensation, at that moment, he could have asked anything of her.

Anything? a sly voice whispered.

Mirrored in his intense brown eyes, unwavering on hers, she saw her weakness, like a spectre, rise up to haunt her. Her mouth went dry and in a wrenching spasm of fear, her throat locked. Too full of emotion to speak, but wanting desperately to tell him how much she loved him back. . . . how very much she wanted him. . . .

Wanted.

In the aftermath of crashing ivories and a thundering crescendo of African drums, a breathless stillness reigned in the room—the moment of truth before whinny cymbals clashed, screamed, and in a tired semblance of a smile, one corner of his mouth lifted. Dropping her hand, Patrice pinched the bridge of his nose, shook his head.

"I'm sorry. I'm kind of tired. I misunderstood." He got up heavily from sofa and went to the hallway closet to get his jacket.

"I'm still holding you to tomorrow. Six o'clock, don't forget." Shrugging into the heavy jacket, he forced a teasing lightness into his voice that failed miserably. Half-turning in the foyer, his hand closed around the door's knob, his eyes focused on her face with a yearning that took Leana's breath.

Staring into his gritty, anguished eyes, long sooty lashes merging wet at the corners, Leana was up from the couch and beside him in a heartbeat.

"Don't go." She gripped the cracked leather covering his broad shoulders. "Please," she appealed in a small urgent voice. "Don't go."

Chapter Nine

Waking to a sense of presence in her bedroom, Leana lay curled beneath the sheets, still on her side. Very still. Her body tense, her every sense acock, one eye eased open, rolled slowly inward, toward her nose; stared at the hairy chest. Tension dissipated, and her face grew soft, content. Rubbing a hand caressively over his hairy, muscular chest, her lashes drifted down; she snuggled her head beneath Patrice's chin, and wriggling her naked body closer into him, purred like a kitten.

She had felt shy, turning her back to him before the dresser, ostensibly to remove her jewelry. Unhooking the pierced earrings from her lobes, her lashes chanced to lift and what she saw reflected in the triple mirrors made her knees go weak. Patrice was standing beside her bed stripping, peeling the sleeveless black Tee from his upper body, exposing to her startled view a mass of wiry, kinky-crispy black hairs that wound down his compact, defined chest into the indented navel of his flat abdomen then out again, disappearing finally into the battered, low-slung jeans that hugged his hips.

The tips of her almond-shaped eyes narrowing, the

lashes fanning their liquid length fluttered. The man was a god. She sucked in a bracing draught of air as a stir of dizzying emotion weakened her limbs. A god would love her. Tonight. Her blood heated up, raced in her veins as the stir of emotion deepened to a shudder of desire.

No, she resolved, the role she must play weighing bittersweet upon her breast. Not so soon. He mustn't think you wanton. Demure. Ladylike. Let him take the lead. Let him take the lead, she reiterated in her mind, almost as a chant, waiting for strength to return to her sagging body against the dresser as she watched, mesmerized by the beauty of the masculine form unfolding before her eyes.

Straining his long torso up, the hard muscles of his back bunching about the curve of his spine, he first pulled his head through the Tee and then his arms, the thin gold chain and cross he wore around his neck that emphasized the muscularity of his shoulders, flopping back on his chest. Unbelting the jeans riding negligently about his hips, Patrice glanced toward the dresser, smiled when he met her intently staring eyes in the mirror. The tenderness in his face squeezing Leana's heart, he stood motionless for a moment before unbuckling his belt and tossing the Tee on her boudoir chair like a rag.

Crossing the room, he came up behind her. He laid his hands on her lightly, hugging her shoulders. Vouchsafing her a long and tender glance in the mirror, there was a husk in his voice when he asked, "Need some help?"

"Yes, please," she said overflowing with emotion in response to his half-naked reflection. Her fingertips touching the nape of her neck, she indicated the long full-length zipper numbly. Feeling a small relentless shiver as the zipper slithered smoothly down her back, ending at the sweet curve of her behind, she stood outwardly still, yet inwardly trembled with emotion as his strong brown fingers massaged the tightness from her neck, kneaded her shrinking shoulders. His hands slipping with seductive ease beneath the fabric of the dress, he coaxed it from her arms to slither across her hips where gravity took hold and with the static sibilance of silk protesting silk, slid it down her long shapely legs to curtain around her ankles in a soft blue puddle.

The soft mellow light of the brass floor lamp reflected in the mirror, illuminating her face, pooling in the soft hollows of bared shoulders, glowing tense, unnaturally still limbs, without recognizing its source, Patrice saw the fear, felt the hesitation.

"Don't be afraid, baby." His voice was persuasive and utterly gentle, as gentle as the love words he breathed silkily in her ear. "I'll take it easy. I want to be with you, but I'd never rush you. What we've got will last." He lifted the hair from her neck, kissed her nape with tender lips. "And we've got all the time in the world to see that it does."

Reaching down to pull her to him lightly by her hips, Leana's eyes closed when his strong arms slipped, then locked round her waist, and her lips softly parted. Feeling the rough rasp of denium against the backs of her thighs, the heavy bulge of his manhood throb through his jeans and the thin silk of her panties, desire so great she could barely stand it, curled in the recess of her thighs and lay there, heavy and pulsing on her sex. Her head tippled back, and an anguished gasp escaped her lips. Shuddering in her self-imposed passivity, then falling limp against him, she snuggled the side of her face yearningly into the warm crook of his neck, her trembling, heavy-limbed form supported by his arms and strong muscular thighs as he rocked them softly, his lips planting feverish, loving kisses along the side of her neck.

"Leana! Leana!" His voice a pulsing, burning ecstasy, he murmured her name like a prayer, like a benediction that washed her ravaged senses with love and fluttered deep within her breast.

Leana clamped her bottom lip between her white teeth, and biting down hard, fought her erotic impulses, steeled herself to not break free, to whip about and with tongue and hungry fingers caress every sinew and muscle bulging the flesh of the demigod who wrapped his dark length about her.

But when his hands rubbed across her stomach, then moved up the curve of her waist and along her sides slowly, caressing her ribs, causing her to gasp and tremble, she felt the first of her resolve crumble. Arching her neck back, her head rolled in slow, anguished frenzy across his shoulder while Patrice kissed her dampening brow, and although the same sense of urgency shook him, held fast to his promise.

No! she sobbed inwardly. She would not show her weakness before this man!

"Leana, love. Love," he whispered in a gentle, beguiling voice when he felt her bones stiffen, her body go rigid.

Her flesh quivered beneath his seductive hand as if in answer to his tone. Waves of pleasure broke across her skin and her eyes drifted closed.

"Love," he whispered softly, stroking slowly, so slowly, exulting in the satiny feel of the meltingly lovely woman beneath his fingertips. "No need to be afraid. No need. You are my dream," he murmured, nuzzling his face into her hair. "A beautiful dream borne full-blown in my heart the moment I saw you. Then at the party, I saw there was more to you. With your gentle eyes and loving heart, you were more than a dream, more than beautiful. You were the one."

Nothing in Leana's structured life had prepared her for such a sensual verbal bath, and even as an inner voice whispered: *Don't,* the muscles in her body relaxed and her flesh again responded. Slowly Patrice smiled, warmly, and although his self-control stretched tight as a bowstring, he held back, consumed in that moment utterly with her seduction. "My beautiful Leana. Beautiful, beautiful Leana. . . . my *love.*"

Her skin was warm satin. Her supple body seemed to have no bones as he dropped his head forward, and gathering her into his virile maleness, caved his body over hers. Nuzzling her throat, his open mouth moved up the warm curve of her cheek and seized the fleshy lobe of her ear, all the while seeking fingers pushed beneath the lacey bra that stretched like a sheer mist over her dark, aroused nipples. Cupping her swollen breasts, he lifted their soft weights in the palms of his hands. When his thumbs rasped roughly across the tiny, chocolate buds, enticing the timid peaks with gentle persuasion to pebble-hard arousal, Leana's breath caught on a sob, and despite her best efforts she moved, swaying in his embrace, her bikini-clad bottom sash-shaying against the bulge of his fully aroused member. As he rolled his hips across her quivering, taut buttocks and worshipped her tumescent mounds with strong, stroking fingers and made sucking sounds in her ear, Leana groaned helplessly, and her back arched. Flinging an arm over her head and hooking it behind his neck, she forced his face into the dimpled curve of her shoulder.

"Oh, God," she whispered, squirming her full length into his nakedness as she re-lived those moments. Earth-shattering moments in which her whole body rejoiced, soul-shattering moments in which she thought she would die of the sheer pleasure of it.

Patrice groaned, her amorous movement bringing him to somewhere between good, satiated slumber and the waking state. Tending toward the latter, he flexed his awesome muscles until he rose from the mattress slightly, and stretching widely, yawned. Whole-body relaxing, the great all-is-good-with-the-world sigh that rolled up his throat, escaped his lips in a moan when her hand brushed across his hairy thighs and stroked his manhood slowly.

"Mmm, baby," he sighed, capturing with a gentle paw the slim hand with bones so fine he could crush it with one good squeeze that was wreaking so much havoc with his sleep.

"Like that?" she whispered, moving his hand covering her slim fingers beneath rumpled sheets in a gentle up and down motion.

"Yes. Oh God, yes!" he murmured ardently, feeling the familiar pleasure-pain tightening in his groin with the first stirring of his flesh.

"If you want," she breathed sultrily, "I'll stop." Although his eyes remained closed, his fingers tightened over her hand, as if afraid she might.

"Does that mean . . ." Her voice was low, soft and purring, as unmercifully, she teased him, for the events of the previous night proved she had no reason to fear for this man, ". . . stop?"

Propped up on an elbow, her hair a shimmering ebony tangle, Leana watched with the lambent eyes of a woman who is loved as his hard stomach heaved under her gentle ministrations, felt his powerful nakedness shudder when she kissed the hollow where his shoulder curved in thick cords into his neck, thrilled to his final waking in a moaning, needy state; lay back compliantly beneath him when Patrice rolled with gentle impatience atop her, her legs, her thighs, her whole life opening to him in consent and welcome.

"Got it on with him, did we?"

"I beg your pardon?"

Brenda laughed at her indignation, then brushing aside the tears trembling on her lashes, suggested, "That good, huh?"

"Really, Brenda!" she whispered, her dark eyes snappish. "Some things are private, you know. And in case you hadn't noticed," she said, indicating with a sweeping glance around the Water Tower Place restaurant on Chicago's Magnificent Mile, a fine insolence came into her tone. "This *is* a public place!"

"Oh, lighten up," Brenda said nonchalantly as she re-arranged the big, rust-red napkin on her lap with dainty fingers. They were seated at a table on a carpeted platform of the light, airy and nice, but expensive, restaurant, its decor a rich, rust-red and white. From their vantage point on the raised dais, they had an enviable birdseye view of the entire dining room area—rust-red carpeting throughout with a high plush nap, heavy white tables covered with white linen, and gilt and white arm-chairs upholstered in rust-red velvet that seated elegantly-dressed diners.

No slouches in the well-dressed department, the two best friends—Brenda sporting a green, blue and shocking pink bolero jacket over a black, high-waisted midi-skirt with gold hoops in her ears, a gold chain bracelet dangling playful gold charms on one wrist, a similarly chained watch with a black dial face circling the other, and smelling of Chanel No. 5—were a credit to the crowd. A beaded, multi-strand orange choker rising from the flawless column of her lovely long neck, Leana looked a knock-out in a reddish-orange coat dress draped elegantly from neckline to waist with covered buttons at the cuffs of full long sleeves.

"So!" Brenda exclaimed cheerily, looking up at her, and straight shooter that she was, square in the eyes. "What's he like in bed?" When Leana sighed, pursed her lips and looked off, Brenda slumped back in the lush velvet chair. "I just wondered," she said out of her petulant plump face. "You don't have to get all bent out of shape about it!"

Leana smiled at her vaguely, then preoccupied herself with the menu. "I think," she said finally, her face brightening even as her stomach growled, "I'll have the tossed salad."

Brenda flashed her an accusing look. "Do you do this on purpose?" she asked suspiciously.

Picking up a cut-glass goblet of water from the table, Leana's eyebrows lifted innocently. "Do what. . . ?" Her attention was drawn to the main floor where a light-skinned man in a distinguished worsted gray suit that played up his premature graying-at-the-temples curly black hair was being seated at a table. Glancing around casually, he unfolded his napkin and laid it neatly across his lap.

"Bernard!" she called, an impetuous smile spreading her lips.

The man twisted his head around the floor, then up. Spying Leana, he hesitated but for a moment, then swept hastily from his seat. After righting the chair he knocked over in his rise, he vaulted lightly the two steps onto the platform. Turning sideways in her own chair, Brenda looked up just as he tripped across Leana's lap.

"I don't believe this!" she muttered, her widened eyes incredulous as she settled back in the graceful armchair into her former slumped attitude. With mouth agape, she watched as a comedy of apologies commenced. Bernard apologizing to Leana; the waiter, hovering nearby awaiting their order, apologizing with solicitousness and the greatest concern to Bernard; and Leana, laughing merrily at the both of them and the profuseness of their regrets.

Once no damage was discerned, all potentially ruffled feathers had been soothed and Leana made the introductions, Bernard, having taken a tableside chair, said in a manner that was intended to be suave, but from his pink, openly grinning lips came off as laughable, even wacky, "I always fall for beautiful women such as yourself and," he added, inclining his head graciously to include Brenda, "your friend here, with her mouth open."

While Brenda's eyebrows rose, Leana's mouth curved in a tolerant smile as she told her, "Bernard is the 'W' partner in the WBBB firm." "You remember, I told you about them. How they've been growing by leaps and bounds this past year?"

"Yeah, we're on a roll," he concurred, grinning at Brenda who, disdaining all feminine subtlety, grinned back.

"Yes, indeed!" Leana set her jaw in loyal approval. This lunch was proving to be fortuitous. WBBB was an electronics firm that besides having a loveable, if clumsy, klutz for a part owner, made small parts for watches, transistor radioes and such, employing welders, solderers and other skilled, as well as assembly line, workers. Rumor had it they had just negotiated a big contract with the government.

Putting on her hat of chief head-hunter for the Blyden Center, she said briskly, "And when you start your expansion . . . as you will," she affirmed stoutly, placing a hand over his in an effort to wrest his grinning attention from Brenda whose face was now glowing with a look of almost silly bliss, "you will, of course, look to the Blyden Center to fulfill any additional personnel needs you may require. Won't you, Bernard?" She smiled her best professional smile.

Bernard stared at her, a baffled look wiping the grin from his face. He tilted his head toward her. "What's that you said?"

"WBBB?" interjected Brenda, seeking to re-divert his attention to her even as Leana prepared to repeat her request. "What does that stand for?"

She succeeded. A playful gleam sparking his eyes, Bernard puffed out his chest, intoned deeply: "We-Be-Black-Builders."

Leana smiled politely when Brenda, pulling herself up in her chair and leaning forward, whooped, and finding her appreciation of his little joke contagious, Bernard laughed along with her. Her tolerance turned to muted resentment when the two of them fell into jolly competition to see who could laugh longest before being thrown out of the posh restaurant. But when the joke wore off, which to Leana's mind, was trite and unwarrantedly long, Bernard reinvented the laughter. Leaning across the table to grasp Brenda's hand, he knocked his water goblet over.

A pained look on her face, Leana put a hand to her throat and fixed her eyes at a point above the curious, up-turning heads of the urbane diners on the lower level.

"Bernard! Bernard!" Brenda whispered quickly, squeezing his arm in an ecstasy, her face yet rosy with mirth. "Shush! Look at Leana. We're embarrassing her!"

"Embarrassed?" Leana turned her head, held haughty on her elegant neck, sharply. "Why would I be embarrassed? So I'm sitting at a table with a woman who was raised in a barn and her new friend, the Klutz! What's to be embarrassed about?"

There was a tense moment when a hound dog expression appeared on Bernard's face. "You're no fun, Leana," he said, shaking his curly head sadly. "You ought to be more like Brenda."

Leana lay stretched out in the jacuzzi in her blue and aqua bathroom. Lounging in the churning, steaming water laced with soothing bath oils, she closed her eyes dreamily. Patrice had left her to return to his 'Case of the Suspicious Boyfriend' right after they'd made love again and showered. Her head lolling on the rim of the tub, she thought it incredible the effect the man had on her. Just thinking of him made her weak. Lying back in the tub and letting the whirling waters do their thing, she felt giddy. No need to worry about being too much for Mr. Patrice to handle. Sighs, caresses, stroke for joyous stroke, he'd matched her. She kicked a refreshed leg through the rushing water, high in the air. Life was wonderful.

Brenda. She sighed. Her high spirits went poof!, and the smooth, hairless brown leg flopped with a lethargic splash into the water. Brenda was another reality. Sometimes, she just did not understand that woman. Brenda was warm, generous, a little nosey but friendly, and even though her humor left a lot to be desired, could actually be funny. They were best friends, and God granting, they would always be so. But why, she wondered despairingly, couldn't she be a little more . . . genteel? Brenda had a good-paying job and her family was loaded. She'd never been poor. Maybe that was why she didn't take things seriously.

A frown creased her tender brow when she recalled how close she had come to making a scene in that restaurant. Brenda could be so dense. Everyone wasn't so fortunate as she. There she was giggling and flirting with Bernard while she was trying to get him to commit to a couple of jobs for people on their last spiritual, not to mention, economic legs. Desperate men and women who looked to the Blyden Center as their last hope for a hand up rather than a hand-out. Young kids just out of high school who couldn't seem to get that first job; older men and women who knew employers were not supposed to turn them away because they were over forty-five, but either had no idea of how to go about fighting age discrimination or were so worn out from a lifetime of trying to get around racial discrimination, they had nothing left with which to fight. There had come a point in all that loud laughter where she had wanted to just scream at Brenda. She, little Leana Claremont who never made scenes; who always tried to be reasonable and fair, who even cringed when she heard a mother yell at her child, had been on the verge of creating a public disturbance! And Bernard—Gawd! Talk about not being able to take a person anywhere!

Biting down on her lip in mild exasperation, Leana sighed. Even in high school Brenda had been a prankster; she'd always pushed at limits. Like the time she borrowed Oletha Goodwin's school pass to go to the basketball game because she'd left hers at home. The game began ninth period; students with passes were excused from class. The next day, when Oletha's ninth period teacher looked over the list of students who went to the game, he had been surprised to see Oletha's name, for he knew she had been present in class. They had wanted to suspend Brenda, so sure Miss-butter-wouldn't-melt-in-her-mouth-Oletha had been misled by her when in fact, it had been Oletha who suggested to Brenda that she use the pass in the first place. Because she was passable pretty, wore nice clothes and could be counted on to laugh louder than anyone else at even the lamest of jokes, Brenda was popular with her peers. Thus, when Oletha refused to own up to her complicity, as she had anticipated, Brenda refused to squeal, preferring suspension to being known around school as a snitch.

But Oletha had not reckoned on Leana. Leana, the skinny, shy girl with the quickly hurt eyes; the little nobody Brenda had befriended simply because she needed someone to blabber with in Trigonometry; Leana, who would rather be known as a wimp than to cause a scene. It was the other Leana—Leana, the do-gooder, the Leana of whom an advanced sense of justice, integrity and loyalty would always be guiding forces in her life— the Leana who had not yet learned that no good deed goes unpunished that went to the principal.

While Brenda was guilty of using another student's pass, she argued earnestly, Oletha as instigator was even more guilty. And if punishment was needed, well, consider her, Leana, as punished, for once it got around school that she'd 'snitched', she would be ostracized.

True to the unwritten code, Marilyn Henderson and Rutha Peabody had met her in the hall between periods the next day, and after blocking her way, tried to get smart with her. Brenda, who had been walking with some of the Chicken Shack gang behind them, saw what was happening and jumped in, straight up.

"You got a problem with my friend? I don't think so. Just keep on going where you're going. Okay?" Marilyn and Ruta took her advice and continued on down the hall, sullen but faster. So no matter how tiresome she could be, Leana knew that Brenda was the best friend a girl could ever want for.

Leana stretched her arms out, let them float on the fast bubbling water. Feeling relaxed and refreshed, she smiled driftingly. Who would have thought it. Brenda and Bernard. Klutz number one and Klutz number two. In different ways, of course, but klutzes, nonetheless. Wanting the whole world to be as happy as she, Leana plucked the tulip-shaped glass filled with cola from the rim of the tub, and toasted to her two friends' future together.

Turning off the jacuzzi and rising from the tub, she

Wish You Were Here?

You can be, every month, with Zebra Historical Romance Novels.

YOU'RE GOING TO LOVE GETTING
4 FREE BOOKS

These books worth almost $20, are yours without cost or obligation when you fill out and mail this certificate.
(If the certificate is missing below, write to: Zebra Home Subscription Service, Inc., 120 Brighton Road, P.O. Box 5214, Clifton, New Jersey 07015-5214

Complete and mail this card to receive 4 Free books!

Yes! Please send me 4 Zebra Historical Romances without cost or obligation. I understand that each month thereafter I will be able to preview 4 new Zebra Historical Romances FREE for 10 days. Then, if I should decide to keep them, I will pay the money-saving preferred publisher's price of just $4.00 each...a total of $16. That's almost $4 less than the publisher's price. (A nominal shipping and handling charge of $1.50 per shipment will be added.) I may return any shipment within 10 days and owe nothing, and I may cancel this subscription at any time. The 4 FREE books will be mine to keep in any case.

Name _____

Address _____ Apt. _____

City _____ State _____ Zip _____

Telephone ( ) _____

Signature _____ LP0395
(If under 18, parent or guardian must sign.)

Terms, offer and prices subject to change without notice. Subscription subject to acceptance by Zebra Books. Zebra Books reserves the right to reject any order or cancel any subscription.

TREAT YOURSELF TO 4 FREE BOOKS.

A $19.96
value.
FREE!

No obligation
to buy
anything, ever.

dried herself off with an oversized towel, then wrapping her body in it, padded barefoot across the floor into the adjacent bedroom. Pulling from her wardrobe a tank top and cardigan in a shimmering, jazzy jade with a black silk overlay and black, silk-velvet pants, she dressed for her date with Patrice. She was decorating her ears with black pearl drop earrings when the telephone rang. Thinking it might be him, she ran into the living room, the sequined top and cardigan flicking from green to silver as she went. Flopping onto the sofa, a leg curling beneath her, she called breathlessly into the receiver, "Hello!"

"Who's dis?"

"I'm sorry." Taken aback, she sat up straight. "Who did you wish to speak to?"

"You, if youse Leana."

"Who is this?!" and even as she asked, she felt a sense of deja vu. Sometime, somewhere, she'd had this conversation before.

"Dis here is Henry. Henry James. You Leana?"

Leana's face softened in her confusion, and then she smiled. Very prettily. "Yes, Henry. I'm Leana."

"So, you is da one I talked to da otha day. I told Mr. Jackson 'bout that. He say since I runs my mouth so much, I'm da one has to call 'n tell you he's sorry, but he caint make hit tanight. Seems some lady's ole man . . . Naw, let me git it right," he said, regrouping. "Said to tell you dat 'da boyfriend' is done left town 'n he gotta follow him. Said he hoped you'd undastand, 'n dat he'd make hit up ta ya."

"Oh, shoot!" Leana said as she fell back on the sofa, her voice ringing with disappointment.

"Aw, don't worry none," Henry James said laughingly. "He love you, too!"

"Henry," she could not help grinning, her face again soft and now flushing. "You are something else! It's just a date, that's all."

"Date, smate! Dat man is crazy 'bout you, girl. You betta latch onto him. He a good man. 'N dat's all I got ta . . ."

"Hello." It was a woman's voice. "Is this Leana?"

Leana felt her stomach muscles tighten. "Yes, it is," she replied equably. "To whom am I speaking?" And when the woman replied, "Mrs. Jackson," she almost dropped the receiver.

"Patrice's mother," she continued.

"Oh, his mother, Mrs. Jackson!" she exclaimed, breathless with relief. "Yes! How are you?"

"I'm fine, thank you," the cultured voice with the slight Southern accent replied. "Dear," she went on, "Patrice told me he had to break a date with you before he left. I've been over here, trying to help out," she explained. "I'm on my way home, now, and since you're not going out tonight, I was wondering if you'd care to join me at my house for a cocktail later on? Patrice has told us so much about you."

Leana paused at the word 'us'. She was sure Patrice had said his parents were divorced. "Yes," she said hesitantly. Then, putting a bright enthusiasm into her tone, said more definitely, "I'd like that."

"Good. Marie and I will see you at seven. Is that all right?"

"Marie?"

"Yes. Patrice's sister."

Oh Lord, Leana thought nervously as she hung up the

telephone. A sister, too! Peeling off the shimmery lounge clothes, she pulled her basic little black dress from the closet, along with a magenta, lightweight nubby wool jacket. Choosing a pair of black patent leather pumps with suede toes to dress up the conservative outfit, she stepped out of her gold party shoes. She checked the overall effect in the mirrors above her dresser, adjusted the shoulders of the jacket. With the black pearl earrings dropping from an antique gold clip centered by a round black pearl in her ears—her only other jewelry a gold dinner ring with a cultured pearl inset—and her straight slim body, she looked classy, not at all intimidating in the simple black dress. Satisfied with the image she presented, she transferred the contents of her silk pouch into a black leather bag, slung the strap over her shoulder, and left the apartment for the Deli in the atrium, ready to conquer her love's family on a full stomach.

Chapter Ten

Mrs. Jackson was a matronly woman. A large pearl brooch pinned across her ample bosom, her hair was brushed off her face and puffed softly into a carefully arranged bun at the nape of her neck. As dark as her son, there were lines of sorrow on her brow, but etched there were lines of sweetness, as well, and neither age nor melancholy could dim the beauty of those deep dark eyes gleaming the gentle sable lights that Leana would have recognized anywhere. She had a calm, easy manner, and although like many transplanted southerners, she tried to hide it, a sweet country girl drawl. Greeted with a true smile of acceptance, Leana was made to feel so at home that she completely forgot the anxiety and trepidations that had so wracked her when she first set out to meet her.

Leana's first surprise had been when she drove through the bright moonlight into the little cul de sac shaded by mature, leafy elms on the near West Side. A pleasant quiet street of one and two-story homes behind carefully groomed hedges and well-kept lawns, the area was in the process of being gentrified by ex-suburbanites who, wanting to live in the city, were pouring tens of thousands of dollars into restoration of the old buildings and townhouses.

While there was nothing glamorous about the Jackson house, a two-story frame, unprepossessing, but with beautiful cornices, two brick chimneys, its exterior painted an incredible café au lait with green shutters and trim, Leana felt the pride and love that had gone into its maintenance as the Mercedes' headlamps swept into the short circular drive, edged by sweet, low-lying ground-cover.

When Mrs. jackson showed her into the living room, Leana came to a dead halt, her eyes growing large in her face and softly gasping, charmed by the room that looked like a page out of a Victorian catalog.

Papered in a spanking gold and gray floral pattern, good maroon carpeting, laid in strips, covered the floor. Two narrow windows, deep-set and seven feet tall that were almost straight-laced in their simplicity, fronted the veranda that wrapped three sides of the house. Heavy green brocade drapes were tied back with center drawstrings dangling old-fashioned gilt tassels so that only the white sheers covering the windows held back the dark. Framed photographs of family members were arranged around heavy crystal candelabras on the dark walnut mantelpieces of two working fireplaces in the long, narrow room. Neither fire was lit, although a gentle warmth pervaded the room.

Mrs. Jackson took a chair facing Leana, sitting on the edge of the gracefully curved sofa opposite and peeking at her surroundings as she tried to steady the cup to keep it from rattling. She felt comfortable and at the same time, in awe of this room. With its eclectic mix of textures and cheery papered walls and china lamps with long-fringed cloth shades, it was a memory from her childhood—not the drab one-room reality of spring-sprung upholstery covered with bedsheets that she and Muh-dear shared; rather the warm one with brothers and sisters and parents who waited up late that carried her through the night.

"I hope you like tea," said Mrs. Jackson. "I didn't remember until after we'd hung up the phone that Patrice said you didn't drink alcohol."

Leana hunched her shoulders like a little child. "No. I don't. No real reason. I just don't see any need to pick up any more bad habits. Although," she assured her, leaning forward apprehensively, "I don't have any really bad habits. At least, none that anyone would consider really bad."

"I'm sure you don't, dear," Mrs. Jackson replied, settling back to a more comfortable position in the tapestry-upholstered side chair. "And believe me," she added, eyeing her tolerantly, "no one expects you to be perfect. None of us are."

Leana smiled, relieved, before lifting her head and blurting, "You have a charming house, Mrs. Jackson! I know your children loved growing up here. I think this might have been the house of my dreams when I was little." She spoke quickly, her breath coming fast and, looking around the restored, spotlessly clean room, in hushed, awed tones.

Mrs. Jackson's full lips curled, primly pleased. "Thank you, dear. Marie feels the same way. She has an apartment in Prairie Shores, but she stays here half the time. Her closet upstairs is chock full of her clothes. She's here so much that I almost listed her on the last census.'' Then, her dark brow crinkling and looking suddenly, very maternal, she sighed. ''Patrice, however, is another story. He moved out when he finished school. Lock, stock and barrel. He's more adventurous—like his father.''

Leana looked down with a quick, uncertain smile as she continued, a tender look sweeping her face, making wistful her softly blurred features. ''My husband always believed in crossing the road, turning the bend, exploring the next town. But then, again,'' she said casually, and in spite of the accompanying smile, Leana sensed tension in her, ''he's well equipped to do so.'' Her voice changed subtly. ''You know I put him through college.''

''Really?'' Leana asked with restrained politeness.

''Yes. When we married, he could hardly write his name, and he went on to graduate—magna cum laude.'' Leana was surprised to see a certain fierce pride come to her eyes. Then, again sighing, she said, ''Whatever he wants . . .'' She gave an eloquent shrug by way of completing the thought.

They sipped their tea in silence. Then, leaning slightly forward, Leana said, ''Patrice didn't tell me he had a sister. You say her name is Marie?''

''Oh yes! My daughter, Marie.'' Mrs. Jackson got to her feet, limberly for a woman of her size, and went to the mantle. ''This is a picture of her when she was a junior in high school.''

Her cup rattling on the saucer as she placed it on the little side table, Leana rose from the sofa and followed her, taking the picture she proffered proudly. It showed a tall girl in a gymsuit, her face and limbs the color of maple syrup, a volleyball held under one arm. Her bangs mussed, but saucy, there was a dimple in one cheek of her cheerful, grinning face. "Oh, she's pretty!" she exclaimed.

"Thank you!"

Leana turned quickly. Looking chic and comfortable in a sleeveless shell-pink jersey that fell to her bare ankles, given shape by a silver concho belt that rested low on her hips, outside of an off-the-face hairdo, Marie had not changed much since high school. The dimple puncturing her left cheek, her smile was as winsome as the sexy long toes on her slender bare feet that she wiggled as she greeted her. Uncomplicated, warm and friendly, there was a playful quality about her one could scarcely avoid liking, and unable to resist, Leana smiled in return while Mrs. Jackson made the introductions.

"So, you're Leana!" Stepping back, hands sassy on her hips in the clingy dress, Marie let an insinuating smile curl her lips as she gave Leana a jaunty once over. "We have been hearing a lot about you," she grinned, mischievousness sparkling her big brown eyes.

"Hushup, Marie!" Mrs. Jackson admonished her, darting a smiling glance in Leana's direction. While her invitation to Leana to visit was impulsive and could be construed as premature, when a beloved, 31 year old, never married son sits his mother down and says quietly, 'She's the one, mom', what mother could resist throwing decorum to the wind when the opportunity for a quick peek at such a rarefied creature as her possible future daughter-in-law presented itself?

"This one was taken on Patrice's sixteenth birthday," the mother said innocently, as she took another picture from the mantelpiece and handed it to Leana. Her head dipping gently to one side and smiling, neither of the Jackson women missed the precious way she handled the frame nor the tender light in her eyes as Leana looked upon her love's youthful likeness. He had not yet taken on the smouldering determination she knew him to possess, but even at sixteen, the full mouth showed passion, and the compelling dark eyes that from the first had stolen her heart with their beauty were there.

"People say he resembles me a bit," said Mrs. Jackson, gently intruding on her thoughts and, although standing right beside her, sidling up even closer, her enjoyment at seeing her son's portrait through the eyes of his beloved, apparent.

"He certainly has your eyes," Leana murmured, smiling as she stared fixedly at the photo.

"And everything else is daddy's—especially the big nose." Playing with her mother's hair as she peered with her over Leana's shoulder, Marie laughed.

Sucking her breath in with an appalled hiss, Leana frowned. "Patrice doesn't have a big nose! It's perfect! It's strong and beau . . . nice," she amended herself quickly, her cheeks taking on a dusky glow. Then, staunchly: "It goes absolutely perfectly with his face!"

Her eyebrows winging at the passionate defence and the serious expression covering Leana's face, turned now fiercely to her, Marie's mouth twitched.

"Marie's just talking," reprimanded Mrs. Jackson, slapping at Marie's hand twisting a strand of her hair, all the while shuttering her dark eyes against a show of amusement, fastened on their guest's flushing face. But when Leana's indignant expression refused to yield, the rounded corners of her own lips twitched. Taking the frame gently from her hands and replacing it over the fireplace, she handed her the remaining photograph.

"This is a picture of me and Patrice's father when we were first married."

Tearing her frowning eyes from Marie, Leana glanced at the black and white photo of the young elder Jacksons. Startled from her indignation, surprise and admiration tangled with the breath in her lungs. "Oh, my. Oh my," she gasped softly, struck by the provocative pairing of sheer, unadulterated beauty with sheer, masculine forcefulness. She hardly knew which to look at first, the two faces were so compelling.

The 8×10 glossy showed a young woman of tender age with an intelligent, hauntingly beautiful dark face. Possessed of long, heavy black eyebrows hung elegantly over silky black lashes smudging deepset dark eyes, her sleek, black hair was parted on the side and finger-waved across her ears to a "V" at her nape. One squiggly strand dangled from a major wave over her high broad forehead.

Demanding her attention, the bold nose, high cheekbones and grim jawline carved on the face of the proud, heavyset man beside her seemed to jump from the picture at Leana. Bristling with a brash, raw energy that appeared to shoot straight out from piercing, heavy-lidded eyes, his hold on the shoulders of the beautiful, brooding woman with the midnight romantic eyes was easy, yet possessive, and Leana got the sense of a man primed for instant action. Lighter complected than his bride, his hands, lying near the junctures of her slim shoulders and neck seemed tense, as if he guarded something precious, while the determined, close-set eyes which only intensified their piercing nature, showed a man who once he makes up his mind he wants something, goes after it, and once gaining it, keeps it.

Leana felt intimidated just in looking at his likeness. She could better appreciate the anger, the frustration, the hurt the son felt at his mother's loss, at his own sense of abandonment. Knowing, however, that she was expected to comment, she did so. Hesitantly.

"He does. . . ." she groped, tingling with an almost electrical tension as she stared mesmerized by the bold-featured face with dark, almost black eyes holding her attention with an expression that seemed dangerous in its tenacity, ". . . kind of reminds you of Patrice. Uh," she shook her head, awed, stretching for words, "the shape of the head. The jawline, maybe?"

"Tell me about it," Marie said dryly. "They're two of a kind." She pulled a small face, impatient, eager to get it on. Her parent's divorce was old news and she had seen the pictures all her life.

"Spades!" She had an idea. "Let's play spades!"

Leana's awe, however, had not quite flattened. Turning to Patrice's mother, she exclaimed, "But you! Mrs. Jackson!" she marveled, her eyes soft, melting, "you look beautiful!"

"Oh, shoot," Mrs. Jackson demurred, her lips pursed in a teeny smile of vanity as, Leana's eyes dwelling upon her in besotted admiration still, she took the picture and replaced it on the mantlepiece lovingly.

"Shoot, nothing! Let's see how beautiful you think she is when you see her play," Marie warned, her smile deepening the dimple in her left cheek. "My mother's a real shark when it comes to cards!"

"Shame on you, Marie," Mrs. Jackson frowned, taking her daughter to task. "You know my game is bridge. I only play Spades because you and your brother never took the time to learn a real card game."

"Oh, momma!" Marie teased. "You know, you like any card game."

"You don't know if this heah chile even plays cards," she chided, lapsing into her southern accent. "She doesn't drink, you know," she intoned significantly.

"Oh, I play," Leana assured them in a hasty, apologetic voice. "And Spades is my favorite."

Marie needed no further prompting. "I'll get the cards." Turning on her heel, she sped from the parlor, her bare feet slapping on the carpeted runner to her upstairs bedroom while Mrs. Jackson and Leana retired to the dining room. It was another charming room in a house where all the rooms charmed. Green brocade drapes tied back with gilt tasseled braid, its sole window opening onto the spacious veranda, pots of leafy green plants dangled from the roofed overhang throwing shadows across the moon-drenched planks.

The green-draped windows were the only constant in the interior decor, Mrs. Jackson proudly informed her as they sat at the drop-leaf walnut table. In all the rooms were different patterned carpets and bold, floral-patterned wallpaper; all as attractive as that found in the parlor. The dining room carpet was squares in a multitude of rich orange and red colors. Fabulous snowy white gardenias on curved green stems covered the walls.

Pulling up a side chair, tenderness for the ecletic textures and colors surrounding her warmed Leana's heart and sinking into a gentle place in her mind, she pictured her, Patrice and a passel of kids belonging to them. She imagined them in the dining room at breakfast, sunlight pouring in through the window, burning a white patch on the floor, as white as the gardenias on the wall, settling over them all like a blessing. Unlike its pink and green exterior, Mrs. Jackson's house inside was just the opposite. It was an old house, she told Leana while they awaited Marie, almost a hundred years old, with swinging glass transoms over the doors of each of the second floor bedrooms.

"My husband bought it for me after he finished college and the business took off. I've been here ever since about fifteen years now," she said, looking fondly around the spotless, busy-patterned room. Her voice changed subtly. "It turned out to be his going-away present, as well."

The subdued way she spoke took Leana unawares, plucking her from her fantasy and she looked up in surprise.

"Well!" Mrs. Jackson exclaimed briskly, giving a quick shiver. "That's that!"

Dear God in heaven. Here she sat in this room dreaming of new beginnings while the dignified woman opposite had presided in this same room over the demise of her own dreams. Her bravery wrenched Leana's heart.

"I'm sorry, Mrs. Jackson. Really and truly."

"It's okay, dear. What's done is done," she said philosophically. "What's past is past."

"I just. . . ." Leana hunched her shoulders, peering out at her from troubled eyes. "I just don't understand. Patrice . . . well, he told me what happened. And after meeting you. . . ." Her slim shoulders moved feelingly. "You're such a nice lady. . . . I just don't understand."

"Oh, my husband felt he'd outgrown me," Mrs. Jackson said primly, her emotions under control. "He was up and coming and I was an old, worn-out homebody. I didn't fit. I wasn't young, anymore, you see. I wasn't glamorous. I was willing to keep on working in the business—don't get me wrong. But I also wanted to raise my kids proper, have supper on the table when my man came home. The way I was raised.

"You see," she went on confidingly, warming to the woman who took on the sufferings of others so readily, "to me, the business was the means to an end. A good life for my family. Crawley now, he enjoyed the game part of it—the wheeling and dealing, the one-upping of the next fellow. He loved the challenge, the excitement of the game. Patrice, you know, shares that with him. He has that same dauntless spirit, that same determination to have it all." She laughed then, and the sound was gentle, but mirthless. "And on *his* terms."

Marie returned with the cards. Smacking her lips and slapping the deck on the table, she flung her limber body in a side chair, tucking one bare foot beneath her. "We playing 'blind nine' or what?" They were sitting around the dining room table engaged in a cutthroat game of Spades when they heard the front door open.

Shuffling the cards, Mrs. Jackson looked up, her head tilted in a listening attitude. "Now who could that be?" She pushed her chair back, but before she could rise from the table, Leana felt her pulse quicken as the voice reached them, her very heart to snatch: "Hey, anybody home?!"

Moving familiarly through the small front foyer and busy-patterned parlor, Patrice turned into the dining room where, upon seeing Leana, he did a double-take. Then, embracing her with a eye look, a slow smile spread his dark-wine lips. "Hi," he said softly.

His sensuous lips pulled back, showing even white

teeth under his mustache, with his shirtsleeves pushed to the elbows, his tie hanging loosely around his neck, the pale blue of his shirt bringing out the dark brilliance of his eyes and clinging limply to his shoulders, emphasizing their breadth. Leana felt the force of his masculinity across the floor, and her heart fluttered in her chest. His voice was low with the tender timbre that made her knees go weak and it took all that she had not to leap from her seat and fling herself upon him.

"Hello," she instead replied softly, and grinning a little stupidly.

He stared at her so warmly and with such melting intensity that Mrs. Jackson coughed gently to remind them that others were present.

"What're you doing here?" Marie asked flippantly. "You're supposed to be on one of your cases."

"Case over, lil sis," he replied with no change of expression. Then breaking the haunting gaze, his denim-clad legs moved across the carpet to mother's side, who with a warm motherly glow smiled when he kissed her.

Turning to Marie on her right, he pulled a wolfish grin. "And you!" he said, bending, and with one hand bracing on the top rung of her chair, planted a kiss on her forehead. "Happy to see you, too!"

"Aren't you going to kiss Leana?" she asked cheekily.

Cuffing her affectionately on the shoulder, then circling the table, he leaned over Leana, who, out of respect for his mother, turned him a hot cheek. To her embarrassment, and secret bliss, he grasped her chin with a careless hand and turning it, gave her a peck on the lips. "Hi sweetheart," he whispered against her mouth.

Her skin tingling from the intimacy of his greeting—
the endearment had slid so easily from his lips—Leana
lowered her head. The smile curving her lips split her
face as she fussed with her hair.

"Hey!" a new voice demanded. "Where is everybody?"

"Oops!" Patrice grinned. "Forgot all about
Mandy." Poking his head through the doorway abutting
the parlor, he called out directionally, "Back here!"

Bouncing into the dining room, Mandy burst upon the
scene, a rich grin for Patrice. The smile faded from
Leana's lips as she noticed he grinned back fondly. She
found it impossible not to notice also the skimpy, openly
sexual black camisole that showed Mandy's belly button
above her skin-tight jeans.

"Mandy, dear!" Mrs. Jackson smiled at the younger
woman. Her eyes beneath her lifting brows warmly encouraging, she held up the cards she was dealing.
"We're playing three-handed Spades. Why don't you
join us and make it partners?"

"Three . . ." The smile ready on her lips, her glance
shifted to the bow-fronted China cabinet before which
sat Leana. Rearing back like a serpent almost in reflex,
bluntly she asked, "What're you doing here!?"

"Have you met Leana, Mandy?" Marie asked quizzi-
cally, shifting in her chair, her head turning at the queru-
lous tone.

Shrugging slim, barely clothed shoulders, Mandy
looked her distaste. "We've met."

Folding her cards on the table, there was nothing girlishly bashful in her demeanor as Leana parried the antagonistic glare with a quiet smile. "Yes, we have. As a

matter of fact," she said, turning her smile to Marie, "we met at my friend Brenda's house last week."

Mandy was disinterested. Her hazel eyes skimmed Leana's person from head to foot, then flicked back disdainfully to her face. Throwing her head back aggressively, she repeated her demand. "So what're you doing here?"

"She's my guest, dear," said Mrs. Jackson amiably, beaming at Mandy a unperturbed smile of such understanding that she flinched. "I invited her over." She stopped shuffling the cards long enough to glance at Leana, a dear, cheek-plumping, country-girl smile.

"And I'm glad I did. She's a very nice young lady." A look of complete approval in her smiling, deep dark eyes, she reached a hand across the table and patted Leana's slender fingers affectionately.

Taking note of the glinting dislike in Mandy's eyes, then swinging her considering gaze to Leana, looking poised and in control of herself and the situation, the dimple in Marie's cheek re-surfaced.

Surveying the cards as she dealt them, in a pleasant, well-modulated tone, devoid of accent, Mrs. Jackson asked, "Won't you join us, Mandy?"

"Why don't you Mandy?" Patrice suggested.

Mandy looked at Leana, sullen. "I guess so. For a minute," she added gracelessly. "We've had a long drive and you still have to take me home."

Patrice quirked an eyebrow at her rudeness. "No sweat. You'll get there. You can take Leana's hand for her. I want you to see my mother's garden," he said, turning to grasping Leana by the hand, pulling her to her feet. "It's not as fancy as Brenda's, but I think you'll like it."

Marie burst out laughing. "The garden? Why don't you just ask her upstairs to see your etchings?!" Looking across the table at her mother, she threw her a waggish look that begged comment on her cleverness.

"Chill, Marie!" big brother, who was not amused, said snappishly. His heavy brows tugging together, he wound a possessive arm around the nubby wool jacket covering Leana's delicate shoulders, he nodded brusquely around table. "Excuse us."

Conscious of his arm curved around her and of the three pairs of eyes she imagined boring like brown lasers into her back, butterflies fluttered in Leana's stomach as she allowed Patrice to steer her through the kitchen and onto the shady back veranda which overlooked the large back yard.

It was a bright night, clear and beautiful, with a full moon that bathed the yard in an eerie silver light. The voices of the women drifting out through the open back door, Leana leaned over the wooden railing. The green manicured lawn, drenched in glittery moonlight, swept back to the two-car garage before a paved alley.

"Where's the garden?" she asked, looking around the yard puzzled.

His answer was to put his arms around her, and hauling her against him, kiss her, a long, consuming kiss that took her breath.

"Oh!" She drew away from him with a little gasp, flicking an uneasy glance back at the house.

Laughing at her sense of propriety, he recaptured Leana in both his arms. "The shades in the kitchen are down and no one can see us under this overhang. Now," he drawled, leaning over her with a lecherous grin, "pucker up, baby!"

Leana giggled. "Silly," she said, pushing at his chest. "We'd better look at your mother's garden. They might ask questions!"

"Why?" he asked, his voice muffled as refusing to release her, he nuzzled her neck. "They know what it looks like."

"Patrice," she remonstrated, planting her hands squarely against his wide shoulders and pushing him away. "Don't embarrass me. Not here. Not in . . . this house."

"Hmm," he murmured, drawing back, one brow lifting. "Seems like my hot momma has turned into a cold fish."

"Come on," she demanded laughingly, pulling him from the veranda. "Let's go look at that garden."

Slipping a cosy arm around her waist, they started down the steps into the yard. The night was warm, the air filled with the scent of freshly mowed lawn, the tinkle of Leana's laughter and his leg brushing against her skirt, Patrice leaned for a whiff of the perfume she dabbed in the hollow behind her ear.

"Oh, this is cute!" she exclaimed, when they reached the object side of the garage and she saw yellow and gold and wine-red marigolds with velvet-petals interspersed gaily between short neat rows of vegetables— lettuce, sweet and hot peppers, and salad tomatoes glowing like drops of blood against the dark tilled earth.

"She should get a pretty good yield out of it," he said, glancing briefly at the colorful small plot. His eyes drifted back to Leana. "Want to see the lawn mower? It's in the garage," he said, his voice taking on a husky edge, a hungry possessive darkening of his already dark eyes. Taking both of her hands and moving slowly backward, pulling her toward the garage, when she balked, he tipped his head to one side, and for a moment, studied her face.

Frowning, she licked her lips. When she raised her lovely eyes filled with reproach, to him, a faintly wry smile coursed his lips.

"You don't think anyone actually believes I brought you out here to see this little two by four garden, do you?"

Leana's gaze flickered, slid away from the passion mingled with a certain amusement smouldering in his eyes. She looked down briefly at her hands, held fast in his, lifted her dark lashes slowly to midnight romantic eyes. Then, twisting her head on her neck, she cocked an eye at the garden. For a long slow moment, she stared down upon it silent contemplation, and when she spoke her voice was low, oddly seductive. "Looks more like six by nine to me." One corner of her mouth curled up, she looked back at Patrice, the sweet gleams in her eyes locking provocatively with his heavy-lidded gaze. "Yes," she said slowly. "I definitely would like to see that lawn mover."

Chapter Eleven

Patrice was seated on an old orange crate; he held Leana nestled in his lap, one hand rubbing the insides of her thighs.

Wiggling her bottom sinuously against him, her voice was thick as she whispered, "Patrice. You mustn't." She moaned softly, shakily, when squeezing high on the soft firmness of her thigh, his knuckles brushed across the sensitive lips of her vulva.

"What?" he murmured, pressing his lips to her long neck, her gentle, embarrassed responsiveness firing his libido, making him feel powerful and sexy. "You're so soft, baby. Your thighs," he sighed, drawing her to him closely, his deep voice tender. "They're so soft, they make me crazy. Crazy." His free hand roamed her back and hips, curving beneath her buttocks in the little black dress. He lifted her higher into his lap.

"Please, Patrice," she cajoled him, her voice ragged under his kneading, knuckling caress. Feeling a surge of heat with the whole body tingling that shuddered her person and caused her bottom to squirm restlessly against him, she planted a frenzy of tiny kisses on his neck.

Patrice captured an earlobe between his teeth and nibbled it lightly. "Please what, baby?" he demanded in a rough, husky whisper, tugging at her lobe with his lips. "Please love me? Like I love you? Let me show you how much I love you, baby." He brought her gently against him, and twisting his hand higher up her thigh, pushed beneath the elastic band of her panties, stroked her quickening sex.

Oh, no! Not here! She couldn't! Not in this dirty garage. It was just too cheap! she thought, even as her slim fingers curved around his neck, her swelling breasts flattened against his chest and she panted moistly, "No. Oh!" She turned her head into his chest and moaned, a soft, shurring sound as the fluids in her body melted against his hardening erection.

"Baby. I missed you," he groaned, gripping one squirming buttock, his voice hoarse as he sucked tenderly the fleshy lobe of her ear. Feeling a tickling bubble up inside her, his hand was sliding down the front of her arm, about to cup her breast when Leana's breaking giggle erupted, derailing his concentration, cooling his ardor.

His head lifting, Patrice leaned back against the wall, tilted her face on his shoulder. Light issuing from a streetlamp, its sodium bulb buried in the branches of an elm in the alley, filtered through bamboo blinds covering the rear windows of the garage and touched dimly Leana's mirthful face.

"What're you laughing at?"

"Nothing," she lied, turning her face back into the warm cove of his shoulder.

He plucked loose a strand of her hair, twirled it carelessly around his finger. "Not going to tell me, huh?"

"It's nothing," she smiled, cradled gently and safe in his big hard body. "I could fall asleep on your lap. For always," she added dreamily.

"You know you can if you want to," he whispered intimately in her ear, tucking the strand of hair he'd played with behind it. "I wouldn't mind."

Leana giggled again.

"What!?" he exclaimed gently and smiling.

"Oh," she began, snuggling against him, deciding an explanation was in order if she was going to keep up this silly giggling. "It's just that you said you missed me," she said mistily, her mind drifting.

She had been so nervous at the thought of meeting Patrice's mother without him. So wired, that by the time she reached Jackson Street and was turning the corner, she had found herself fiddling with the radio, trying to find a station with music more soothing than Rap. Her nerves were stretched taut and questions worried her mind. That slightly nasal tone she heard in Mrs. Jackson's voice. Was it Southern in origin? Did she always invite Patrice's new girlfriends over for after-dinner drinks? Why not dinner? Had Patrice told his mother she ate funny, or something?

When she shifted on his lap and giggled all over at the thought, Patrice sighed, and cuddling her close, very gently rubbed her back.

Oh, I hate this! She had bawled in her mind. Talking to strangers was one thing. Sitting across a table looking at the mother of the source of her life, her breath, her reason for being, was something different. Every insecurity she ever harbored had risen up to taunt her.

Miss Classy, hot-shot executive would be exposed for the little nappy-headed girl from 35th Street she'd always been.

'Patrice should be with me' she thought, taking deep breaths to calm her nerves. He made her feel strong, capable, good about herself. Rotating the feminine muscles in her shoulders, she heaved a deep, tension-relieving sigh. So very good. Strong and passionate. Liberatingly passionate, allowing her to be herself without censure, she realized, feeling a tingling of the whole skin of her body. Where he'd touched her. Kissed her. Like he was kissing her now, she thought dreamily, feeling his lips nuzzle in her hair.

Uncurling her body in his lap and tipping her head back on shoulders broad enough to hold her forever, she lifted a languid hand, felt for his face in the darkness and finding it, stroked his rough cheek lovingly.

"You're wonderful," she sighed.

"You think so?" he asked lazily, taking her hand and nibbling on her knuckles. "It's not true, but . . ." She heard a strangling sound vibrate in his throat before he cleared it, then continued. ". . . I'm glad you feel that way." He lifted his head and although she could not see his expression, it altered, and his voice sobered.

"I've never met a woman like you, Leana. When it comes to wonderful, you're everything wonderful to me. You're everything wonderful a man could want in a woman," he said extravagantly, his words flowing in the darkness full of love and quiet conviction. "You're sweet and warm and you soothe my emotions. I feel more connected to you than I've felt to any woman. I love you Leanna Claremont, and I want to protect you."

Leana lay quiet, listening to the rhythmic flow of his

words. She took a deep breath and exhaled slowly. Protect her? An incredible thought, but he sounded so serious . . .

"From what?" Her tone was joshing, but breathless, a husky tremble flowing back in the dark to meet him. She had never thought of herself in terms of needing protection. She was young. She was healthy. She had a good job and a little set aside. And with the state the world was in, she couldn't. It would be emotional suicide to permit such a notion to enter her head.

"I'm a big girl. I can take care of myself."

"Can you take care of me?"

His breath had slowed. She could tell from its fanning warmth across her skin. Oh my, she thought. This man was so full of mysteries she could spend a lifetime unraveling them if only he would let her.

"*Would* you take care of me?" he persisted.

Leana almost laughed in her giddiness. Take care of him? She'd cook for him. She'd clean for him. She'd . . . *Dear God in Heaven!* What was he trying to tell her? Was something wrong with him?! Was he sick? Was he going to *die?*

"Is there a light in here?" she asked, wanting to see his face suddenly. She *had* to see his face. Bolting from his lap, she fumbled along the wall until she found the light switch. She moved back warily in the glare of a flickering bulb to where Patrice remained seated on the orange crate, his hands dangling between his knees and grinning up at her.

"Oh . . . *you!*" she laughed, relieved, and poking him in the chest with a finger.

Unfazed by her puny finger, he pulled her back onto his lap. "See what I mean, sweetheart?" He wrapped his arms around her and held her close. "I'll protect you from the boogy-man.

"Leana." His voice was husky with conviction. "Any man worth a dime wants to protect the woman he loves. Other than my mother and baby sister, you're the only woman I love. And I want to protect you. Full time."

Her eyes glazing with tears, Leana bit down on her lower lip to keep it from trembling, at the same time pressing two fingers to his mouth to still the source of her heart's breaking from happiness and joy.

But there were things Patrice wanted to say, things he had to say. Kissing the tips of her quivering fingers gently, he put her hand aside.

"A man needs a woman to need him," he said, his voice taking on a caressing, almost hypnotic quality. "As woman's instinct is to nurture, man's instinct is to protect." He tilted her face on his shoulder. "I offer my protection to you, Leana," he said, a dark emotion in his eyes as he gazed at her humbly, with no ego. "I would be so honored if you would accept it."

The air between them changed, thickened. Leana was suddenly acutely conscious that she had been holding her breath for the past few moments. She gulped air, then swallowed.

"Thank you," she whispered moistly. Flinching at the woeful inadequacy of her response, she arched back from his embrace and looked searchingly into his glittering dark eyes, somber on her face and tender.

"You have beautiful eyes," the man who stole her heart with his own whispered. "Really beautiful."

Although others saw her as tender-hearted, Leana had always thought of herself as a strong person, emotionally. She knew there were those who would prey on her sympathy, but in her climb to the top of her profession, she had erected barriers, developed defenses against the hustlers, the cons, those with hidden agendas who would use her tender regard for their own self-serving purposes. Looking into his serious dark eyes, turned so directly and exclusively on her, she recognized her barriers for what they were—mere tricks, illusions. By the force of his love, Patrice laid waste to her emotional defenses, laid bare her fragile heart, and what breath was left in her lungs exploded in words from between her lips: "Not everyone likes my eyes 'cause they're not really almond-shaped, you know, they're a little too oval and some people even accuse me of having cat's eyes!"

At her rushed, evasive words and breathless voice, a tiny smile kicked up one corner of Patrice's mouth. His eyes held hers for a brief and tender moment, then deliberately, he cuffed her on the chin.

"I like cats," he grinned, lifting the intense mood with humor.

"Silly."

"But it's the truth."

"Amazing. A truthful man," she said, her neck curving in a graceful incline as she smiled down shyly, thinking back on when she'd last heard that.

"Okay. A blind man, then."

Her head snapped back dubiously. "Blind?"

"I'm in love," he said, gathering her up with a sigh, returning her to his arms. ". . . with you."

Pressing her face into his neck, Leana smothered another nervous giggle when the flickering bulb gave up the ghost, plunging them back into darkness. "See there," Patrice chuckled. "Told you I was blind."

Falling blissfully mute as well as blind, she rested her head on his chest. When she felt a gentle hand smooth back her hair, then his lips caress the top of her head, Leana tipped her face up and allowed him to kiss her. Their lips sealing gently, rolling about, exploring with a freshness the generous contours of each other's mouth, it was an affirming, incredibly satisfying kiss.

At some point, Leana did not know when, passion reared its hungry head. Her hands sliding across the thick warmth of his hair, she embraced his head, and with his unspoken permission, kissed him again. Kissed him softly, urgently, the dusty floor, the cobwebs she'd spied in the corner, the close, slightly musty smell of a place where the windows did not open and the door seldom was, forgotten. His response as swift, he joined her new kiss with bruising force before his lips slowed, melted into her compliant softness, moved druggingly across her mouth.

Sighing and trembling, feeling little thrills and shocks race through her blood, prickling her skin, her arm was hooked around his neck, the hem of her dress was tangled high on her hips, one foot was on his thigh, the knee turned into his chest and his stroking hand returned inside her panties when the garage door creaked.

Oblivious of her environment and kissing his face, Leana aligned her lips again and again with the full, royal lips of Patrice. His tongue a thick, raspy-textured force plumbing the sweet, warm offering of her mouth, her hand was unzippering, moving inside his jeans when a shaft of moonlight spilled like water across the floor of the garage. Leana tensed. Her head lifting, she sat up on his lap, alert and tingling. When the creaking intensified and the wedge of silvered light widened, she pushed his hand from her hastily and scrambled to her feet. "Who's there?" Zippering his jeans with clumsy fingers, passion mingled hoarsely in his voice with frustration, and tension hardened his face.

"Me," came the tentative reply. "Mandy." There was a silence, a hesitation, before she stepped over the portal. Thanking the darkness, Leana was standing, nervously smoothing her dress when she entered the garage fully. Rising from the orange crate, Patrice moved edgily to the door. Stopped in the pale wedge of moonlight, his tension-hardened features appeared cold, eerie.

"Just what is so urgent that you felt the need to come bursting in here without knocking?" he asked Mandy in a deceptively quiet voice. "What exactly were you looking for?"

"I have to go, Patrice," she said, her voice little girl-like. "You promised to take me home."

His broad muscular shoulders hunched forward, seeming to fill the door, when Mandy took an apprehensive step back, the tension in the aftermath of aborted passion abruptly fled Patrice's body, leaving him feeling drained. He blew a deep sigh through his nostrils; turned his head laboriously.

"Look baby," he said, glancing back at Leana with a weary air of apology, "If you haven't made any other plans, I can always come back."

"But you need your rest!" Mandy objected swiftly. "We were on the road a long time."

Swiveling his head on his neck slowly, and leveling a glare on his assistant, the tension in Patrice re-surfaced. "I have a mother, Mandy," he said in a soft, lethal drawl. "I don't need another. Come on, baby," he said, drawing Leana, who in an augre of shame, was trying hard to melt into the woodwork, lightly against him, "I've got to tell my mother and sister goodbye. And you!" he snarled, flashing a hard look at Mandy. "I'll talk to you later . . . in the car!"

Poking her bottom lip out, Mandy darted out of the garage, angry.

The moon was a pale sphere high in the sky, its glow over the quiet street lighting their passage along the walkway. Leana passed an arm through his and clasped his hand. His fingers sliding through hers, they strolled, hands entwined, to the house. Passing the redwood fence beyond which grew bushes of lilac, a waft of floral perfume caught on a velvet night breeze, blew across Leana's face and lifting her head, she inhaled deeply.

Slowing in the walkway, Patrice smiled at his fanciful companion. Her face tilted moonward, as if inviting the silver beams to bathe her face, to wash her with its spiritual sheen, his expression softened and his touch on the smaller hand held loosely in his altered. Sharing with her a more earthy magic, he caressed the inside of her wrist, traced with the ball of his thumb love messages on her palm. When her heart gave a curious little thump, and he felt her shiver, he put an arm around her. "That better?" he asked gently.

She murmured in reply, relaxing against him. Her head resting on his shoulder, Patrice, she thought with a whimsical smile, was an easy man to love. The kind of man a woman could feel safe with, grow gracefully old with. When he looked at her with those luminous, sooty-lashed eyes, the sheer beauty of him made her tremble. When his lips kissed hers, she trembled. A potent mix of strength and tenderness with a heavy dose of sensuality that any woman would covet, she was thinking dreamily before her vision focused and a concerned look rose to trouble her brow.

"If you're tired, maybe you should go home," she suggested quietly, drawing back to look at him.

"No sweat, baby," he murmured lowly in her ear, hugging her warm body, scented with her perfume and a whiff of their passion, back to him. "I'll never be too tired for you."

Although her heart expanded near to bursting, and she felt a renewed tingling right down to her toes, the mind of the woman who could not leave well enough alone was not at ease. "Where did you go?"

"Ohio. Dayton, Ohio." He sighed, his body against hers slumping, feeling the after-effects of the drive all at once.

"Why, you must be exhausted!" Squeezing his waist, dismay for him widened her eyes. "That's at least 500 miles!"

"And worth every one. I got togeth . . ." Rearing back a little, and turning half-way around, he looked at her sharply, the skin around his eyes tightening. It was a wary, almost challenging look, one she had come to know only too well. It seemed to grow with their every encounter. Some regret, some misgiving, some fear? "Let's just say it was worth it," he mumbled uneasily.

The air was warm, drifting the scent of lilacs from across the fence, the moon making crystal moondrops of the late evening dew on the lush green lawn; otherwise, only shadows, and a gentle sheath of silence, surrounded them. Leana stood on the smooth cold pavement, stared at his averted face and felt fear, real fear. Silence and shadows, always between them. Love was there too in the strained silence, but secrets cloaked in shadows and shrouded in silence take love away, eat love alive, banish love to 'what could have been. . . .'

Silence and shadows, she thought despairingly. Striving always for transcendence in her life over the evils of the world, Leana's first impulse was toward love, harmony. Most people saw that in her, even if they had not the words, and gave her their trust instinctively. Why couldn't he? she wondered sadly. Why not him?

"Patrice," she ventured in an attempt to breach the awful strain threatening to settle completely between them as they moved further up the walk. "There's a man at work. His name is Horry Grant. I promised I'd try to get him a job. He's done security work before and. . . ."

A sudden tension clenched Patrice's jaw, surged with anger in his voice. *"No!"*

They were beneath the overhang of the veranda. Her back to one of the wooden supports, Leana fell back blindly against it. Her slender hands clasping together lightly across her chest, astonishment altered her features, made her eyes larger, her mouth softer. Weakly, she asked, "I beg your pardon?"

"Will you give it a *rest?"* His lush lips thinning with impatience, he threw her a look of supreme irritation. Why was she so persistent? Why wouldn't she take no for an answer? "I don't have time for this," he snapped, turning an angry face toward the house. "I've got to get some sleep!"

Leana's heart dropped to her stomach; her hand flew out. "But . . ."

A muscular arm snaked out, grabbed her by the upper arms. The light was stark on his face. The tendons stood out in his neck, and around them the silence suddenly was deafening. For long seconds, he simply glared, the pupils of his eyes dilated to pinpoints. When he did speak, his voice was low, hissing.

"*Listen* to me. Listen to me *real* good. This *my* business. I will run *my* business in the way *I* choose. *Do you understand?*"

The effulgence of the moon washing one side of his face in a cold, perlescent light, his deep-set eyes flashed, diamond-bright, from between their sooty setting of narrowed lashes as he pushed his face, the vein snaking across his temple bulged with blood, close. "Do you?!" he ground out brutally.

"Stop," Leana whimpered. "Let go of me."

"Let . . . !" Patrice looked down at his hands, clenched like manacles on her arms. An expression of agonized disbelief swept his face, he dropped her arms. Reeling back as if drunk, he whirled about, puffed his cheeks and blew through his nostrils. The muscles of his broad back shaking, when Patrice turned back to face her, his voice was thick, bitter, and grating through his clenched teeth. "I told you I loved you! Now just trust me!!"

Leana drew in a confused breath, her soft mouth trembling. Trust him? Trust was a two-way street. What about her? Not five minutes ago, he was loving and needing her and wanting to protect her. Now he's jumping down her throat like she's his worst enemy! What was wrong with him? She stared in silent despair into the face of the man she loved. 'Silence and shadows' she thought with sick chagrin.

Seeing the way the shock of his outburst quivered her body, the shattered expression on her delicately shaped face, Patrice passed a heavy hand across his forehead. There was a moment when their eyes met, and she glimpsed in the adamant face before her, a softening, a silent appeal in the lustrous eyes, and instinctively leaning toward him, she laid gentle hands on his shoulders. Leaning into her caress briefly, he reached a hand out, ran trembling fingers down her cheek, then traced her lips with his thumb before his hand dropped, fell twitching down his side, and he turned away. "Don't get in my business," he told her wearily. "Just don't get in my business."

Snatching bleak eyes away from the cloud of hurt he saw fill hers, his voice changed; it became rough, shuddery. "I'm taking Mandy home now. You can stay or go. It's up to you."

Crossing her arms over her chest and gripping her shoulders, rubbing where he had held them so bruisingly, Leana sagged against the rail, hot tears blurring her eyes. The sky had turned to shades of cobalt and purple, and the veranda was webbed with shadows. Following with pain-filled eyes his retreating back, she felt as if all the sorrows of the world had settled upon her heart. She was turning her gaze over the lawn so that her tears might fall unnoticed when she heard Patrice catch his breath, a shurring shuddering sound.

Turning, through an upwelling of tears, she surprised a frightened look on his face, a torment of desperation in the deep lines radiating from the corners of his brilliant eyes gazing at her in mute agony, as if knowing the decision was now hers, and he was terrified of the verdict.

Confused by his words, battered by his actions and then, that fearful look as he jerked through the door, Leana could not think straight. She stumbled across the veranda, headed for a porchswing beside some begonias in artfully arranged pots. Her brain numb, she felt stupid, and wierdly off-balance, as though with any step she might plunge forward on her face. Fetching up against the swing, she was lowering herself gingerly into it when the back door opened, and Mandy came onto the porch.

The two women stared at each other, the one feeling fragile and half-dazed, but at the look of loathing in the other's eyes, rousing herself internally to do battle.

Mandy spoke first. "I dropped my keys. Did you find them?"

Stalling for time to recover her wits, for while men count notches, she knew that as a woman, Mandy would have nothing less than her scalp, Leana lifted her shoulder in a careless shrug. "I wasn't looking for them."

Slanting her an antagonistic glare and brushing her by, Mandy started down the steps, then turned and stared, an openly speculative light in her eyes. Tilting her head consideringly, she gazed at the tracks of the tears she saw staining Leana's cheeks.

"I hate to mention this," she said smilingly after a moment's contemplation, and Leana braced herself, for there was not a smidgen of 'sorry' in either her purring voice or the sly expression on her face, "but you really shouldn't wear black. You're so thin as is that black makes you look positively skinny."

As women are wont, Mandy had centered her attack on the physical level. A large part of Leana's attractiveness came from knowing that she was attractive. As a student of human nature, she had learned long ago that the world believes who you say you are and treats you accordingly. Disparagement of her fashion sense? Who did Mandy think she was? The fool who bought the pumpkin? Her eyes never flinching from Mandy's hard stare, Leana's lips spread in the slow smile of the woman who brought the pumpkin to town in the first place. It was a melting smile, one of complete feminine understanding.

"Don't let me keep you from your hunt," she advised her, twitching aside to let her pass. She rested her two hands on the railing and smiling that madding smile, looked at her.

Frowning at that knowing smile, Mandy backed up a step before taking up a stance of aggressive defensiveness and flinging her head high. Spitefully and out of sheer exasperation, she threw at her: "You know that Patrice and I went to Ohio together!"

Leana gave the old news the bored sigh it deserved. "Yes. Patrice told me," she said, raising a shoulder indifferently and falling languidly against the post. "I hope your trip was fruitful."

Tossing her head, as if she couldn't care one way or the other, Mandy flounced down the last of three moon-washed steps into the yard. As Leana straightened away from the railing and started for the door, she spun about on the pavement.

"Patrice needs me!" she flung at her back. "I'm the one who found that detective's school in Ohio for him! And I'm the one who set up appointments for him to interview new security guards next week! Me!" She jabbed at her chest with a defiant finger. *"I'm* the one!"

Mandy's words going through her like a shock of cold water, Leana's back stiffened, and mentally, she reeled. "Se . . . security guards?"

"Yes!" Scenting blood, Mandy drew nearer into the shadows of the veranda, her voice low, caustic. "I wouldn't count on any man-catching dinners next week

if I were you. *All* of our appointments will be *after* working hours. *Our* appointments," she repeated, and at the ashen look on Leana's face, with lip-smacking satisfaction. *"I* help him to decide who he should and who he should not hire. As I said," she purred, and there was an equally feline quality to her smile, "Patrice needs me." Then, her voice lowering to a sibilant hiss, she added, *"Only me."*

Leana turned into the house just as Mrs. Jackson was entering the kitchen, a cup and saucer in each hand. Her mouth gaped open when she saw her. Leana stood drunkenly, ashen and wan, eyes huge and liquid in her face. Placing the dirty dishes on the counter with a clatter, she rushed across the narrow-planked chestnut floor to her side, put a comforting arm around Leana's shoulder and gave it a warm squeeze.

"What is it, dear?" she asked, compassion in her dark eyes.

Regaining her composure in the embracing tenderness of her gesture, Leana managed a weak smile. "I'm all right. Oh! Is . . . is Patrice still here? I don't want to see him!" she blurted, feeling another onslaught of tears. Tears she would be unable to fight off if she came face to face with him.

"Sit, child!" Mrs. Jackson ordered, her dark brows swooping in a concerned, 'no-foolishness-now' frown.

Doing meekly as she was bidded, Leana pulled up a kitchen chair and sat down heavily. Mrs. Jackson pulled up another beside her, settling herself comfortably sideways in order to view her. She studied her slender beauty, her somber, tilted eyes. Patrice had said she was a beauty, refined and sophisticated, but she'd turned out to be nothing like stuck-up. Taller than most girls, she was, indeed, lovely to look at. Her flawless cheeks were plump and her soft eyes matched her voice. She looked exactly as he'd described her. Of course, 'with a figure shaped like music' was a bit fanciful to her way of thinking, but then, she wasn't in love with the girl.

"Now tell me. What is wrong here?"

Propping her elbows on the tabletop, Leana dropped her head in her hands. "I don't know. I just don't know. Mrs. Jackson," she said awkwardly, her throat throbbing with grief. She turned her a tearful face. "I . . . I don't want to sound silly . . ."

Her lined brow reflecting maternal strength, Mrs. Jackson leaned over and with motherly tenderness in her hands and eyes, embraced her. She had started trembling again. She placed a hand on Leana's forehead. It felt warm, but not feverish.

"I'm sorry," Leana sniffled, resting her head on her shoulder.

Patting her on the back she comforted Leana. "It'll be all right, dear. These things always work themselves out. Is it Patrice?"

Her face somber and painfully strained, Leana's head wobbled up, and when she nodded miserably, Mrs. Jackson said kindly, a sympathetic look on her face, "I don't pry into my children's business, Leana, but if the way Patrice talks about you and the way he looked at you when he saw you sitting in the dining room are any indication, I'd say you have nothing to worry about."

"Well . . ." Leana swallowed. She felt awful, pumping Patrice's mother for information, but was unable to stop herself. "Wha . . . what about Mandy?" she asked, cringing inwardly. "I know he cares for me," she said earnestly to Mrs. Jackson's quickly shuttered eyes, "but

he takes her everywhere with him! I mean, he asks. . . ."
Her voice faltered. She bowed her head and shook it,
ashamed. The whole conversation was shameful. She
had been better raised.

"I'm sorry," she murmured in a faint, chastened
voice.

Her dark eyes, so much like her son's, from underneath the wings of her brows unfathomable, Mrs. Jackson regarded her steadily.

"Mandy has been Patrice's assistant for nearly two
years now," she said in a curiously flat, reluctant voice.
"As far as I know, there's never been anything between
them. I always felt that she would like for something to
happen, but never has Patrice shown the slightest interest. She's helped his business to grow. He praises her for
that. But you're the only woman he's acted silly about.
Patrice is like his father in that respect."

"Patrice's father . . ." Leana looked up quickly,
tipped her head to one side. "I get the impression Patrice is a lot like him," she said, some of the awe she'd
felt in looking at his picture was in her soft inquiry.
"What's he like?"

Mrs. Jackson smiled, almost preened. "Oh, he's an
unusual man, very intelligent. That's why he wanted to
own his own business. He was working for a white man,
Mr. Joshua Hoxley. He was a big bear of a man, tall,
heavy-set, not too bright. But he was making good
money in that little printing shop on 35th Street. Crawley said that one day it just kind of dawned on him—
why should he be taking orders from a man dumber than
him?" The corners of her mouth deepened, and she
chuckled, looking past Leana to a younger, happier time.
"People said 'What!' " She laughed out loud, her once

shapely figure gone the way of the flesh, shaking. Then, just as quickly, she sobered, and her eyes grew hard.

"He was ambitious; he wanted something. That was what the black people of that time couldn't understand. They scoffed at him; they mocked him; they said, 'dat man's crazy!'. They said that behind his back," she added quickly. "Now, I was soft in those days, but Crawley ain't never been no man to fun with. Not my husband, he ain't," she said with a sort of happy pride in her voice, unaware that Leana had stiffened, pulled back, and was now frowning at her, a concerned look on her face. Crawley was someone else's husband now.

"When we finally got on top," she said mistily, caught up in the glory days, "all those that had laughed at him tried their best to get some of that money we made—borrow it, good-time with it, you name it. Yeah," she breathed smugly. "They came around; like a pack of slobbering hyenas round the lion that made the kill, they all came around. Crawley told them that he'd go to the top if he had to do it by himself. And he did." She chuckled heartily. "Course, you know, men are vain. But for my sacrifices, while he might not still be sweeping up in Mr. Hoxley's office, he sho nuff wouldn't be where he is today! It was with me behind him that he beat them. But no matter how hard it got for us—me, the children and him, too—he beat them with his head held high."

She paused, and as if just remembering Leana, her eyes searched her, suddenly tense and watchful. "You're right to think that about Patrice. He's as hard-headed as his father ever was. It's strange, though," she mused, her voice as soft and gentle as Patrice's could be in a like moment. "For all his hard-headed ways, unlike his father, Patrice will bend. But then again, just like his daddy, he won't bow down to nobody.''

When her lips rounded to form an ''oh'', Mrs. Jackson smiled—right up to her crinkling eyes.

''I didn't really think . . .'' Leana began hopefully. ''It's . . .''

Mrs. Jackson smiled. ''Leana,'' she said, bending toward her like a mother to her child, ''Trust me. He loves you.''

Chapter Twelve

The leaves from the trees faded from green to lime to tarnished gold then drifted to the ground like sighing memories as summer rolled round to autumn. By mid-October, Patrice had ceased calling and Leana could turn off her answering machine and stop screening her calls. Still, flowers came occasionally, and once he had even waited for her outside the Blyden Center. Lying in the foaming white waters churned up by the jacuzzi, her muscles slowly relaxing as its silky warmth swirled around and soothed the tenseness from her body, Leana saluted the memory with a smile, a sad, wistful smile.

It had been a hectic, wonderfully stimulating day. Horry Grant had dropped by her office. She had had to do some fast talking and a lot of stroking, but she'd finally convinced one of her corporate contacts to honor her promise and hire him. Keeping her fingers crossed, when word came through the grapevine that he was doing well on the job, she had breathed a sigh of relief.

Someone once said that the only reason there are so many counterfeiters is because there is real gold. Horry, her instincts told her, was real gold. He had worked out

so well that he had earned a raise. Unbeknownst to
Horry, and because Leana believed in him, the raise had
come upon an inflated starting salary that she had negotiated on his behalf, as well.

In order not to break down and cry when he handed
her the African Violet plant his wife had sent to express
her gratitude, she had chided him severely. But Horry
was wise to Leana's ploys. He grinned when she let him
press the plant upon her, his rough, worn hands squeezing on hers trembling around the plant as she scolded
him, insisting, "I don't take bribes!" But when her
lashes lifted and she admitted of the good heart behind
the broad grin, a wetness had come to Leana's eyes. Her
voice was no more than a misty whisper as she graciously thanked him, even when all she really wanted
was to grab and hug him to her for justifying her faith in
humanity.

Earlier that day, she had lunched with Evan Snow,
head buyer for one of the city's largest and most fash-
ionable department stores, with branches in the more af-
fluent suburbs. Spying the nattily dressed man in a
pastel shirt and mottled burgundy tie beneath his sharply
tailored gray suit, she moved briskly in soft Italian
pumps across the floor of the restaurant, tossing a suede,
elbow length, gloved hand up in greeting.

Her hair falling like lacquered ebony from a center
seam part straight down and curving beneath her cheeks,
she was wearing a camel pantsuit with flap pockets and
big, pearl gray buttons. Her silky, similarly colored
blouse closed in white pearl buttons at the high collared
neck. Carrying a camel-colored, cashmere trench coat
over one arm, a brilliant scarf pulled through its mili-
tary-style shoulder-flap, she looked exactly what she

was—a high-powered businesswoman out to woo an important client.

The Christmas season was only months away and Leana was there to remind Evan that the Blyden Center had trained people ready and able to fill any openings the stores might have. Before she could begin her sales pitch, however, he had complimented her on how chic she looked, and instead of discussing temporary help, offered her a job as buyer for a pilot store they were about to open in the Southwest. Looking radiant and breathing rarefied air, when she returned to the office with a commitment for ten temporary sales positions and, if they worked out, a possibility of five becoming permanent. Horry was there, waiting for her, bearing gifts.

Leaving work on a high, her leather-strapped bag slipped jauntily over one shoulder, she and LaDonna were filing through a side entrance of the Center with other employees when shock made her legs weak, and she gripped the stone bannister for support. Paused on the porch, obstructing foot traffic, fear, as soft and caressive as a dove's wing, flitted over her dark face when she saw the Harley. A surge of excitement chased by shivers of dread racing down her spine, and she took an instinctive step back before being swept irresistibly forward by the exiting five o'clock crowd. Going with the flow of humanity down the steps to the cracked asphalt pavement, just as she thought to break free and make a mad dash for the parking lot, LaDonna's big eyes spied Patrice.

Squinting in an openly inquisitive manner at the lean, leather-jacketed figure straddling the Harley, she stopped dead in her tracks, clapped her hands to her

mouth and after squealing through her fingers, grabbed
Leana's arm. Even in steel-lashed boots and heavy
leather recognizing Patrice, she waved cheerily, calling
out immediately and loud enough that his head lifted,
dark eyes sharpening when he saw Leana.

Moving slowly toward him, a serene smile pasted to
her face, before she could fix her mouth to graciously
refuse his offer of coffee, LaDonna had gone and put in
her two cents. Chuckling and wagging a coy finger at
her perspicacity, she pointed out with sparkling eyes that
Leana almost always wore skirts to work, but because
she wore pants that day, she could straddle the bike.
What luck!

Leana had wanted desperately to refuse, as well as to
strangle LaDonna's skinny little neck, but the Harley
was beautiful, gleaming black and buffed chrome, its
cushiony, black leather saddle slung low—and half-ob-
scured by the press of her co-workers crowding around
it—with a high-riding, smaller bottomed passenger seat
behind it. Shading their eyes with cupped palms against
the late afternoon sun glinting off the big bike's chrome,
they were admiring the instrument panel with raised
"USA" decals stamped in gold on round, gleaming
chrome medallions at either side of the panel.

'Slick', 'fresh', 'powerful', were among whispered
exclamations of envy and admiration. Following
Leana's approach behind dark glasses, Patrice did not
seem to mind that they caressed the mirror on the han-
dlebar, nor the roofed headlamp. Unwilling to cause a
scene—looking into the hard handsome face beneath the
beret, she saw the determined, squared jaw—Leana
lifted her coat, gathered her pants' legs up, and climbed
gingerly aboard the passenger seat behind him.

Leana rose from the jacuzzi and toweled off. The skin on her body was ruddy and softly glowing. Wrapping herself in the satin kimono, she went into her bedroom. She sat down before a little ivory dressing table, covered in green silk. It glistened with mirror brilliance, reflecting the aqua venetian blinds at the window and the creamy-white filigrees of the high-ceilinged room, as delicate and sophisticated as the woman herself. She pushed herself forward, her elbows leaned on the table, and took a deep breath to focus herself. Sectioning her thick mop of hair, layered in loose ebony curls, part by part, she fingered Ultrasheen on her scalp, then massaged it doggedly until her crown glowed with a fragrant sheen. Still, despite her concentration, her thoughts inexorably retreated, back in time.

Approaching the Harley, memories of her disastrous visit to the Jackson home flickered like holiday slides through her mind: Mrs. Jackson, slumped in a kitchen chair, her eyes hard in defeat; Mandy, chin jutted on a stiffly held head, her eyes hard in triumph; Marie, her expression wry as she looked upon her parents' youthful likenesses. All of them, like slides from a bad vacation, crowded her memory; even she, the catalyst for all that happened, was a still-life, paralyzed by confusion. Only Patrice, of the fierce and threatening postures, was alive, breathing fire through his nostrils like a woman-eating dragon.

Against all logic, merely because he asked her to, she trusted him. Even on the veranda, merely because he offered her his protection, she not once feared for her safety. She trusted him in a way he seemed incapable of comprehending. Her faith rose out of her love for him.

She loved him, and true love does not require reason for its defense. It is above reason, beyond logic.

But compassion, a sympathetic heart and, foremost, trust were important, too. Without them, love, like a flower deprived of water, withers, dies. Or in the case of women like Mrs. Jackson, nurturing memories in a desert, living on in a stunted, deformed, sadly perverted state, keeping curative, transcending perfume, a poison.

Coming upon him, her intentions were pure. She would tell him it was over. Perhaps not as effectively as a Brenda might—bluntness simply was not her style—but gently, and with the utmost consideration of his feelings. Her greatest treasures were always of the spirit, to set him free would be her last act of love.

As always, it was her flesh that was her undoing. Looking into his hungry hard face, she experienced a bout of dizzying, profound emotion. Her response was immediate, so sudden and shattering that in any sort of confrontation she knew she would be unable to cope.

She had wanted to go to Gladys' Restaurant where there was always a big crowd of people to try and pull her scattered emotions together, but Patrice preferred a more intimate setting. Settling on a compromise, they took a back booth at Chili Mac's on nearby 47th Street.

Leana had never before ridden the back of a motorcycle, and as they barreled through the streets, she found herself as excited as she had been when she'd first looked into his eyes the day Patrice fell into her lap at Gladys's. Her cheek pressed against his broad back and squeezing his waist, with the smell of old leather from his battered jacket, the freshening wind and his potent male pheromones stinging in her nostrils, the trip over had been exhilarating.

Gripping his wide shoulders for support when they arrived at the restaurant, Leana clambered from her seat behind Patrice, laughing out of sheer exhilaration. Throwing her a quick reciprocatory grin, he swung a leg over the saddle of the bike, then lifting her against his chest, swept her into his arms and kissed her full on the mouth. The achingly tender feel of his too-long-absent lips on hers intensely warm and satisfying, she pressed the whole of her body against him, joining the kiss before a burst of applause cut through her senses and she jerked abruptly away.

They were in the heart of the 47th Street shopping district, a cacophonious open air market, equally notorious as a red light district, and the street was jumping—cars cruising, horns honking, unsavory types mingling with idling pedestrians on the sidewalks, clapping and hooting at the free show. Humiliated and feeling more than a little chagrinned at the capriciousness of her body, another of those awkward silences developed between them as they entered Chili Mac's.

Over her protestations, Patrice ordered not only coffee, but plates of the house speciality for two. Resentful of a repeat of his high-handed manner—along with her recent embarrassment on the outside pavement, his hurtful behavior at his mother's house kept cropping up in her mind—Leana ate in silence, only picking at what was reputed to be the best chili mac in the city.

Sipping the strong coffee, Patrice looked across the rim of his cup at his subdued companion with soft eyes. Gently, he placed the thick mug on the table. "I'm sorry."

They were in the dim, L-shaped section of the restaurant so small it could properly be called a diner, most of the light coming from the big storefront window in front. Along with a silent jukebox, there were two other booths in the rear that could seat four, both empty. People came to Chili Mac's for chili in all its hot varieties, not romantic conversation. Most ate at the lunch counter in front; a few sat at small tables for two cramping alongside the front wall, but as most of its clientele were men, only when the dozen or so stools at the counter were taken.

Bringing forth a groan from the crinkling, creotone-covered seat striped with duct tape when he slid into the booth opposite her, in the cool mirrored gloom, Patrice seemed bigger than she remembered. Bigger, and in his heavy biker's leather, more powerful. Still, after a nearly two month's absence, the first shock of seeing him was slowly fading, to be replaced by the invisible barrier of their last verbal altercation, buttressed by a dull ache she had felt sure would last forever.

Shrugging out of her coat and fiddling with the paper napkin beside her plate, she said dully, "You shouldn't have kissed me."

Shifting on the patched creotone which buckled up slightly and let out a sigh as air was forced out, Patrice stretched his long legs out into the aisle and settled against the booth. Studying him from under her veil of shadowing lashes, Leana thought again what a handsome, manly man he was. From the high winging brows to the lean, tightly muscled physique to the virile, bristly mustache above his sensual, chiseled lips. Especially his lips. Dark, luscious lips, browner than the skin of his face with a healthy purplish tint that dared a man to mess with him, and a woman to sample them. Feeling in spite of her reservations, the old electrifying, at times dizzying turbulence tingle deep inside her, Leana, trying hard not to focus on his mouth, added dolefully, "It was uncalled for."

"I'm not sorry about kissing you. I'll never be sorry for that. What I am sorry for is causing you embarrassment," he said, looking at her out of eyes so grave and beautiful that Leana cringed. "I've missed, you," he added softly into the tense silence that followed.

He's closing in on me, she thought, resolutely not answering. She continued to play with her food, moving it aimlessly about her plate.

Gently, he persisted. "You haven't missed me?"

Refusing to meet his gaze, she said sharply, "Why should I? You made yourself perfectly clear the last time we met." And, as if to refresh his memory, she added defiantly, "At your mother's house."

Long heavy brows swooping low, Patrice turned his head, stared broodingly at the backs of the male customers at the counter. "That's another thing I'm sorry for. I know I came off like Conan the Barbarian or something. . . . Even my mom is mad at me!" he exclaimed gruffly, as though shocked, swinging his glance filled with wonder for the woman whose gentle and circumspect intelligence had so captivated his mother. But when she refused to respond, he said lamely, "I was tired. I'd just come off a long trip."

Tapping her fork with inch-long red fingernails and looking off at nothing, she said with quiet firmness, "Yes. So Mandy said."

Surprise flitted across his face before his mouth grew hard, and he frowned. "Mandy told you what?"

Leana dropped the fork into the steaming spaghetti, heavy with even hotter chili, all pretense at eating abandoned. "Nothing. I mean, she just said what you said. That it had been a long trip. For the *both* of you." Her mouth tightening at the memory, she stared resolutely down.

Patrice looked at her with a searching regard. "And that's all it was. I don't mix business with pleasure. If I did, it would have been you with me on that trip, not Mandy."

Her eyes glued to her plate, Leana swallowed a sob when she felt the joyous leap of her heart. Fighting to stop the sudden, hopeful trembling, her fingers on both hands clenched themselves to fists.

"There are things . . ." Dropping his chin to his chest, Patrice uttered a heavy, whistling sigh. Then, to Leana's complete astonishment, he burst out impassioned: "Why?! Why did I have to meet you now? Why couldn't it have been later?"

The torment of his gaze, the jerking violence in his voice were startling. Caught unawares, Leana raised tender eyes to him. Like quick-silver, his mood changed, and he chuckled. Low, shuddery and vibrating off his palate from deep inside his chest, it was a bitter, almost diabolical sound that chuckle, thought Leana, an electrical feeling slicing through her. The glimmer in his eyes was disturbing, even a little crazy. She was unconsciously scrunching up in a corner, her spine pressing between the wall and the back of the booth when Patrice drawled bitterly: "*The sins of the fathers. . . .*"

Patrice closed his eyes for a space and Leana was releasing the gasp she'd smothered when he straightened, then strained ominously forward. Suddenly, sharply, he flexed a hand into a fist that came down hard on the table, leaping cutlery and saucers in the air, and

Leana's heart in her chest. With a scowl that tugged his heavy brows to meeting, he glowered at those men seated at the counter who, able to see into the L-shaped section, had turned on their stools and were looking in on them curious.

Giving them a daunting, "what you messin' in my business for?" look, then snorting his contempt when they turned away quickly, he swung his glittering glance back to Leana. The hardness around his mouth softened, and slowly, his jaws unclenched. Hunching over the table, he pulled her hands into his, rubbed the calloused pads of his thumbs gently, intimately, over her trembling, delicately boned knuckles.

"I acted badly and I'm sorry." His eyes were warm, his husky voice pleading. "I should never have spoken to you that way. But some things, baby, please, you've simply got to trust me on! I believe in you. Please believe in me."

Slanting him a look through silky lashes which lent a tender girlishness to her dusky beauty, Leana's slender, gracefully boned hands tensed in his. The gloom of the corner intensifying the poignancy of his plea, the ache she felt in her heart was reflected in his eyes, and as her gaze met his and clung, her racing heart slowed and she felt the first underpinnings of her resolve crumble.

Confounded by him, by her weakness for him, she wanted to run, to cry. Was it because the most dangerous man she'd ever known could touch her with eyes holding so much tenderness that her will turned to mush when she looked deeply into them? Here sat a man who asked her to take huge leaps of faith for him, yet didn't trust her judgment enough to give one aging, very capable man a job. If any other man had treated her so abominably she would have told him to kiss off without a second's hesitation. Yet . . . It was undeniable. He excited her. He fascinated her. He awoke in her a craven sensuality. She wanted to be with him. . . .

Snatching away her hand in a sudden agony of torment, and propping her elbows on the table, Leana dropped her head in her cupped palms, as if she were about to be sick.

"Leana."

He pulled her hands gently from her face. "Don't shut me out. I've no where else to go," he whispered, his voice pulsing with emotion. "There's no one else I'd even want to go to," he said, the huskiness of his voice plucking at the chinks of her resistance, overwhelming her with its warm flow. "I've been in hell these past weeks. Trying to reach you and you not answering the phone. This wasn't the first time I waited outside your job, either. I almost screwed up my last assignment trying to catch up with you before you came to work, hanging around until everyone had gone." Hunched forward over the table, he spoke quietly, persuasively, but in spite of all that, she heard in his voice the growing intensity of one who fears his words will not be believed. "I even called your office. Your secre . . ."

With an effort, she flicked her eyes from his. "I got the messages."

"Then you know, so . . ." Quick hurt flared in his eyes. "Why, baby?"

Leana tried to be strong. "I've got to think about this. I . . . I . . . Oh, what's the use?" She sighed dejectedly, a gentle, weary sound. But when she tried to pull back, he entwined his strong fingers tighter with hers.

"Please, baby. *Please.*" The captain of his ship, the

master of his fate, manly dignity had always been Patrice's strong suit, but his tone now was hoarse, and a gentle supplication shone in his eyes. He had been reduced to begging.

A muscle worked in Leana's throat. Oh God, what this must be costing him! And why was *she* being so difficult? Something had happened . . . She couldn't think. God! The man had robbed her of the power to think! But she didn't want to think. She wanted to take him in her arms. She wanted to soothe his troubled brow, to kiss the hurt from his eyes. Wanted . . .

"You . . . you hurt me. And you yelled at me."

"I'm sorry," he said in a throaty quaver. "I've always had a bad temper, and I sometimes forget my own strength. But I swear it won't happen again. Please, baby. I swear on my life. No, give me something better than my life to swear on. Please, I'll do it."

Her emotions threatening to tear her to shreds, Leana felt tears gather in the back of her throat. He was not forthcoming on why he had become so angry with her in the first place, and she had too much pride to ask him again. "Can we leave?" she asked instead. "I'm not hungry."

His gaze held hers a brief moment more, then dejectedly, he nodded. Looking at him through the tears mottling her eyes, watching his face collapse in folds of sadness, it came to her that this was no con. He was sincere. She felt suddenly, totally out of whack. Blinking back the tears puddling in the wells of her eyes, she wondered if maybe it was her clothes. Maybe because she dressed like a fashion plate he thought her to be an airhead. Maybe if she were to dress in more sturdy clothes . . . like, maybe, blue jeans. . . . Leana's head swam. But he knew what kind of job she had, she thought, frustration pitting in her stomach making her insides clench, the kind of people she had to associate with. He had even commented on how important it was to blend in with the people with whom you do business.

Sitting there mute, dumb, loving him and wanting him and not knowing why—the man had an incredibly hard head!—her gaze locked with midnight romantic eyes so sad and beautiful that she could not have looked away to save her life. She just didn't understand what drove him. But of one thing was her heart certain, he was not conning her. As loving as it was tormented, that despairing look on his face was real, so real that Leana felt love well up inside her like a fist and squeeze her heart. She wanted to take him by the arms and just shake him, and at the same time, she wanted to hold this big, powerfully built man, cradle his head in her arms gently and while he suckled contentedly at her breast, whisper incantations of love to drive from him the demons that pursued him. He looked so bereft, so heart-breakingly sincere, that the harsh pain of their last encounter faded.

The drawn-up muscles in her abdomen clenching with frustration, relaxed. Looking at him, she could almost forget his lack of faith in her, that he didn't need her. She wanted to forget, to start over. But, if she did, she knew she'd be lost. Temptation passing through her like a sigh, Leana smiled, a low, lovely smile.

"My car is back at the Center," she said quietly, gathering her things together.

As if he'd read her thoughts, there was a flash of anguish in his eyes, and then it was gone. Rolling reluctantly to his feet, Patrice dropped two bills for the waiter on the table. "I'll take you back, then follow you on my bike," he acceded, his voice heavy with unhappiness as he assisted her into her coat. "It's almost dark and that parking lot in your building never seems to have anyone in it."

Although it was unnecessary, she had allowed him to escort her into the building, tantalyzed by the alternating pressure of his fingers on her waist as they navigated the corridor to her apartment. Lines of unhappiness edging his sensuous mouth, he had taken the key she scrabbled from her shoulder bag when her fingers fumbled nervously at the lock, and opened the door, refusing, however, any attempt to enter.

Another awkward moment. The apartment was empty, sheathed in a silence of darkness. Should she or should she not invite him in? As if her thoughts were transparent, he let go of the door handle and rubbed gently, the rough back of his hand down her cheek before he stooped and kissed her.

"I love you," he said softly against her lips. "Know that always. No matter what." Straightening to smile down on her from his great height and broad shoulders, his expression was so bleak that Leana's heart wrenched when he drew back and, slipping his beret from his head to his heart, with a languid sadness, said, "Thank you for coming into my life."

Having dressed, combed and brushed her hair into a becoming, upswept crown of waves, Leana slipped into a lustrous print evening gown draped from the hip and slit down one side. Trailing her fingers over the whispery sigh of silk, she studied her three-sided reflection in the mirrors over her bureau.

Tilting her head, as if not quite satisfied with her image, she went to the bed where she picked up a filmy concoction of soft azure blue in which she enfolded her slim body carefully. Her figure shimmering in corals and reds, blues, aquas and silvers, the transparent azure shawl bringing out in her hair soft, heretofore unseen blue-black highlights, with a pair of heavy ridged gold hoops in her ears, a trio of gold bracelets on her arm, and gold-dusted stockings on her long shapely legs, she looked fetching.

Strangely, she didn't really care. She was on her way to a party. For her, it would be a business as well as a social occasion. There were over a hundred people on the Center's employable list who needed jobs: some not really about anything, but most like Horry, sincere people who would work hard.

It was a small businessman's ball. Chaired by her friend, Bernard, it was being held at Brenda's family home outside Momence. Misery stabbing her like a knife, it was ironic. 'Or is it poetic justice', she mused as she brushed mascara on her eyelashes, 'turnabout is fair play'? She knew only that Brenda and Bernard had hit it off, and that for once, she, little Leana Claremont, had played the match-maker. God knew she was happy for them. Then why, Leana thought, daubing on bright red lipstick then stepping back from the mirror to examine the results, did she feel so blue? Her thoughts again drifted, the answers to be found in the last time she saw Patrice.

Standing there and smiling down at her from his advantage of six or seven inches, there was a sorrowing in his eyes beneath the lustrous brows that broke her heart. He looked so lost and forlorn that she had invited him in. And back into her heart.

Be it business, personal or romantic, trust was the

foundation for all Leana's relationships. Even though she would have died of shame to admit it, she took an almost hedonistic pleasure in being able to pick up a telephone, call an officer of a major corporation and have them hire on the spot a friend or even one of the Center's trainees, based solely on her recommendation.

A virtual repository of other people's secrets, she was accustomed to the phenomenon of strangers telling her their life stories. That Patrice trusted her enough to tell her the intimate personal details of his life was not remarkable. What was remarkable was that she had said or done nothing since that time that he should abandon his initial trust.

Had he been, as his mother so quaintly put it, 'fly', she would have closed the door on him, because she would have known his only interest in her was sexual. But standing in her hallway, stripped of his pride and tough guy veneer, his eyes begging her trust once more, and with literally his hat in his hands, the woman who wore her trustworthiness like a halo on her clothes put her qualms aside and stepped into his arms on faith.

One thing led to another, and soon he was holding her. Holding her in his arms and kissing her, desperately, as if there were no tomorrow. She had clung to him, needing him, believing that he needed her. Believing with all her heart that he needed her. They had wound up in the bedroom. In her bed. Although their blood rippled hot with desire and the romance of separation, it had not been a frantic, frenetic coupling. It had been tender, beautiful.

Leana looked at herself in the mirror. Why did she torture herself like this? After nearly two weeks in this mad, despondent state, memories of that night still seethed in her brain. One moment she would be beating herself up emotionally for loving a man she wanted to spend time with, to share with her the issues of his life, to tell her things, important things, but who thought her an airhead; the next would find her growing weak as she recalled his relentless, gentle passion and her rapturous response. Kissing her lips, his hands reaching out to touch her, to warm her with the blood-heat of his body—these things, sadly, she remembered.

Chapter Thirteen

When she started to undress, Patrice told Leana to wait, then to her bemusement, stripped himself bare to the waist. Risking an uncertain glance through silky lashes up at him she followed his lead, fumbling at the buttons on her blouse. Before she knew it, his hands were on her shoulders. Pulling her close, he covered her trembling hands with his, bringing them gently to her sides. With a loving glance and a slow hand, he began wordlessly to undress her.

Not one to disrobe in a dark closet, Leana had never before either had a man to undress her. She felt awkward, vulnerable, but the warm shuddery feel of his hands gliding across her skin as he removed her garments, one by one, pitched reason aside, rushed the blood to her head, and she felt dizzy.

Left only in panties and her bra, a tingle of excitement mingled with the glow of desire to flush the curves of her cheeks dusky. His eyes half-closing, they glittered for a space on the swell of her softly heaving breasts then traveled the satiny brown line of her ribs to the gentle flare of her hips. At the fleecy private hairs escaping the champagne-laced elastic edging her pink bikini panties, a fully wicked gleam lit his eyes.

"Please, Patrice," she said lowly, her thighs quivering under his scrutiny.

Patrice stirred. He smiled. "Not yet, baby."

Paused in the burnishing glow of the ruddy shade that washed illumination full upon his face, etching his bold dark features and glittering the narrowed eyes that stroked her slender form like a firm but caressing hand, he gently took her arms and pushed her hands down when she sought to embrace him. "Let me look at you. You're beautiful," breathed the man with a body to rival the railroad man, John Henry, his dark gaze worshipful on her face, her body. "So very beautiful."

Finding his dark compulsion riveting, Leana closed her eyes and because the skin around her nostrils pinched, cutting off air, she licked, then parted her softly lush red lips, and as he continued his visual exploration of every swell of her tense, honey-brown body, Patrice heard her breathing quicken.

Moving close, he curved his hands across nubile hips and drew her to him. His splaying fingers moving to the small of her back, running in an erotic ticklish caress up her sides, he unhooked her brassiere. The tiny bikini panties left her only shield, Leana felt naked, exposed. Her shoulders shrinking slightly, she leaned tremblingly into the circle of his arms, and breathing in her sweet woman's scent, Patrice brushed his lips against the side of her neck. Clasping the softness of her lissome length to his hard form, he rocked them slowly, all the while murmuring love words in her ear.

What was he doing? she wondered, clasping her arms around his heavy shoulders. Why didn't he just take her to bed where they could make love like before? It had been so good, that sweet rushing race to fulfill their mutual need. This was sheer torture. Not to mention embarrassing.

But when she felt his big hands slip into her lace-edged panties, palm her round, quivering bare buttocks, and draw her between his legs, and his thick masculine part commence to move slowly against her hot belly, conscious thought ceased and her back arching, Leana whimpered.

When she murmured a sibilant sigh, with a hoarse throaty groan, Patrice slid down her nearly nude body, leaving burning spots on her breasts where he kissed her, a wet trail on her stomach where he tasted her, goosebumps on the backs of her strong legs where he caressed her, and on her thighs where he wrapped his hands around them and eased her pink panties down with a shockingly intimate kiss that made her knees go weak.

Kicking her feet through the sheer lacey garment almost in reflex, she stood tremblingly as he moved heavily back up her, the hairs on his chest tickling the fronts of her thighs to her stomach, quivering where his nose had just nuzzled it and stopping at a full perky breast. It was warm and ripe and her heart thundered beneath his palms. Kissing its swollen undersides lightly, he licked the shadowed aureole of flesh surrounding the dark chocolate of its nipple, the flickering tip of his tongue closing in tiny circles, teasing the raised, aching bud until she thought she would go mad. But when his hand cupped the swollen globe and his wet warm mouth opening, possessed himself of the tormented nipple with his lips, her self-control broke, and with a soft moan,

Leana folded her arms round his head and clasped him to her like a baby, lovingly at her breast.

He released her breast and swept her easily into his arms. Patrice carried Leana to the bed and laid her gently upon it. Straightening, his chest heaving as if he'd just run a marathon, he stepped back to look upon her sleek, lissome body, sprawled in sinuous sienna, her slender neck relaxed, her ebony mop of hair splayed like a sibyl of his fate, across the sea of quilted white satin of the pulled back covers.

The sable lights of his deep-set eyes flicking hot with arousal, he drank in her sultry, half-closed lids, her smudged, pouty lips, the soft belly caving in and out with the rise and fall of her swollen, kiss-bruised breasts. His vision darkening, his eyelids drooped, and as if suddenly light-headed, he weaved on his feet when his gaze shifted to the soft triangle of ebony hairs where her firm thighs met. Pulling his belt from its loops and unzippering the faded jeans, then bending quickly to yank their casings from his legs, he dropped to his knees on the bed.

Daring a glance from between quivering lashes, Leana saw a blurred vision of ruggedly handsome male with strong taut loins centered by a black bush of hair, staring raptly down on her. God, but he was beautiful! Never in her life had she seen a man so beautiful! All hard brown muscle and wiry black hair, she knew she would never again. Her lashes drifting to his sex thrusting from a tangled bush of dark hairs, the tip of her tongue licking across her bottom red lip, and covering her chest bashfully with her arms, she turned her head.

Smiling his amusement at her demurely averted eyes, Patrice eased his magnificent body sinuously across the bed to lay beside her. "Lovely Leana," he whispered. "I'll love you for all of my life." Lifting her arms from her chest gently, he spread them wide, like wings across the covers, then kissed both trembling nipples slowly, gently, his mouth an agony of tenderness.

A pulsing current of desire jerked Leana's legs on the bed, and the muscles of her stomach contracted.

"I do love you," he murmured, kissing the skin on her tingling flushed face, his lips a caress on her quickly fluttering lids. "I can't be around you and not want you. I can't think, I can't plan, I go crazy. I'm too weak for you, baby. Don't you know that?"

Her eyes opening, her lashes lifted lambently to his. He was watching her out of those beautiful, heavily-lashed eyes that could melt butter, causing her to stammer. "I love you, t-too."

Sparks seemed to flash from his riveting black gaze, then were gone as he very quietly bent, and shaping his lips to hers, delicately explored the contours of her mouth. Every bone in her body seeming to melt, her lips a warm soft tremble, infinitely tender, quivered beneath his like a breath, a prayer, a sigh. Urging toward him, when they parted to receive the sweet scalding juices of his searching tongue in a hungry caress, Patrice moaned, clenched his whole body rigid against the fist tightening in his groin.

"Oh, hell! I want to love you . . . *right*!" he hissed before he hauled her unresisting body against him and his full, purple-passion lips covered her mouth in a drugging, devouring kiss.

"Oh baby," he said raspingly, as he cradled her head in his arms and threaded strong trembling fingers through her disheveled hair gently. "I missed you. I missed you so much! Don't ever run away from me again.''

Leana slicked her tongue over bruised lips, and her eyes glistened. She could feel his breath warm in her hair, and with a sigh as soft, whispered, ''I love you so, Patrice. Let me show you,'' she said, drawing his head to hers. ''Let me show you how much I love you.''

''I . . . Oh God in heaven!'' he muttered hoarsely, jerking his head from her grasp and pressing his face to the junction where the slim column of her throat curved into the warm brown slope of her shoulder.

Leana lifted his head, even as he resisted, cradling it in the palms of her hands, stared at his strong, anguished features that startled her, as if he were a wonder to behold. A wetness rose, welled in her eyes as she wiped with a gentle thumb the moisture streaming from his.

Taking one of the hands that caressed his cheek, Patrice brought it to his lips. He closed his eyes painfully and kissed it, and then her wrist. His Adam's apple bobbing in his throat, he said moistly, ''I didn't want you to see me like this. I love you. I loved you from the first. I love you so much it hurts!''

Gazing at him with melting adoration, her smile was angelic, her tenderly plumped cheeks so beautiful to his eyes that Patrice groaned, deep in his throat. Rolling on his back and in a rough, husky voice, murmuring, ''Come here,'' he pulled Leana atop him, and when her nubile body arranged itself softly around him, trapped her with his arms close to his chest. His hands moved in a luxurious run down her slender supple back. ''You're soft,'' he husked, his eyes heavy-lidded with passion as he moved his big hands with smooth dexterity over the satiny, round cheeks he trapped between his muscular thighs in a seemingly random pattern. "Ahhhh, you are so soft," he whispered, and his voice had changed; it had become hoarse, gutteral. "Your skin feels like a baby's."

Grasping a fleshy cheek in each hand then, he pressed her softness to him. When his hips began a slow, strong grind, Leana lifted her head from his chest and kissed him. Kissed him adoringly, her lips clinging, sighing over his beautifully crafted mouth. When she began to mimick his movements, swaying her naked pelvis gently, insistently, against his raw sex, Patrice thrust his tongue between her wet lips which parted to receive him. Alternately smoothing and caressing her buttocks in a two-handed grasp, when her tongue tentatively tasted, then sucked his own in a way that he favored, he hurtled them over tongue-locked and sealed to probe hungrily, even more thoroughly, the soft recesses of her mouth.

"Patrice!"

Leana broke the kiss, her head falling next to his on the pillows, quivering and panting for air.

"Tell me you love me," he demanded in a whisper. His hands bracing her shoulders, he kissed her passion-flushed face. "Tell me you love me. That you'll be patient with me," he murmured against her skin in a velvety rush. "Tell me that no matter how long, you'll wait for me, that you'll always love me."

"Always," Leana breathed rapturously into his ear, running her hands across the hard flesh of his back, sighing with pleasure at the feel of hard male muscle bunching and flexing about his spine, reveling in his taut male buttocks, hot and tight under her palms, as she caressed him. The thrill of desireable womanhood rippled through Leana's veins. Her hair kinking up in reversal, her cheeks warm with the red blood of passion and dusky from their kisses, never had she felt so alive, so feminine, so glad to be a woman.

"Baby," he breathed, rolling to his side, one leg sliding across her stomach, pushing his hand into her hair, forcing her head gently upward from his chest. "Show me you love me, baby. Show me!"

All the frustrations, all the shame, all the old insecurities were gone, banished by his acceptance. Never had she known it could be so good between a man and a woman. Without fear, without reservation, her delicate, tender young heart could accept the fire, the power and intensity of his love-making and lavish on Patrice her love in all its delights. Her warm lips planting slow, feverish kisses on his neck and chest, when she slipped a hand beneath the outstretched leg to embrace his hairy, engorged balls and caress them in the curve of her palm, Patrice let go a tortured hiss.

"Does this please you?" she asked softly, loosening her gentle hold to unashamedly stroke his shaft, enclosing his fully erect sex with her hand. Stroking the thick, throbbing flesh in a gentle up and down motion, her voice was soft, like the pink glow through the shade of the brass floor lamp rosying the walls and floor.

"Yes! Yes! Oh baby," he moaned into her neck, his voice husky, his words thickening, and cupping her neck, kissing the top of her head. "Don't ever leave me, again," he begged her. You're my woman. You belong to me. . . ." He shuddered as he felt the ball of her thumb brush over his sensitive peak.

"Like what, Patrice?" she persisted in the throaty, whispery voice, her eyes closing, glorying in the trembling of his virile male body beneath her slender hand. "Like that, darling?"

Groaning inside an inferno of feeling, he removed her hand from him gently. "Slow down, baby," he grinned weakly. "We don't want this to be over before we begin. You're the one who has to be convinced, not me."

Turning her liquid gaze, heavy with passion and not a little confusion to him, Leana looked into his face, and gasped at the look of perfect love she saw etched in his face. "Oh, Patrice," she moaned meltingly.

"I know baby," he said, and although the need to possess her was great, exercising restraint as he propped himself on an elbow above her. "But it's not enough. I want more. I want you . . ." he said on a husk, lowering his face to kiss the anxious furrow from her brow, "to be my woman. . . ."

When in relief she tried to embrace his neck, Patrice quickly grasped her seeking hand, turning it palm up to his lips, and kissed where the pulse jumped in her wrist. ". . . my lover," he continued tenderly in the same, fluid tone, and nuzzling her soft cheek with his nose, his breath a warm breeze in her ear, ". . . my friend."

Leana's lashes fluttered up like a hummingbird, and her heart like to burst with happiness. A groan of pleasure broke from her throat.

"I want to make love with you," he whispered, pulling her into his arms and although glorying in her responsive trusting as she laid her head on his chest, clasping handsful of hair to lift her face to his.

"I want to make love to you so that you'll never want any other man," he told her, the compelling sable glitter in his eyes belying the plea in the gently spoke words.

Leana's heart skipped a beat; watching his thick lashes drift over his eyes with his lips to her face, her breath tangled in her lungs. Wrapping an arm around her waist, a hand behind her head, his lush lips melted into the welcoming softness of her mouth as he crushed her to him, molded her against him, imprinted his hard arousal on her stomach. Falling limp to the bed she sighed the sigh of pleasure one feels when all is right with the world. He left her lips to lift her full breasts in the palms of his hands, kissing their tops, their dampening undersides and curves. As he lapped in long rough strokes the dew pebbling between them, sponging her moist heat with his tongue, she felt a burst of raw passion shoot like adrenalin through her veins.

Twisting anxiously, writhing against him, her long fingers ran riot across his thick springy hair, coarse, damp with the feel of lamb's wool against her skin as he devoured one passion-swollen breast in his mouth, his nimble tongue flickering the rigid little bud until her back arched like a bow and something exploded inside her and she sobbed softly his name.

Moaning long and mournfully through his nostrils, her tiny cries of pleasure igniting a fire in his loins. Patrice pulled at her defenseless little nipple, tugging it with his lips, nibbling it with the edge of his teeth, suckling at her breast with a pure, desperate delight, like a child too early weaned. Her stomach heaved, and he caressed her belly, but when his fingers pushed through the springy soft hairs of her pubic mound and clasped her gently, she gave a sharp gasp and fell flat on her back. Her legs falling open and quivering, when he spread the fleshy lips between her thighs and in a gentle probe stroked her sex, she moaned sublimely and arching her hips, pressed her hand over his.

Sweat popped out on Patrice's brow, covered his chest. She was arching frantically. Closing his eyes and breathing deeply, a groaning welled up in his chest, rumbled through his throat. He wedged heavy masculine thighs between her shapely, sweat-slicked legs. Stretching her slightly with his fingers, blood pounding in his ears with the sweet music of her sighs, he descended between the damp of her thighs. Undulating his hips while holding her smaller form in his strong arms carefully, he pushed himself slowly, gently into her body.

"Oh, Patrice!" she whimpered, her hands moving restlessly across his back, long magenta nails grazing his rugged male beauty as with slow, measured strokes, he delved deeply inside her, again and again.

"Oh, darling! I love you! I love you!" she sobbed. Their legs entwined, her hips rolling upward to meet his quickening thrusts, matching her rhythm to his, she cried blissfully, "Oh Patrice, you fill me up!"

"God, baby!" he whispered, flexing his hips to drive deeper inside her. "As tight as you are . . . Leana!" he cried in a protracted groan when he felt the force of her womb contract tightly around him.

"Oh, darling, Patrice. Darling, Patrice. Darling," she babbled in soft cries of ecstasy as sensation continued to soar, lifting her higher and higher until in shattering cataclysmic oblivion, she came.

The doorbell chimed. Leana drew a shaky breath, threw her head back. Taking one last look into the mirror, she adjusted the wide chiffon shawl to off-the-shoulders; plastered a big smile on her face. Kerry was there to escort her to the ball.

She had called Patrice the following day to thank him when the flowers arrived. So excited she would have been happy to speak to old Henry, disappointment marred her pretty features when a tape recording clicked on. Made nervous speaking to a machine, briefly, she gave her name and number. The call was not returned. Two days later, she tried again.

A woman who identified herself as his secretary answered. She was friendly and courteous with an excellent speaking voice, but when her caller's identity became known she turned incredibly vague. She thought he might be on a case. Where, she didn't know. Whether in Chicago or out of town, she wasn't sure—he left no itinerary. But if she wanted to leave her number, she stammered, and Leana could almost see the perspiration on her upper lip, she'd be surer than sure that he got the message.

Leana hung up. Henry was right. The woman couldn't lie worth a nickel.

Leana tried waiting until Patrice called her, but the call never came. And then, a week later, she called Patrice again. When the ringing stopped and she blurted, "Hello, may I speak to Mr. Jackson, please?" there was a fumbling on the other end, and then, the tape recording came on. Stung to her quick, for she had heard breathing on the line, she replaced the receiver gently.

She did not understand. She sat back on the sofa, hands folding one over the other in her lap, dazed. What was going on? Her head tilted and her eyes clouded over. Aside from his obvious sexual desire, was it all really just a con? She sat up straight, suddenly alert.

Something was wrong here. Terribly wrong. She went over their last encounter in her mind. He had said strange things. Something about waiting, being patient. But then, there had been that moment when she had looked in his eyes and was sure she had seen all the way into his heart. Hanging onto that belief, she decided she would wait. By the end of the second week, however, she swallowed her pride and called his mother.

Mrs. Jackson was happy to hear from Leana, but seemed surprised she didn't know that Patrice was back in Ohio. He had a big contract and he was on his second interview with prospective detectives. This was not unknown to Leana. It was Bernard's company. He had complained that someone was stealing parts and he thought the thefts were an inside job. She had strongly recommended Patrice. A professional with a good reputation for having an instinct about people, as well as a friend, Bernard had taken her referral and immediately contracted with the Jackson agency for security. Although it had been on the tip of her tongue numerous times, something had kept her from mentioning it to Patrice. She did not really know why, but some breath of caution had always held her back.

Mandy, Mrs. Jackson went on, was with him, interviewing security guards. Her brother ran an employment agency there, and since Mandy had always been able to talk Patrice into anything—here she laughed—he was hiring from that agency. But when she heard the sudden, strangled sob at the end of the line, she realized this was no casual call. Hurriedly, she assured Leana that Patrice had no romantic interest in his assistant.

"Still," she added in a hesitant, yet temperate tone, "only a fool would say who a man will have and who he won't. I love Patrice and I've tried to raise him right, but,'' she said, and her voice unconsciously lowered, ''*the sins of the fathers* . . .''

Leana was devastated. She managed a weak laugh at Mrs. Jackson's observation before excusing herself from the telephone. Before she could gather her thoughts, the instrument of her undoing rang, commanded her attention. It was Brenda, telling her about the ball. She asked if Patrice would be taking her. When Leana broke down and told her all that had happened, Brenda became incensed on her friend's behalf, and demanded that she come. If necessary, she told her angrily, she should call Kerry. While a selfish pig, she judged him harshly, he liked Leana. Their breakup had been amicable, and knowing how appearance-conscious he was, there was nothing he'd love more than to parade his little fashion doll off at the party.

The smile on Leana's face turned wry as she thought about her call to Kerry. She had thought he might be angry or, since it had a good six months since their breakup, he might be disinterested. Or, worst scenario, gloat. His first words, however, were of complaint.

''You should see some of the women who have embarrassed me. They don't know how to dress. I finally found one girl who could dress almost as good as you. She looked real good! Talked nice, had a college degree. I thought she was okay, you know? I thought she could hang with me. But when I took her out for dinner, right before the waiter, she looks at the table and says, 'Why do I have so many knives?' I mean, the chick didn't even know what eating utensils to use! Leana,'' he went on urgently, ''We've got to patch things up. You're a classy lady. I need someone like you to make me look good.''

I, I, I. Me, me, me. Good old Kerry. Well, she thought, rummaging through the velvet-lined box that held her jewelry, what man wasn't selfish? Taking out a gold serpentine necklace, she draped it behind her neck and fastened a matching bracelet around her bare arm. Patrice got what he wanted and now she couldn't get hold of him. Why? Whatever the reason, it was a selfish one. At least, she could count on Kerry. She could call him at his office; she always knew where he was. He never just 'disappeared'. He was selfish, but dependable. It might be hard getting him to do something that didn't benefit him personally, but if he said he'd do something, he could be counted on to follow through. So hold your chin up, girl, she told herself. Throw your head back, and when the bell chimed again, cutting in on her thoughts, as she swung open the door with a big smile on her face, she resolved to love the one she was with.

Chapter Fourteen

"Leana! Don't you look *love-ly*!"

"Lea-na! That dress is just *darling*!"

"Leana! Leana! Come here in that beautiful gown you're wearing and introduce me to your friend!"

Stepping lightly by Kerry's side, Leana had changed into a heavy, claret velvet gown with a portrait collar, dropped waist and full gathered skirt. His stern look of disapproval at the side-split, multi-colored frock had caused her to have second thoughts about its suitability. The silk jersey that felt so luxurious against her skin was too daring, too sensual. The shimmering colors of the diaphanous shawl that wrapped her in a brilliant cocoon bounced too playfully off the light; it was too bright for Kerry. When he made a tight, irritated little movement with his mouth, she cringed at the realization that subconsciously, she had chosen a 'Patrice' dress.

Rummaging through her wardrobe, she found and stepped into the off-the-shoulder, red velvet gown. A triple strand necklace secured by a five cluster pearl pendant, each cluster shaped into a heart and three times as large as any individual string pearl, graced her fair, brown throat. With the flick of a slender finger tucking a curl behind one ear, she looked tres elegant, tres riche, the kind of woman Kerry would feel comfortable escorting, be proud to show off.

Colored light glanced off her head and to one side on her lengthy neck beneath the tinted quadrangular chandeliers. It was in the beautiful but traditional gown that Leana glided into the press of the party, her hand tucked beneath Kerry's arm. There was a placid little smile for perfunctory compliments curving her soft red lips that widened prettily at those subdued murmurs of admiration she thought sincere. It went with the territory, as did Kerry, strutting self-importantly through the crowd one step ahead of her. He was with, if not the most beautiful woman at the party, certainly the most elegant. His chest sedately puffed, he made it a point to cruise the entirety of the vintage room, glamorous with its paneled oak walls, muted chandeliers and smartly dressed couples in ever shifting clusters, given a further touch of elegance by youthful, sloe-eyed waiters in plum dinner jackets, with Leana carried along ostentatiously on his arm.

"Leana!"

The clear laughing voice floated out, reaching Leana's ears before she turned, eyebrows raised, to see Brenda, glittering in a heavily sequined gown, come upon them. Always handsome, even more so tonight in an exquisitely cut powder blue tuxedo over a pleated, white silk shirt and a friendly grin, Bernard loped along lankily beside her.

"Hi, girlfriend!" Brenda exclaimed chummily, giving her a kissy-cheek. Her welcoming eyes moved to Kerry, turned cool. "Hello Kerry."

Kerry inclined his head slightly. "Brenda." As there was no love lost between them, his tone was as distant as her look. At the sound of a throat clearing loudly beside her, Brenda hunched her shoulders and giggled. "Oops! Bernard," she said, tilting her head up at him, her cheeks plumping in an adoring grin before her glance again shifted, and like her voice, turned cool, "this is Leana's friend, Kerry. Kerry," she said, looking back at him and unashamedly dimpling, "my friend, Bernard."

He shook Bernard's ready hand in a stiff ceremonial fashion. He suspected Brenda was behind his and Leana's breakup. Kerry then turned abruptly to Leana. "I saw the Johnsons over by the fireplace. Let's go introduce ourselves."

"Kerry!" Although her glance was tender, Leana's tone was chiding. Kerry obviously had rough edges still to be smoothed—not to mention manners to be learned. "Don't be so gung-ho. We'll get around to them. I want to talk to my friends."

Kerry's lips contorted. His cheeks puffed out. Dark splotches appeared on the sides of his neck. "Excuse me," he said huffily when he found his voice. "If you feel that way, I'll just go and introduce *myself.*"

"Kerry," she said quietly and with a gentle expression, "don't be mad. We have all night to meet people. "Look," she smiled, her dusky cheeks filling out sweetly. "Why don't you find Miss Eulalia and ask her to fix me my *special* drink?"

"And while you're at it," Brenda threw after him, once he was safely out of hearing, "why don't you go jump in the lake?"

Leana rolled her eyes to the ceiling. "Do not insult my date, Brenda."

"Insults only count when you say them to the insulted person's face," she retorted blithely. "Hey!" she arched her brows slyly, winked. "How about me introducing you to the Johnsons," she said, her voice lowering in devilish conspiracy. "They're real people. Down to earth. Nothing like your stuffy ole boyfriend."

"Oh, please," she said drily and sighed. While Brenda was grinning at her own cleverness, something flickered in Leana's eyes and a change came over her demeanor. Her face had come alive; hope warred with despair in her glistening brown eyes. Brenda followed her liquid gaze to the double doors where she saw Patrice. Standing there. Staring at her. Midnight romantic eyes in a sooty setting of heavy black lashes staring at Leana. Her eyebrows again lifting when she saw Mandy, barely covered in a pale yellow gown cut low and draped so that it shaped her lissome body, glide up to his side, she turned to share a hard glance with Leana.

Not out of impoliteness did Leana ignore her, but because she couldn't help herself. Every bone in her neck, indeed, every limb in her body seemed to have calcified. Staring across the crowded floor at her with a night dark compulsion, Leana could feel the magic of his nearness vibrate in the air, the sheer power of his presence ripple through her senses in sweet, feather-soft waves.

He had come for her. When he couldn't get her on the telephone, he had been frantic, figuring finally that she'd be at the dance and had come for her. Impervious to Brenda's apprehensiveness, blind to the glamor of her surroundings, to all save the fantasy she'd concocted out of nothing at all, her lips softly parted, and the eyes in her suddenly solemn face looked yet a darker hue as they locked with his.

"Come on, girlfriend," Brenda said quickly. "Let's go see the Johnsons. That ole Center of yours will give you a raise if you hook up with them."

Leana looked at her blankly, a small frown on her face. "I'm sorry. What's that you said?" Her voice was vague, her eyes, as with a magnet, drawn back to Patrice.

For all that his clothes held not the Italiante stamp of Bernard's, a fitted black tux rode Patrice's broad shoulders masterfully as he came through the smartly-dressed populace in the room lavish in oak, artglass and decked with summer flowers, neck slightly bent, looking neither left nor right, his eyes homed in on Leana.

"Leana. He has that gir-rl with him," Brenda practically snarled, tugging at her arm. "Come on!"

Her tunnel vision unlocking, Leana's gaze enlarged to take in Mandy by his side and the tender fantasy of reconciliation with no recrimination flaring full-blown inside her burst. Fighting a sudden sickness in her stomach, and with the last of her reserves, the force of his thick-lashed compulsion, she lifted her chin, sluffed Brenda's hand from her arm. She stood tall, quiet, and erect. There was no reason she should run from him. She had done nothing wrong. If there was an injured party it was she, not he.

Her light-pointed gaze following his purposeful, loose-hipped stride, his lean physique and aggressive, street-wise virility only enhancing the formal evening attire, Leana felt a fierce riptide of emotion move within her when Mandy, mincing in quick steps on four-inch spiked heels and looking adoringly up at him, looped a possessive arm through his arm.

"Hello, Patrice." Hating the flaw within her that

raced her heart and made clammy her palms before the carnal life-force that emanated from his granite-hard body and midnight eyes, she forced calm into her greeting when he stopped short before her.

"Hello, Leana."

For a space, they seemingly swarm in silent solitude, linked only by their eyes.

"Patrice," said Brenda, casting him a jaundiced eye. "You know Bernard, don't you?"

"Hello Brenda," he said casually, never taking his eyes from Leana's. When, failing to shift his gaze he nodded his head and added absently, "Bernard," Brenda flicked a sidelong glance at Mandy.

Tight-lipped, her small face was a darkening squall of anger.

A spark of devilishness glinted Brenda's eyes. Turning to Bernard, she exclaimed brightly, "Bernard! Do you know . . . Uh, what was it again, dear?" she asked in the dagger-sweet tone she seemed unable to resist when addressing the woman who would move in on her friend, "Sandy? Andy? Man . . . Mandy! Yes, I do believe that's it," she confirmed herself as Mandy swung round her glance, grim as death, to glare her displeasure.

"Ask Mandy to dance, Bernard," Brenda smiled, unperturbed. "She looks like a good dancer and Patrice can't hardly match you on the floor!"

Throwing her a street-smart smirk, Mandy ran her hand caressingly up Patrice's muscular arm through his coat sleeve. "He dances well enough for me."

His eyes sultry on Leana, Patrice demured. "Go ahead. We have all night to dance."

"Well," she said doubtfully, looking from one to the other. They were close, standing so very close, his head

inclined, her neck arched, her eyes wide and soft. "No."
She threw her head defiantly. "I'm saving the last and
the first dance for my handsome date." Tightening her
grip on Patrice's arm, the words came from between her
lips purringly, and the smile she threw Brenda was
flinty.

Deliberately, his deep voice resonating with author-
ity, Patrice removed her arm from his. "Dance with the
man."

Patrice had not raised his voice, but there was a
roughness in his tone that brooked no argument, and
took Mandy by surprise. Her thin lips contracting, she
lifted an irritable eyebrow, then feigning a shrug of in-
difference, proffered a graceless hand to Bernard.

His eyes darting around him, Bernard shifted on his
feet. There were strange undercurrents here—jealousy,
hostility, even a measure of sexuality—and of such
stinging intensity they disturbed him, but the lady was
waiting, and ever the gentleman, he took her hand ami-
cably. Once they were safely on the dance floor, Brenda
did her famous 'disappearing hostess' act. It was as well,
for Patrice's smouldering eyes never once wavered from
Leana's face. Alone, however, a subtle change came
over him.

"Where is he?" he inquired with sudden silky menace.

Plucked from her dreaminess by his tone of voice,
Leana was taken aback. "I beg your pardon?"

"The one you came with," he pursued ruthlessly.
"The one you just had to come to this party with."

Leana frowned as her bewilderment deepened. She
did not like the aggressive tone she heard in his voice.

Uneasily, she replied, "His name is Kerry. He went to get me a drink. He's an old friend."

His dark eyes glittering, Patrice studied her with such concentrated intensity that she began to feel uncomfortable. "An old friend? As in an old boyfriend?"

Leana flinched from the sharpness, the ugly jeer in his tone and voice. But when he lifted his head and with insulting eyes looked around the room, as if seeking the bum out, the vulnerability in her brown eyes changed to sullen resentment. "I don't have to answer to you. Considering that you did not come here alone, I really don't think it's any of your business."

"You couldn't wait, could you?" he said in a whipping whisper, leveling a harsh glance upon her. "I'm not gone three weeks and you take up with your old boyfriend!"

Startled by the unexpected bitterness edging his tone, Leana quailed, her knees quaking against the folds of the heavy velvet gown. Then, as if backed against the proverbial wall, her spine stiffened, and she raised an outraged face to his.

"Of all the nerve! You brought your old girlfriend!"

The skin around his eyes tightened; a black brow arched in surprise.

"Girlfriend!?"

There was a name for that innocent look. She couldn't remember it at the moment, but the thought of his head being chopped off at the neck was sufficient to stoke Leana's long-banked ire. "Everywhere you go you take her! Who do you think you are? You . . . stay at my house," she stuttered, flushing at the memory of him holding her, touching her, carrying her to the waiting bed; his mustache deliciously tickly on her face as he tumbled her against his chest and kissed her, "and then you don't even call! And, you have the nerve to think I'm supposed to wait around by the phone!? You don't call—fine! But don't you dare try to chastise me for coming to a party with a man I can depend upon!"

His neck stiffening, Patrice's eyes darkened, then shifting on his feet, flashed. "You know what kind of work I do. You know it takes me out of town for weeks, even months, at a time. I'm finally getting this business going to the point where I can stay in town and court you properly," he snarled, his nostrils flaring with each breath. Had there not been such an aura of menace about him, she would have sneered at his use of the old-fashioned word, "and what do I find? My woman out with the first man she sees!"

"Maybe if you had let me know you were going to be out of town, I would have waited for you. You didn't ask me to be your date. You asked Mandy!" She retorted, her gaze dark and snappish. "I am not a child, Patrice Jackson! All you had to say was, 'Leana, I'm going away for a few weeks. You can't call me, but I'll call you every once in a while to see if you're still alive'!"

The hostility radiating from their bodies charged the atmosphere, reached like sizzling tentacles throughout the country classy room. A passing waist-coated waiter felt it and siddled closer in their direction. Suspending conversation, several couples networking beside an oak planter, were inching their way, too.

Catching hold of her arm, his strong fingers digging into the tender flesh, Patrice pulled Leana to one side, away from the unwelcome attention. Lowering his voice to a raspy whisper, he charged her, "Don't act like a child if you want to be treated like an adult! Mandy is nothing to me other than an employee! She works for me and she does a damn good job! But that's it! Nothing more!"

She turned up her nose. "Oh puh-leese!"

"Okay! I'm no fool. I'm not blind. So she has a thing for me. So what? Have I ever denied you before her? Tell me that! Have I ever withheld my feelings for you just because she was around?"

Leana snatched away, the heavy velvet of her gown making a angry, rustling sound. "Why do you have to take her everywhere you go?" she asked tensely, determined not to let him off the hook. "Why don't you take . . ." she fumbled for a name in her agitation, ". . . . Henry with you if you need company so badly?"

Patrice stiffened. He glanced sharply at Leana. "Henry?" he asked uncomprehendingly. "The janitor?"

"Oh, forget it!" She blinked back tears of frustration. "Just don't come in here playing Mr. Wronged when it's you who wronged me. And why," she asked, her voice shaking, but moving inexorably to the crux, "did you take her to Ohio *this* time!?"

"I don't know where you get your information from, lady," he said, boring into her reproachful glare with a hard look of his own, "but I did not take her anywhere. I was out of town by myself. Mandy was at work, interviewing people in Chicago. We have some big contracts on the line. We have to have personnel hired and ready for them to go through, and Mandy's brother runs a day labor place. She got him to supply us with some men we could train quickly as security guards so that we could secure the contracts."

Security. There it was again, that slap in her face. Experiencing a sudden, sick churning in her stomach, Leana's slim shoulders slumped. It was out in the open. Her real antipathy to Mandy. Swallowing the lump formed in her throat, she said moistly, "I guess she was right. You do need her. *Only* her."

A woman's low throaty laughter amid a clinking of glasses coming across the room to them, Patrice eyed her with a keen, candid look. "You don't like her."

Whether it was the sense of loss, the feeling of betrayal, or the understatement of his observation, something evil moved up Leana's spine. The man had the nerve of ten fools. He was the one at fault here. How dare he try to throw the onus on her? The skin on her whole face stiffened. Her voice, re-energized, rang out: "Obviously, you do!"

A look of supreme irritation contorted the bold sensuality of his face as Patrice thrust it close to hers. "You're talking trash!" he said sharply, his hold on his temper snapping. "It's business. Pure and simple business! Will you get that through your head?" he asked, tapping his temple, the face of his jeweled watch sparkling in the light furiously.

Leana's brow furrowed, her red lips pursed. Her eyes were tilting when she felt a wild thrumming rush with her blood, beating hot and salty through her veins.

"Get out of my face!" Whirling in the heavy dress indignantly, her spine arched and her gentle eyes flashed fire. "Don't you ever, in life, put your face in mine again!" Her voice was low, intense, and she stood her ground.

Standing toe to toe, his brow lowered ominously, but looking into her flashing tip-tilted eyes, Patrice yielded, and his midnight eyes turned velvet. The last time he'd seen that look on her face, he had felt compelled to touch those dusky cheeks with his hand, to gentle those furiously pouted lips with his own. His hands spread in a supplicating gesture and in a tender utterly tortured voice, he said her name.

"Leana . . ."

"Here's your lady! Oh, uh . . ." The dance had ended. Bernard's glance flitted from Patrice to Leana. They were staring deeply into each other's eyes, troubled and tense. But it was Patrice, his thick brows pulling together, that looked away first. Leana's face suddenly crumpled, and when her eyes began to puddle, he reached blindly for Mandy's arm. "Let's get moving," he said gruffly. "There are a lot of people here we need to meet."

"Yeah," Bernard interposed drily, his mild eyes snapping. "The place is chock full of new folk to meet."

Patrice's head jerked, on his neck. He looked hard at Bernard, as if just seeing him. His face relaxed.

"So there are. But none so important as old friends. Thanks for the invite. And for recommending me to the boys downtown. A couple more contracts like that and I can sit in my office all week . . . and play president," he added, narrowing an odd pleading/harsh look on Leana. He glanced back. His face again relaxed, and white teeth flashing in a smile, he took Bernard's hand in an open-palmed slap, thumbs locking in the black handshake. "I won't forget it. Thanks again, man."

Bernard's mollified eyes crinkled with unexpected laughter. "Don't thank me. Thank Leana."

Patrice threw him a startled look.

Bernard's smile enlarged to an open-faced grin.

"She's the one who recommended you to us in the first place. That undercover work you did was great. Alphonso was ripping us off good. You sure flushed him out. So I guess we both should thank our pretty little Leana, here," he indicated, reaching out a careless hand to pat her arm affectionately, "for what I'm sure will be a long and mutually profitable relationship."

Leana waved her hand in a small gesture of dismissal. Her serious eyes focused, then misted again, hurt, when she saw Patrice take a step back, away from her, and looking into his unguarded eyes she seemed to find some sense of horror there, horror mingled with exasperation. Horror? Exasperation? About what? Her? Why? Why? she cried inside. What was wrong with her!?

"Hey," Bernard said softly when with mumbled apologies, Patrice terminated the conversation and took Mandy's arm, who looked back over a bare shoulder at Leana, her face crinkled into a sexy, smug smile, "something between you two? I didn't know. Damn! You should have said something!"

Her dark and lovely face looked tragic, and listening to Mandy's low throaty laughter as Patrice led her off with no word of explanation, the brown eyes grew soft, and infinitely sad. "There's nothing to say. He obviously thinks I'm some kind of airhead. A barbie doll you play with, but when it comes to important things, you go to strangers." She gave a despairing shrug of her shoulders.

"I'm going to set him straight!"

"No, don't." Leana laid a gentle, restraining hand on his arm when Bernard would have started off. She trembled a smile up at him, soft and brave. "It'll be all right.

Excuse me, please, Bernard,'' she said moving free of him.

Bernard watched with troubled eyes as Leana, looking like the little cast-off princess in her regal velvet gown, wended her way through the crush of handsomely suited and frocked party-goers.

Chapter Fifteen

Brenda found her before the fireplace in the little sitting room opposite the family room. Tiled in brown, tan and black mosaic, its grate was lit and Leana was gazing fixedly into the flames. Easing onto the arm of the leather sofa she occupied, Brenda laid a quiet hand on her shoulder.

"What's wrong?" she asked gently at the feathering of unhappiness she saw ringing her eyes. "Was it that old Mandy girl?" When Leana lowered her head and with the fingertips of both hands wearily massaged her temples, Brenda started, and in a sudden flash of clarity, sat up.

"That's it!" she snapped smartly. "It was her! What'd she do?!" Her tone was aggressive, scalding on her friend's behalf and although Leana loved her for it, she only shook her head.

It wasn't Mandy. It never was. It was her. Brenda, God love her, had forgotten, but Patrice had seen through her to the little nobody girl from 35th Street, and treated her accordingly. And yet, even knowing that, she felt the emptiness he left with his departure, arrogant head in the air, yawn like a corroding hole in her heart.

"Oh, Brenda!" she moaned, looking up and turning to her with a helpless gesture. "What am I to do?"

"Come on, girlfriend," Brenda said with a brisk exhalation of breath, tugging her from the sofa. "It is too open in here. And take your hands off your face! You're going to mess up your makeup. Come one, now," she insisted, and putting an arm around her slumped shoulders, drew her through the darkened corridor into the big, asthetically pleasing dining room. Leana sank down onto one of the handsome ladderback chairs cushioned in mellow Corinthian leather before the buffed oak table.

Rushing up a steep flight of narrow stairs to her second floor bedroom when Leana complained of a headache, Brenda was returning with a bottle of aspirin when through the glass window-wall that presented a panoramic view of the dining room she saw Leana. Her heart lurched in pity.

Looking like one of those pretty Jamaican dolls one finds at rummage sales, their chocolate-painted porcelain splashed in fiery, tropical finery, she was sagged over in her chair. Looking beautifully disheveled in ruby-red velvet and utterly forlorn, her head was propped in her hands and her shoulders were shaking, as if racked with sobs. Instead of the sunny Carribean smile, there was a distinct look of sorrow about the tiny figure, bent like a willow over the glossy mahogany table softly weeping.

Concealed behind wooden friezes at the curving of the walls in the vast, cathedral-like room that soared sixteen feet up, were gas lights that cast a soft yellow glow upon the burnt orange and ochre earth-tone ceiling, washing it with a false leathery patina that reflected its muted glow upon the ebony curls feathering Leana's bent head. The dark, jeweltone images of asters and goldenrods fired into the skylight twelve feet up the back wall enhanced the almost brooding solemnity of the place. Had Leana been on her knees, she would have looked holy.

Returning to the dining room, she watched as Leana downed the two white tablets with a swallow of water. Once the deed was done, Brenda settled back, crossed her legs, and with a look of bright interest on her face, asked cheerily, "So, what happened?"

Leana moved her head sadly, numbly. It was too painful. Brenda would eventually find out—she always did—but Leana was not yet ready for girl-to-girl confidences. Her voice was muffled, cutting in its self-condemnation as she muttered, "I should have minded my own business. I should have waited to see if he would call."

"Crap on your own business. Truth is everybody's business. And the truth is, he didn't call. So if that offends Mr. Jackson, well, more power to him. Here, have another drink of water. It's good for the digestion."

Leana picked up the glass Brenda pushed back at her.

"Probably wouldn't know the truth if he heard it, anyhow," she mumbled contemptuously, picking an imaginary piece of lint from her glittery bodice.

But the problem was not that Leana got into everyone's business—for she did—but that the pain was too recent; the wound was too fresh. This was not news to Brenda. She knew her friend. Leana would wait until she was alone to think things over fully. When she felt she could handle it, then and only then, would she open up. As a teenager, it used to drive Brenda crazy, but she was used to her moody ways now and oddly, she reflected, uncrossing her legs and smoothing the expensive gown over her large thighs, she respected them. In hanging with Leana, patience had overtaken Brenda, and her watchful expression was inviting her to confide when before them came a crash and a cry. Bolted upright in their seats, the two women looked to the doorway. Bernard, righting the chair he stubbed his big toe against, and Kerry, fisting a brandy snifter in one hand and a cocktail in the other, hurried into the skylit room. The after-pain of Bernard's stubbed toe left him limping. Bustling Kerry reached them first.

"Where did you go?" Frowning, he gestured with the brandy snifter at Leana. "I've been carying this thing around all night." Placing the glass on the table, he looked at her sharply. "What's wrong you? Your face looks puffy, like you've been crying or something."

Her dark eyes smudged with delicate shadows and drooping under too heavy lids, Leana made a conscious effort to smile. "I'm all right, Kerry. Thank you. And for this drink, too." She took a sip.

"It's nothing but watered down tea," Bernard scoffed lightly, limping up to them. "My lady takes a real drink," he boasted, grinning an unabashed, friendly grin as he bent to peck Brenda on the cheek. Then, he caressed that cheek.

Leana watched enviously as Brenda gazed up at him, her heart in her eyes, holding his hand against her face for a few seconds longer.

Downing his cocktail in one gulp, Kerry smacked his lips, then objected, "I personally disapprove of women drinking."

"Oh, give it a rest, Kerry!" Brenda said waspishly, releasing Bernard's hand.

Fingering the rim of his glass, oblivious of the slightly keening hum the good crystal produced, Bernard looked from Kerry to Leana as if something worried his mind. "Uh, Kerry," he began. "I was just talking to Volk. He knows your boss at Eritechnic. Says their kids went to school together. I kinda let your name drop a few times."

"You did?" His voice squeaking a bit with excitement, Kerry turned to Bernard with quickened interest. "What'd he say?"

Bernard's eyebrows rose. "Nothing, naturally. He doesn't know you. But, if I were you," he went on, looking at his fingernails with an intense frown of concentration, "I'd make it a point to make sure that he does get to know me."

A rivetingly serious look blanketed his face. Where self-interest was involved, he needed no second prompting. Kerry turned to Leana. "You want to come with me? You're good with these higher level people."

Bernard looked up, surprised, his eyes narrowing, Brenda looked away with distain.

Leana was rising from the table, her lips curling in a smile, happy to be of assistance, when Bernard put a restraining hand on her shoulder.

"Sit down," he commanded in an uncharacteristic, stern tone of voice. "Look man," he said, his voice deep, turning to Kerry. "Leana's a fine woman—in every way"—and in turning his head to smile down on her, he missed Brenda's frown. "But it's your career. Let the man know who you are, what you've got to offer. Impress him with you, not your woman."

A caustic look tightening the skin on his face. Kerry leveled a suspicious glare on Bernard, unsure of whether to thank him or to be offended.

"He's right, you know," Leana said gently, giving him a placatory smile. "You've got so much going for you, Kerry. You can do it. Start off by telling him you're a good friend of Brenda's. He likes her. And, you know her father's story. Tell him how you admire him for pulling himself up by his bootstraps, his talent and perserverance. Then, tie that in to your background and accomplishments."

Kerry beamed. "That's good." Turning circumspect, he rubbed his chin musingly, turned his back to her. "Yeah, that's real good. I can do that. Yeah, I can do that," they could hear him muttering, psyching himself up as he moved quickly through the open door.

Lifting a mordant eyebrow, once he was gone, Brenda remarked, "Tell him he's *my* friend?"

"Any friend of mine is a friend of yours," Leana said solemnly.

Brenda swung a wry look to Bernard. Bernard, however, was looking at Leana. He seemed perfectly perplexed.

"Leana," he said, catching her attention. "What's going on between you and Patrice?"

Leana lifted her head warily. "What do you mean?"

"He backed out of our contract."

"Was it you who invited him here?" Brenda interjected, suddenly fierce.

"Yeah, what about it?" said Bernard, his head jerking to Brenda, bemused, then when she only pouted in reply, swinging back to answer Leana.

"Our contract was for three months with an option to renew. You remember I told you how we were losing merchandise. It was on the strength of your recommendation that we hired Patrice. Well, it turned out the guy we were considering promoting to foreman on the swing shift was loading up on our watches and transistors. While we were watching this desperate-looking character, Alphonso was mailing whole crates of small parts to his relatives—right out of the shipping room." He shook his curly head, floored by the audacity. "The man had heart. I got to give him that. Patrice palsyed around with some of the guys and finally flushed him out. We were offering him a two year retainer worth close to a hundred grand. With perks."

Brenda's eyebrows raised, impressed. "That's not shabby!"

"Tell me about it," he said dryly. "My man is a hard bargainer."

Leana felt an uneasiness creep over her as he spoke. "But what does that have to do with me?" she asked woodenly.

"That's what I'm asking you. Until he saw you tonight, he was gung ho for the thing. A few minutes after you left, he pulls me over and tells me to inform my partners that he's pulling out. He can't do it." He pursed his heartshaped lips thoughtfully. Slowly, he asked, "You don't think he thinks I'm trying to move in on you, do you?"

At the beginnings of outrage on Brenda's face, he added quickly, "You know, I was just being friendly. I mean, all I said was that you were the one who recommended him to us, that's all.'' He screwed his face up. ''And just where does Kerry fit in all this? I know he's kind of a jerk and all, but he seems to really like you. He sure as hell depends on you,'' he observed, and wagging his boyishly curly head slowly, with confused laughter. ''I don't understand this. One man depends on you; the other, he finds out you touched his deal and he pulls out. What does it mean?''

''Leana!'' There was panic in Brenda's voice. She scrambled hurriedly to her feet.

Leana shook her head, as if ordering her not to follow. She finger-waved them good-bye as she walked slowly to the door, her heart aching, the heavy velvet swishing, the eyes in her devastated face streaming copious, bitter tears.

Chapter Sixteen

On Monday, Leana called in sick. She had cried all weekend, beating up the pillows and emotionally, on herself. That, coupled with lack of sleep, had her on the verge of being truly ill. When the flowers came, she sent them back. And then again the next day, refusing even to read the notes attached. She was in the grips of a deep, deep funk when Kerry buzzed her on the intercom from the lobby.

Sitting in a slumped position in the middle of her bed, long legs curled beneath her and clad only in a beige teddy with champagne lace edges on the satin tap pants, Leana let him ring five times before wearily, she uncrossed her legs and went to answer the summons of the intercom in the front hallway. In her weakened emotional state, she allowed him to talk her into letting him come up. She slipped her feet into a pair of beige satin and feather mules, threw on her blue silk kimono, and pulled the door open, when he knocked.

It had been raining outside. She waited as he shrugged out of his damp overcoat, shook it out—precisely three times—then folded it methodically in half before giving it into her hands. Seeing him suitably seated on the cushioned white sofa in the living room, then slouching into the easy chair beside it, she began to feel a small stirring of pleasure in her decision to admit him. Dressed in a 3-piece blue worsted suit, light blue, button-down shirt, blue and white striped tie knotted carefully around his throat, and long black loafers buffed and shiny, Kerry was middle class stability personified. Crossing one knee precisely over the other and sitting back primly so that his profile was turned to her, she was struck by how average his face was. No bold, heart-stopping eyes, no black, romantic sweep of brow, no killer smile, just a nice average face with eyes that looked out on the world with a strait-laced sensibility. This was a man with whom a woman could build a future, filtered the thought through her despondent haze. Kerry would come home nights for dinner. Kerry would come home nights, period. He could be depended upon; and if they got together again, would depend upon her. He needed her social sense, her people savvy. He valued highly her business contacts and advice. And, she needed so desperately to be needed.

Leana felt the fog of the gloom in which she had wallowed in, that she had wrapped like a fleecy blanket around her, lift. She would never have to worry about Kerry. He would work at McDonald's before he'd walk a lonely Southern highway at midnight just to get the goods on some criminal. Kerry would have nice, sensible children, too. They would go to the right schools, associate with the right kids. He would plan their futures for them. Keep them from harm. Life might become a little predictable, even fall into ruts in places, but where was it written that everyone had to fly? Earthbound was good, too, and with his cautious, persnickety nature, Kerry would keep pain from them—and her.

"What's that you have on?" he asked suddenly, an expression of distaste hovering on his face. "That *thing* you're wearing under your robe?"

Plucked by the heels from her comforting thoughts, Leana looked down. Her kimono had slid open. A patch of silk and lace from her tap pants were showing above one creamy brown thigh, gleaming in the overhead lights. Secretly delighted that she felt no hot smouldering gaze burn her flesh nor a rush of blood to her head, she pulled the kimono together carefully, then smoothed it over her legs. "Just my teddy. I . . . I was in bed."

"But it's brown!" he exclaimed, looking at her in dismay. "Your robe is blue!"

Leana smiled inwardly. Good ole color-coded Kerry. He'd keep her safe, she thought, feeling a small surge of satisfaction as she retired into her bedroom to fetch her sensible white terry-cloth robe.

The next day, Leana returned to work. There was not much spring in her step and while not wide or filled with bliss, her smile was sweetly shy when she announced she might be getting married soon.

LaDonna was ecstatic. "Oooooh, Leana!" she cried, clasping her in a tight hug. "Hurry up and get pregnant! I can't wait to see your babies. They'll have the most beautiful eyes!"

"Thank you, LaDonna," she sighed, extricating herself from the exuberant girl's suit-wrinkling embrace. "I never knew you were so taken by my eyes." How foolish of her to wear linen, she reflected, when announcing any kind of news to LaDonna.

"Yes!" she said emphatically. "Black, almond-shaped eyes with thick black lashes. Aw!'' she squealed, and because Leana didn't have sense enough to do so, jumped with joy for her. ''Have a boy first,'' she said, gripping her shoulders and staring her in the face eagerly. ''That way, he can wait for me!''

Leana stiffened, then gave a single exclamation of laughter. ''You?''

''Yes!'' She bobbed her head vigorously. ''Yes! Somebody's got to marry me sometime! And when we do, I'll have a girl. Then she can marry little Patrice and I'll have grandchildren with beautiful, black eyes!!''

Leana's lips parted softly. Her expression took on a doleful look. She hadn't the heart to tell her. ''We'll discuss all that later,'' she said. Picking up the morning's correspondance from LaDonna's desk, she smiled, adding, ''When you calm down.''

Walking into her office, rifling absently through the mail, just before she closed the door behind her, Leana lowered the letters and looked back at LaDonna, her head tipped sadly to one side. LaDonna thought she detected tears in Leana's eyes when enlarging on her earlier observation, she said moistly, ''. . . and when you realize that at a certain age, you have to make choices; that life is not a fairy tale.''

LaDonna screened her calls while Leana telephoned her mother. A weak smile on her face, she propped her chin on one hand and listened as her mother went into paroxysms of ecstasy at the news. Like LaDonna, if for different reasons, she looked forward to grandchildren. She didn't want to hear that Leana had not yet given Kerry an answer. She assumed it. Leana mustn't be like her, she said, and have an only child. She must have at least two.

Leana sighed, the smile still in place, widening gently at her mother's happiness, as she went on, giving names to the boy and the girl that Leana would provide for her old age; where they would live, how she should raise them to be nice and polite and that they should love their grandmother.

"Oh muh-dere!" Leana exclaimed finally into the receiver. "You should be the one marrying Kerry. You think just alike!"

"I'm not being funny, Leana," Mrs. Claremont said tersely into her ear pressed to the receiver. "You just don't know how unfortunate you are and I don't mean in just losing your father."

In the pause that followed, Leana sighed inwardly with compassion when she heard Mrs. Claremont gulp back tears, compose herself.

"Leana," she said in her firm mother's voice, "I never told you this. I didn't want you to feel even more badly than you did. I always felt you were the most deprived child I'd ever known. Hush, girl!" she said snappishly at her shocked 'muh-dere!'

"Leana, you were deprived of grandparents. My parents and your daddy's parents died before you were born. I was an only child and he was an outcast from his people. They went around behind his back, running him down and scandalizing his name 'cause he was about something and they weren't. They made fun of him, scorned him when times got bad and he'd work at any job to take care of his family rather than making me go to the welfare office and lie and say he'd left us. It finally got to the point where they hated him. Of course, that didn't stop them from borrowing whatever we had," she added bitterly. "But, that's the reason you had to come up alone. I didn't want you to be raised around his low-lifed people and I had nobody but me.''

Leana felt tears come to her eyes when the hand hit to receiver too late. The hand that washed her baby's bottom; the gentle, work-weary hand that wiped her childish tears when she cried for her daddy; the trembling, work-calloused hand that cradled her face with such reverence when she became the first person in her family to graduate from high school.

''Muh-dere . . .'' she began, for she'd heard the choking sob in her mother's voice.

''No. Let me finish. I had it hard. I was ignorant . . .''

''No! You didn't have the schooling, but . . .''

''Hushup, girl! I know who am and who I used to be! And number one, I'm your mother so you just set quiet and let me talk!''

''Yes ma'm,'' she replied meekly.

''Like I said, I had it hard. I had it real hard. People mess with women raising kids by themselves. And, if the woman is strong and can take care of herself, they mess with her kids.''

Leana's lashes drooped; her expression fell tender. Fighting an unexpected onslaught of tears, she smiled grimly instead. More than her mother suspected, she knew the truth of her words. Mrs. Morgan, who lived across the street with her husband and six sons, crowded into her mind. Mrs. Moore, who muh-dere had faced down alone, when out of pure spite she called the Department of Children and Family Services out to their house, claiming muh-dere was an unfit mother because she ran a policy wheel out of their tiny apartment. Muh-dere had not only faced her down, right in front of her husband and without fear of her sons, she had backed her down. But, Mrs. Moore had had her revenge—On Leana. She was twelve years old at the time, walking home from school, minding her own business. For no reason at all that she knew of at the time, Mrs. Morgan had leaned out of her first floor window when she saw her coming and yelled, "Quit walking in the streets! Somebody hit you, they go to jail, you stupid little bitch!"

"Leana," her mother was saying, "I was raised with both my grandparents alive. What I needed that ma and pa couldn't give me, they scraped together and got me. When I felt life was too hard or ma and pa was being too mean, I could always go to grandma or grandpa, and they would hug me or get on them for me. I had some uncles but they upped and run off like no-good men do, but my great-auntie Hazel was our little country school's schoolteacher. If I was just feeling blue, I could go to her. She was such a cheerful old lady, just being around her could lift your spirits. So what I'm trying to tell you is that one child ain't enough. I feel so bad about that for you."

"Muh-dere, please," Leana said tenderly, pressing the fingers of her free hand to her temple.

"That's why I never told you," Mrs. Claremont said, trying to sound disapproving, but failing miserably. "I know it was hard on you. I was hard on you. But I did my best."

"I know you did, muh-dere."

"That's good, baby."

Leana listened to her mother's breathing, her mother's sniffles before the thin voice again grew strong.

"Leana, I want you to know this. I want you to understand. It's very hard for a woman to raise a child alone. It's not so much she ain't qualified. It's the burden the world puts on a woman alone. It's a real heavy burden. And it's worse today. A woman needs a man. But children need some other family they can go to when ma and pa got too many problems of their own to be bothered. That's the way it used to be; that's the way I want it for my grandkids. Do you understand that Leana? Teach your babies to love their grandmother. Just a mother and a father ain't enough. They need other relatives, too.'' Her voice took on a sharp, prying tone. ''Kerry ain't no only child, is he?''

Leana laughed. ''Kerry only has three sisters and four brothers.''

''How they fixed?''

Knowing what she meant, Leana began the litany of achievements solemnly, trying to keep the tender amusement from her voice. ''Kerry's the only one with a college degree. But, two of his brothers make more money than he does and one of the others is thinking about starting his own business. Oh, yeah!'' she giggled sweetly into the receiver. ''His sister that dropped out of high school is a model. She's not high fashion, like on magazine covers or anything. It turned out that even at 5'7″ she was too short. So the poor thing is just an ole runway model in Paris.''

Muh-dere was unimpressed by her attempt at humor. This was serious business. ''Good! They want something. But,'' she hesitated, ''what about the other brother and the two sisters? They ain't illegal, are they? You know how these kids are into drugs these days.''

''Oh God, muh-dere no!'' she laughed. ''They're just regular people with regular jobs. And come to think of it," she said dryly, "they're more fun to be around than Kerry."

"Don't worry about that. You need a serious, hard-working man. With his college diploma, Kerry can make a lot of money. And you be a good wife and help him get it."

"Yes, muh-dere," she sighed, thinking again how much Kerry and his would-be mother-in-law had in common.

After she hung up, or rather muh-dere, for Mrs. Claremont had a million preparations to make for the wedding—she generously left to Leana and Kerry the honeymoon details—Leana leaned back in her swivel chair, her head tilted to one side, exhausted.

"Oh, muh-dere," she murmured. "I love daddy's memory like life. But you really should have married again." She jumped at the jangling sound when the phone rang.

"Yes?" Her voice was eager, riveting, yet strangely apprehensive.

"Leana? It's Mr. Grant."

"Oh."

At the disappointment in her voice, LaDonna reminded her hesitantly, "The one you got that job for?"

"Thank you, LaDonna," she said, her tone subdued. Shaking her head then as if shaking off childish dreams, she added briskly, "I'll take it."

"Miss Leana!"

"Horry. What's wrong?" she cried alarmed. His voice was choked and he had taken to calling her Miss Leana again.

"Nothing," he gasped, and there was a joyful lilt to his voice. "Nothing wrong."

"Mrs. Grant?" she asked, unconvinced. "Is something wrong with her?"

"Yeah," Horry laughed. "Woman's too well if you ask me! She's buying everything in sight. New furniture, school clothes for the kids . . ."

"Horry!" Leana's eyes grew wide, and then she grinned—her biggest grin of the day. "Good news! It's good news! What happened? Oh, my God! You didn't win the lottery, did you?!"

"Yes ma'm," he said, his voice again teary, and she nearly dropped receiver. "The day I took my heart in my hands and went to see Miss Leana Claremont, I did. You has been a godsend. First, you gits me a good job, then, I gits a call and the man says you rec'mends me for another, even better job! God bless you, Miss Leana," he said, choking again. "Me and my wife, we prays for you every night."

Leana's mouth gaped. Her mind whirled back. She couldn't remember two recommendations. "Who? Wha . . . ?" she stammered.

"The Jackson Agency," he told her happily. "Mr. Jackson talked to me person'ly. He's hiring me to be the captain of his security guards. Miss Leana," he said, and his voice lowered as if fearful he might jinx his good luck, "you won't believe the money he's giving me. You won't believe it!"

Horry paused when the line seemingly went dead. "Miss Leana? You still there?"

"Horry," she said tentatively. "Are you sure?"

Horry became circumspect. She could hear the fear enter his voice.

"You didn't . . . git this job for me?" His voice cracked. "It's some kinda joke?"

"Oh no, no Horry," she hastened to reassure him. "I did talk to Mr. Jackson. As a matter of fact, he was the first person I talked to. Well," she said, totally confused. "I . . . I'm just so happy for you. I really am."

"Thank you, Miss . . ."

"Leana!" she interrupted him, her old chiding self once more. "My name is Leana. 'Miss' does not appear anywhere on my birth certificate."

"Leana!" he laughed again, that happy laugh that bubbled up from the soul. "I never in my whole life had anybody help me before. Thank you. Thank you," he said with such quiet sincerity that Leana's eyes filled with tears.

"Thank you, Horry," she said gently. "And, your wife for her prayers."

Leana was less sanguine, however, after she placed the receiver in its cradle. Gray thoughts, fears, like shadows, flitted one after another across the landscape of her mind and re-surfaced as doubts. What did Patrice think he was doing? she wondered. How many times had she asked him to hire Horry? How many times had he hurt her feelings when he said 'no'? And Bernard—he had humiliated her with Bernard.

Leana put a hand over her eyes, recalling how sick she'd felt inside. Now there were no tears left. Now there was only emptiness. 'Why?' a little voice whispered. Why give Horry a job now? What was going on? An inward tension building, she rose from behind the desk and as she paced back and forth the small space before it, the emptiness she felt inside her filled with fury.

She flung around, slapped the big desk with an open palm. "That's why I'm marrying Kerry!" she shouted in a loud, angry voice. "The man is totally unpredict-able! And callous about it, too. He doesn't care about people's feelings at all!"

LaDonna peeked in the door, her small face frowning, worried. "Leana? Is anything the wrong?"

Whirling, Leana stared, the anger inside her shooting from the tip-tilted eyes, those sweet doelike eyes that so surprised transgressors when they got, as now, quite sharp.

LaDonna gasped, backed tensely against the wall, when with long, determined strides, Leana brushed past her. "I'm leaving. If anyone wants me, they can call back tomorrow," she said grimly. "Take messages!"

Chapter Seventeen

Although she had never been to Patrice's office, Leana found it easily enough in one of the new professional office buildings, wedged between a Donut shop and an insurance company, on east 87th Street. Entering one of two upholstered elevators, Leana's palms were clammy and her chest felt tight. Taking its own good time, she struggled to remain calm while the elevator crept snail-like to the Fourth floor.

The corridor it decanted her into was narrow, but well-lit, illuminated by a tall, plate glass window, located at the far end of the wall. Pushing through the first door to the left, a blond, steel-reinforced door bearing the legend 'The Jackson Agency—Private Investigators', she halted mid-stride and looked around her. The waiting room was a mess. There were workmen everywhere, plastering and painting, a roll of carpet lay unfurled in one corner. Other workmen and one lone woman were breaking through one of the walls, enlarging the office. Patrice must be doing well, her practical mind deduced, if he needed to expand.

Patrice. Her heart gave a peculiar little thump at the

thought that within minutes she would see him, face to
face. A strange warmth rippled through her. And then,
the strain of the past months, taking their toll, produced
tears. She propped her shoulder against the door frame,
leaned gratefully against its solidness. Her eyes closed
painfully.

How could you? she implored him silently. At every
turn, you slap me in the face. At every turn. All I ever
wanted was to help you. And by helping you, I could
help others. That was all. What did you want from me?
Why did you torment me so? At every turn, Patrice? I
loved you. I gave you everything I had and you threw it
back at me. Except. . . . except my body.

Her eyes squeezed shut and leaning her head against
the door frame, a shudder traversed Leana's body.
Memories, with the effervescence of champagne, bubbled up in her consciousness. She thought of his reaction
when she held the male member of his infinitely beautiful body in her hand. He had kissed her lips, but when
she tried to lift her hand to put it around his neck, he
begged her not to.

*I love this, baby. Don't let me go. Ah, yes! Ooooo,
baby. It feels so good. Oh, hold me. Hold me!*

A warm glow had seeped through her body, bringing
with it a delicious sense of power, a heady surge of
being needed, of confidence in herself as a woman. *This
is exciting,* she had thought. Kerry never talked during
love-making, never let her know how he felt, whether
what she did pleased him or not. Her temples throbbed
painfully at the memory. How could he? It had meant
everything to her. And then Horry calls to let her know
that, once again, he acts with no consideration toward
her at all.

She felt the tears fall, wet the lace on her silk blouse. Is that all I am to you? Someone to sleep with? Why, Patrice? Why? I thought, after that night, I thought that you loved me, too. Oh God! Love hurts. Its hurts so bad.

Well, she thought, a renewed surge of anger pushing her upright, Mr. Patrice was going to answer some of those questions. Today. Who did he think he was? She was not a child, and she was no man's fool. Fumbling with her handbag, she pulled forth a compact and lipstick and with shaky hands, applied a generous sheen to her mouth. Running her tongue over her lips and drawing a deep breath, she picked her way gingerly across the torn-up floor, the cheap tile, broken and scattered across it, to be replaced by the new carpeting along the wall.

Stopping behind a partition at a long, polished oak desk, a gray vase filled with burgundy and rust dried flowers decorating its slick newness, she asked the receptionist for Mr. Jackson.

A stout, prim-mouthed woman of about sixty, wearing chunky faux pearls was rifling through a rolodex. She looked up with startled rebuking eyes.

"Mr. Jackson is in a business conference now. Do you have an appointment?" she asked with fussy self-importance.

"No." Betraying nothing of her inner turmoil, Leana's features were composed, and her tone was crisp. "I do not. Please inform him that Ms. Leana Claremont is here to see him."

Her navy blue suit with a puff of ivory lace at the neckline, a duplicate of the lime-green suit which had captured so much attention at the VIP lounge, her appearance and voice resonated confidence.

Looking up sharply from her card index, as if re-evaluating Leana's importance, a minute frown twitched the receptionist's pencil-thin brows.

She set her mouth primly. Taking orders from Mr. Jackson's secretary, Tracy, thirty years her junior, was bad enough. Now this snippy little thing with her fine clothes and arrogant airs presumed to order her around? Indicating the impossibility of her request by notching her penciled brows an inch higher, she suggested cooly, "If you wish to wait?"

Her face retaining its own cool expression, Leana said evenly, "No, I do not. I wish to see Mr. Jackson. *Now.*"

"Without an appointment? Mr. Jackson could hardly run a business seeing everyone who just walks in off the street, now could he?" Her eyes opening wide, the receptionist looked positively scandalized.

The delicate muscles in Leana's jaw flexed. She circled the desk.

"You'll have to. . . . Wait! You can't go in th. . . ."

The elderly woman's protestations were lost in space as Leana burst through the door labeled 'President'.

It was a handsome office, simple and masculine, with leather and black lacquered furniture. Seated behind a glass top desk, impressive in its size and newness, Patrice looked up sharply. Seeing Leana, her eyes tilting at the corners, he came quickly to his feet, nearly knocking a handsome gray vase, identical to the one on the front office desk but filled with white flowers, to the floor in his surprise.

"What're you doing here, Leana? Getting more jobs for the downtrodden?"

Jerking her head on her neck at the amused note in the voice coming from beside her, Leana's eyes locked with the puppy-dog friendly eyes of Bernard. Startled into awareness of her surroundings by his presence, her eyes swept the room warily. So intent had she been on having it out with Patrice, it was only now that she noticed there were three other men in the office, all looking in her direction. The two expensively suited strangers returning her stare coldly, she felt all of a sudden foolish, fearful; her mouth dry as cotton.

Bernard was watching her, his head tipped to one side amiably, but curious at her unannounced presence. And, although no introductions had passed between them, she recognized the tall, distinguished-looking man on Patrice's right as Thaddeus 'Tad' Meadows, Personnel Director for BPX, Inc., a multinational computer corporation. He had risen quickly upon her entrance; his bright blue eyes now watched her sharply.

His nose in the air, as if looking down on her from a high place, she recognized the third man as Michael Dermus, a city hall bureaucrat from whom one big municipal contract could make a man or woman a millionaire overnight. Two other men she had not noticed appeared miraculously, as if they were waiting in the woodwork, one to stand beside Tad Meadows; the other, a big tawny-headed man, built like a wrestler and with the stealth of a lion stalking, ominously approached her.

Oh, no! she thought, brushing her fingertips across her trembling lips, her eyes popping like a frightened rabbit. What have I done?! She took an instinctive step back as the burly blond bruiser, with not a trace of human sympathy in his expression, stalked nearer.

Planting his broad shoulders, rolling with taut muscle beneath his shirt, foresquare before her, Patrice got to her first. "Gentlemen," he said, smiling his best funereal smile at the approaching tawny-haired giant whom Leana had rightly assumed to be a body-guard, "this is Ms. Leana Claremont.

"Ms. Claremont is Vice President of the Edward Blyden Center, one of the city's oldest social agencies," he went on suavely when the blond giant resumed his post next to Tad Meadows. "Excuse us a moment, please." His eyes moving a cool apology around the room, he grasped Leana's elbow lightly, and turning, piloted her through the door.

"It's all right, Mrs. Lovitt," he said to the receptionist rushing to get in her side of the story as he led Leana around the corner into an empty office. "Miss Claremont is my fiancee."

Ushering her across the portal into the square, brown and gray office, Patrice's executive-suave tone turned brisk, "I'll be right back, baby. This thing is almost wrapped up." Then, without even a 'by your leave' he left, pulling the door to firmly shut behind him.

There was a smile on his face and a spring in his step when Patrice left Leana to return to his office. He could have been had for a penny, when he had looked up and saw her. His eyes crinkling at the corners, the smile expanded at the corners of his mouth. His Leana. His sweet, persistent, bedeviling angel, Leana. Sweet recollection glazing his eyes, he was remembering how crazy he'd been when it had dawned on him just how relentless she could be in upsetting his carefully laid plans, his carefully plotted life. . . .

He would never forget the first time he saw her. It had been a long day. He had gone to Gladys' to drop off his report to a client. He had eaten just enough to be sociable and it was time to go. He had accepted the check, declined dessert, and was standing, making the appropriate noises of farewell, when he saw her. The tables around them were filled with men, and even women, stealing glances in her direction. And with good reason. She was a knockout. Long, girlish bangs, as black as Cleopatra and in that style, framed her clear, smooth brow. Silky lashes, delicately curved, ringed her large almond-shaped eyes. There was an aura of radiance around her that caused him to catch his breath.

She was seated on the far wall of the restaurant, sipping mineral water and talking with Brenda. Her large, exotic eyes looked out from a serene oval face. Her complexion was flawless, with the mellifluous translucency of age-darkened honey. Her beauty of the sort that one look was not enough, she was in the most literal sense of the word, stunning. Patrice stood transfixed. He unconsciously began walking toward her, stopping briefly to return the greeting of a woman who turned out to be a former client. Mrs. Jones. He had helped her son out when he was accused of industrial spying. When he finally reached the fringe of her booth, he went and fell over Brenda's handbag.

Unusual for one so lithe, so agile, so sure of his bearings and aware of his surroundings. Unusual—or an omen. Still, it was not until he left his surveillance of the 'boyfriend' to take her to Bill's lounge that he had known that he was losing it. He had had to see her.

Oh God! he remembered thinking. Oh God, he was losing himself. Everything he had worked for, every promise he had made himself, this madness coursing his veins whether near or roaming far—all began and ended with Leana. Leana of the winsome shy smiles, the heart-aching flushes that stained baby-soft cheeks like the last harrah of summer on the petals of dusky red roses.

To hear once more lest he die, the oh-so-faint tinkle of her loopy earrings, the sweet, slightly nasal, Southside Chicago accents of her voice, to see her legs, shaped like music, trim and graceful, her breasts heave, their full ripe thrusts on the gossamer blouses, and from behind, her own, gently swelling the linen suits she wore with such femininity, he longed to leave imprints of his worshipful hands, to breathe in her perfume, her breath as it left her throat; to prostrate himself before her flesh and blood altar, to humble his proud manhood before the alpha of love.

He was mad. He was insane. His father's perfidy, his mother's frustration, his sense of betrayal, the bitter goads to his will to success were as nothing to the needs that she, who was beautiful, inspired in him. He had been in love before, or had thought he was, which amounted to the same thing, but never, ever, with this passion, this woman, this Leana.

Sitting across the table from her in Bill's lounge, his eyes, brilliant gleams of darkness and luminosity smudged by thick black lashes, had gentled to a velvet blackness as they swept her face, catalogued the bangs brushing her tender forehead, the feathery tips kissing her even jet brows, the uptilt of liquid brown eyes, the straight short bridge of nose that flared softly at the nostrils, the small soft mouth that spread in gentle smiles, her perfume like Circe's song, wafting across the circular table to bind him.

Little did Leana know, but since that fateful day in Glady's his every waking hour had been taken with thoughts of her. And he had hated himself for it. Every man needed a woman, but this mental seige—for God's sake! he even had imaginary conversations with her— was stupid, it was sophomoric, and damn distracting! He had too little time, too much to accomplish. His work was suffering from his obsession with the cool classy lady only an arm-full away. God, but she was beautiful. Everything about her. Even her knees, he frowned, crossed one over the other and poking through the slit in her skirt, were cute.

Feeling the weight of her eyes upon him, he glanced up.

"Is anything wrong, Patrice? We can leave if you want."

Leave? His heart had leapt. Would she take him with her? The lounge suddenly came into focus. He had been scowling. His mind fierce in its concentration on her, had made tunnel vision of his sight. No wonder she thought something bothered him. As if anything could intrude upon the space she held claim to in his thoughts!

She had smiled, uncertain. God, but he could look at a person. A burning tension had hardened his face. His strong shoulders beneath the fine suede blazer were bunched and taut. So uptight, she could actually feel the bow-tight tension emanating from his body, she wished she could get him into a warm sudsy tub and massage the . . .

Patrice blinked. That conversation never took place. Oh hell! he spat mentally as he opened the door to his office. Even with her in the next room, he carried on imaginary conversations with the woman!

* * *

Left alone in the room, Leana had unconsciously been holding her breath. Now she expelled it in a gasp. He had tricked her! He had pretended to come to her rescue and then shuffled her off once more. This time, physically. Well, if he thought she was going to just forget his bad behavior and walk away meekly, he was dead wrong. His fiancee! Of all the nerve! The anger that brought her there in the first place flared. She had things to say and Mr. Patrice was going to listen! Twisting, turning, her mind racing, and with anger roiling inside her, but with no place to go, nor one on whom to vent that anger, she realized with a sigh of frustration that there was little she could do but wait. Deciding to take stock of her surroundings, meagre though they were, she walked around the office where the smell of paint was new to pass the time.

There were lightening-white venetian blinds over the undraped window with a southern view that let in the room's light. A steel filing cabinet—another of those attractive-in-a-masculine-kind-of-way gray vases sitting atop it—this one empty—was shoved flush against the wall in one corner. A wood-grained desk similar to the receptionist's, only square, and from its clean surface, never before used, hugged a space on the newly carpeted floor before the window. The tufted-leather chair behind it looked not just handsome, but inviting, so she went over and sank into it, crossing her legs, the new springs squeaking under her sudden weight.

Swinging around in the chair to the big south-view window at the back of the paneled office, she had rocked, swiveled and tapped her foot impatiently for less than ten minutes when Patrice re-entered the room with what looked to be a bottle of champagne, two glasses appropriated from the sideboard in his office, and a flashing white smile of triumph on a quietly exuberant face.

Obviously the 'wrapping up' he spoke of had gone his way, Leana reflected wryly as she watched him pour the clear sparkling liquid. It was on the tip of her tongue to remind him that she did not drink when she glanced up to wonder at that expression of restrained eagerness on his face. It was as if he were hugging some news to his chest tightly that he was dying to share with her.

In bed?

Blanching in surprise at the cynical thought, she gave him a watery little smile and took the glass he offered silently. Fluttering her exotic eyes in a curious shy way as she clinked her glass against his, Patrice watched her take a sip, then shift the position of her long, slender legs. He was deciding he liked the way she sat, too, when she exclaimed, "Why . . . it's water!"

Patrice stared, sharply disappointed, at Leana. He frowned. "Of course, it's water. Perrier. You said you didn't drink." His frown deepened. "I would never ask you to do anything you didn't want to do. You should know me better than that."

Her head wobbled up. She gave him an uncertain look. "Do I know you at all? I mean," she said nervously, gripping the stem of the glass tightly. "You told your secretary that I'm your fiancee."

Anger again flared. She came to her feet agitatedly.

"Your fiancee! Tossing her head stiffly, sunlight struck her hair into a satiny cloud of ebony that slid across the dark delicate flush of her cheeks. Pushing the glass to one side and leaning on her fingertips over the desk, she demanded, "And, since when did I become your fiancee?!" Then remembering why she came, her hands clenched themselves into fists and battened on her hips. "About the same time, I suppose," she accused, her sloe-eyed gaze burning, "that you decided to hire Horry Grant!"

"As a matter of fact," he said quietly, "yes."

The steam taken from her sails, her fists unclenched. Her hands dropped to her sides, her fingers fumbled vaguely. She watched, slack-jawed, as Patrice drained his glass, then placed it carefully on the desk. She sputtered, "Wha . . . what?"

The thickly-lashed eyes squinted at her puzzled, as if maybe he'd misunderstood. "You're the one who wanted me to hire him."

"Well, yeah," she said weakly, her eyes darting in confusion. "But, he said you hired him as captain of your security guards. You didn't ask for references. Nothing. Just called him up, sight unseen, and hired him."

Patrice shrugged. "You recommended him. I knew you wouldn't steer me wrong."

"But . . ." She dragged a deep breath into her lungs. Moments ago, she'd been trembling with the strength of her conviction, the bravado of her anger. Now there was only confusion. Exhaling the forcefully held air slowly, she came from behind the desk to pace the length of the dark paneled room. Glancing up from her pacing with quickly narrowed eyes, she asked, "Whose office is this? Mandy's?"

Patrice rubbed a hand over his forehead. "Mandy no longer works here."

"What?"

"You didn't like her." Coming around the desk, he hiked up a pant's leg, sat on the edge and sighed. "Too bad. She really knew her stuff. Still . . ." He shook his head. "It was for the best. I set her up in her own agency. I felt I owed her that. She's going to Mobile to work with The Mabry Agency that I told you about. They'll share office space. She can handle it." He gave a low amused laugh. "And Richard's not married. Good-looking guy, too," he said with a quick wink.

"Patrice. I don't understand."

"What's to understand? This office is for your friend, Horry. After all, the captain deserves his own office."

Leana sat down hard on the desk beside him, outdone.

"And the other room they're opening will be for the three new operatives I hired. Thanks to Bernard introducing me to Dermus, I'm going to be on easy street."

"Why is Bernard here? In your office? He said you backed out of a contract with him. I thought it was be . . . be . . ." Her voice faltered, quavered as fresh pain ripped through her, ". . . because I sent him to you."

His face hardened. He stalked to the window and pulling up the blinds, stared uneasily at the street scene below. "That's true, too."

At her muffled sob, he circled the desk. Pulling her to her feet, he enfolded Leana in his arms. "Baby," he murmured, running his hands over her face and neck, stroking her hair tenderly, dotingly. "I didn't do it to hurt you. I hated hurting you, but I had to."

"You don't trust me," she sniffed, unconsciously rubbing her palms over the powerful muscles of his chest. "You trusted. . . . Mandy, but not me. The one you say you love!"

"Leana, baby," he whispered, anguished. "Sweet, beautiful baby, Leana. That's not true. I do love you, and I would trust you with my life. You are my life. But at the time. . . . before now, I couldn't." He held her by her arms before him, gently insistent. "Leana. I told you about my parents. How my father used my mother to get ahead, then dumped her.

"All my life I've heard about how men use women to get to the top, then dump them. Some woman drops out of college to work to put her husband through, then on the day he graduates, he divorces her. Some woman who sacrifices her career to push her husband's. He gets on top and divorces her. Some housewife who gave her husband a nice home, a bunch of kids and the best years of her life, he meets a younger woman and divorces her. I don't know why. I don't know if its the male ego or what. I only know that I carry the genes and temperament of a man who did do such a thing to a woman—a woman that I love."

Looking off, his jaw clenched, harshly he said, "The sins of the father." Swinging his gaze, his eyes stared into hers fiercely pleading. "Baby, I swear to God I haven't had another woman since you. I knew that I loved you the first time I saw you. I knew I wanted you for my wife. That's why from the beginning, I turned my back on you. I just couldn't take the chance!"

"Chance?" Raising her face and shaking her head, puzzled, she repeated herself. "What chance?"

"The chance of letting you help me to build up my business, then getting a big head and leaving you for someone who looked at me like a god because they didn't know me 'when . . .' "

Leana gave a low moaning cry. Was this what it was all about? His father? Good grief! How much pain could one man inflict?! How many lives could one man screw around? Feeling a surge of tenderness, she stepped forward, her hands cupping his cheeks. "Oh, Patrice!"

"I see the way my father's wife looks at him." Staring into her eyes, his tender gaze was anguished. "He's never told her how he got to be a big shot. She never knew him when he could barely read and write his own name, when the bulk of his business was church programs. She acts like he was born educated, wealthy, king of the damn molehill!"

Leana's worried expression was soft, tender. "You wanted me to look at you that way?"

"No!" He threw her hands down. His glance was furious. "I'm glad you saw me doing my own detective work, glad you saw me doing the dirty work, scrambling for contracts! But don't you see, baby?" Taking her by the hand, he kissed it, then drew her down on the desk beside him.

"You knew me 'when', and you know me now. You know I made it, and how I made it. And on my own! I can never feel I've outgrown you, that I'm not really a big shot because somehow I owe you. When you take me, if you'll take me," he said, looking searchingly into her eyes, "it will be as I am. I will never have to feel like I've got anything to prove."

"But, Patrice," she said tremblingly, understanding washing over her in sickening waves. "I'm a woman. A full grown woman. I've got a heart," she pushed on even as the booming of that heart quaked her insides, screamed at her 'let it be!' ". . . and I've got a mind. I ca-can't.. be with you," she stuttered, dying a little with each word, "if you can't trust me, yourself, *us* to grow together! I love you. I love you so much! But you've got to trust us, Patrice. What if your business fails? Would you divorce me, throw away my love because you were no longer, as you put it, 'a big shot'?"

Patrice looked at her as if wondering how she could fix her mouth to say such a thing. Drawing back a little, his voice was stunned, whispery when he asked, "You have no idea how much I love you, do you? I'd lay down my life for you. I . . ." He licked his lips, confounded. "Maybe I was wrong. But don't you see?!" he cried, impassioned, his father's perfidy riding him like an evil thing. "I couldn't take that chance!

"Everything I did," he moaned, kissing her hand, her fingers, each one feverishly, "I did it for you. When Brenda told me your name, I thought, 'Leana. Leana. That for the love of Leana, I would do anything. Even hurt her pride," he admitted softly, pressing her voluptuously kissed hand to his cheek. "And I'm sorry. But I would rather lose you than that you ended up like my mom—disillusioned and even," his voice shurred softly, "a little bitter.

"Leana," he said huskily. There was a spark of anguish in his eyes, so private and stark that she cringed to see it. "Do you really think I work as hard as I've been doing for the past months? I knew I had to hurry up. Get it together so that I could . . ."

He took a deep breath. "Leana, I want to be with you. I want to be with you forever. Will you.. would you consider . . . marrying me?" His voice trembled, and his lips, too.

Her face softened. She looked at him, soft and gentle and pretty. With a teary tenderness in eyes as bright as the light coming in through the windows, her head began to slowly nod, her smile singularly sweet.

"I'm sorry I don't have a ring," he said, frowning, nearly unmanned by her expression. "I was going to pick one up, a big one, once I got the contract with BPX.

I . . . Excuse me.'' Leaving Leana, a watery smile on her lips, he walked to the door quickly and left. Returning in less than the time it took her to repair her makeup, he presented her with a clump of white flowers taken from the vase in his office.

"I only have these wildflowers to offer you, right now. He laughed. somewhat shamefacedly. "I saw some on my way to Brenda's party. They looked so pretty in the moonlight. It was like they were just daring me to pick them. And you know me," he grinned crookedly, the sensuous sable lights of his night-dark eyes flickering uncertainly. "I'm, well, my mom says I'm a little hard-headed," and when Leana giggled, he went on, explaining himself in a rush, "I mean, I don't always do things by the book. Like these," he said, holding the flowers out to her pleadingly. "They're not even roses, but I'm no rose either, all sweet-smelling in some neat little garden. But I can learn," he amended his nature hastily, "I can learn not to be so hard-headed. Just give me a chance! I swear I'll make you a good husband."

In the light that shone through the south window, Leana took the flowers, gathering the sun's fire in its feathery white petals, in the soft hollow of her palm and eyeing them with a reverence, sat back quietly on the desk's edge. She had recognized the yarrows immediately. Raising her face to Patrice and nodding her head, she smiled full into his eyes. "Yes," she said softly.

Patrice dropped down to the desk, embraced her. "You'll have me?" he asked hopefully, pressing his face to her soft brown neck, his voice muffled.

Leana looked down shyly, touched the yarrow with a gentle finger. "If you can learn not to be so hard-headed, I can learn to fly."